14 WAYS TO DIE

14 WAYS TO DIE

VINCENT RALPH

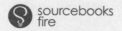
sourcebooks
fire

Published by Sourcebooks Fire, an imprint of Sourcebooks
P.O. Box 4410, Naperville, Illinois 60567-4410
(630) 961-3900
sourcebooks.com

Originally published as *Are You Watching?* in 2020 in the United Kingdom by
Penguin Books, an imprint of Penguin Random House UK.

Library of Congress Cataloging-in-Publication Data
Names: Ralph, Vincent, author.
Title: 14 ways to die / Vincent Ralph.
Other titles: Are you watching? | Fourteen ways to die
Description: Naperville, Illinois : Sourcebooks Fire, [2021] | Originally
    published in the United Kingdom by Penguin Books, an imprint of Penguin
    Random House UK, in 2020 under title: Are you watching? | Audience: Ages
    14. | Audience: Grades 10-12. | Summary: Seventeen-year-old Jessica
    Simmons becomes the star of a YouTube reality series, and she uses her
    fame to catch her mother's murderer.
Identifiers: LCCN 2021001025 (print) | LCCN 2021001026 (ebook)
Subjects: CYAC: Social media--Fiction. | Serial murderers--Fiction. |
    Grief--Fiction. | Justice--Fiction. | YouTube (Electronic
    resource)--Fiction. | Suspense fiction.
Classification: LCC PZ7.1.R3487 Aak 2021 (print) | LCC PZ7.1.R3487
    (ebook) | DDC [Fic]--dc23
LC record available at https://lccn.loc.gov/2021001025
LC ebook record available at https://lccn.loc.gov/2021001026

Printed and bound in Canada.
MBP 10 9 8 7

For my mother

14 WAYS TO DIE

1

"My mom was killed by the Magpie Man."

The guy nods, and I wait for him to reply.

When he doesn't, I say, "Fifty-one seconds from home, she was strangled to death and left to be rained on all night."

They say to start with a bang, and that's the biggest one I've got.

The man types words I can't see while the woman stares at me.

"I was seven," I say. I'm seventeen now.

The man clears his throat and asks, "Do you think you're the only applicant to have lost a parent?"

I shrug.

"You're not. But you *are* the only applicant whose mother was the victim of a serial killer."

The woman writes something on a notepad and pushes it toward him.

He nods and says, "We'll be in touch."

2

My name is Jessica Simmons, and I'm not your average internet star. But then I guess this isn't your average internet show.

The ads say it's something different—a real look inside the lives of real people. No scripts, no airbrushing, no scenes set up for your entertainment. Just you and a camera crew and whatever you want to show.

If this was halfway through the story rather than the start, I guess you'd call it a twist, because I'm not the kind of person to stream their life on YouTube. You'll have to take my word for it that this is out of character for me.

Mom was thirty-two when she died, the first victim of a man they still haven't caught. Number one on a list that now stretches to thirteen.

So if you ask why I want to be one of the five people to star in a new online show about them and only them, it's pretty simple.

I want to catch the Magpie Man, and this is how I'm going to do it.

3

It's been so long since Mom died that sometimes I doubt my own memories, even though the house is full of her pictures and her echoes live in the cracks on Dad's face.

It was Dad who gave the murderer his name. He said the Magpie Man liked shiny things and Mom was the shiniest of all. He said she'd been borrowed.

"Like a library book?" I'd asked, and he'd said sort of, but without a date to bring her back.

Now I realize it was for his benefit as much as mine: when a husband loses his wife, the last thing he needs is a kid asking questions.

When you're seven, you don't think your dad's full of shit, because he's the person who hugs you and kisses you and keeps you safe. Why would he lie?

He should have said that was our little secret. But he didn't, so I told everyone at school that the pretty moms would all be taken eventually, and Dad got called in for that.

Then when I was eleven, taking the bus home from school for the first time, we passed the shop where Mom used to work. The bus ride lasts twelve minutes and twenty-nine seconds, then it's fifteen footsteps to the alley.

I dared myself to walk through but refused every time.

When I finally found the courage, I counted one minute and forty-two seconds from one end to the other...from the shortcut to home.

She made it halfway, less than a minute from safety.

4

There are no rules for mourning.

When Mom died, the house felt gray and haunted, and Dad didn't look like himself anymore.

One day, all the pictures of her disappeared, gone as suddenly as she was.

It was Dad's way of preparing me for a truth he couldn't speak.

People told him to move, that it was unhealthy to live near the alley where your wife was murdered. But he ignored them.

I heard him on the phone once, saying he had already lost so much of her, why would he sell his remaining memories? And that night, the photos returned, filling every surface.

She was everywhere and nowhere all at once.

I cried, but they weren't real tears. I was copying the sadness of others rather than feeling my own.

I believed Mom would come back, convinced she would be

the next knock at the door, the next phone call, the next hug from the line of strangers whose touch felt so different from hers.

People told Dad to send me to a therapist, but again he ignored them. Grief makes what you have more precious, and by then, I was all he had left. So he held me tight through his refusal to make our loss any bigger than it had to be.

It was my grandma Nan who changed that. She got tired of Dad's stories and cried if I asked when we could visit Mom in the museum for shiny things. She said I would find out eventually, and the sooner the better, so she told me Mom was gone forever.

I called her a liar. I hated her. And then I cried the sharpest, heaviest, most unbearable tears of my life.

Your grief journey changes when you aren't looking. It moves in fractions: black shifting through a thousand shades of gray. It transforms into something else: a dull ache, a numbness that becomes the norm.

Websites told me to write a note and put it in a balloon and release it to heaven. Or make a memory quilt and fall asleep wrapped in Mom's best parts. Or make a wish list of all the things to do before *I* died.

I took pictures and hoarded the ones my parents had taken. I drew and painted and wrote shitty poetry and started a feelings journal. None of it worked, but I tried.

When I was fourteen, I got angry and took it out on a dad who refused to fight back.

Seven years after Mom was murdered and he was still a body carrying around a shattered soul, like the newspaper you wrap broken glass in. But it was more than that. He let himself be my punching bag. I treated him terribly, and he took it, because he loved me and because he knew that when the anger comes, it is vicious and all-consuming.

He hid his anger because he had to. I couldn't because I didn't know how.

When I googled "the Magpie Man," I got hundreds of articles but no answers, just the names of all the people he has murdered and comments from frustrated detectives.

He's still out there somewhere, still killing—the monster who took my mother.

And that is why the cameras can't start rolling soon enough.

5

My phone rings with a number I don't recognize, and when I answer, a man says, "Miss Simmons? It's Adrian...from *The Eye*. We've reviewed your application, and although the competition was fierce, we'd like you to be Monday."

This means that on the first day of every week for a month, I will be live online from the moment I wake up until midnight. If I'm not a complete flop, one month will become three.

The show is about real lives with unique twists—that's what the application form said. It claimed audiences have had enough of the same old formats.

I don't know if that's true, but I need to give it my best shot.

I see myself smiling in the mirror and stop, because this isn't supposed to be a happy moment. It's just the beginning.

"When do I start?" I ask.

Adrian says, "Three weeks. We have a few briefing sessions for you to attend where you'll get to meet the others." He sounds like he's reading off a sheet.

I don't particularly want to see them, but what choice do I have? I'm guessing they want to be famous rather than get justice, but I'll go and smile and do whatever has to be done to get my story across.

Anyone can put themselves online these days, but most get lost in the crowd. The trick is to find a stage big enough to be remembered, and this show offers that.

"We need to meet your father," Adrian says. "There are some things for him to sign."

That's what I'm afraid of, because Dad doesn't know I've applied. He thought my interview was a shopping trip.

"You'll have to come here," I say. "He doesn't like leaving the house in the daytime."

This isn't a lie. Dad prefers it when it's quiet outside. He shops when the supermarket is empty. He doesn't like crowds or conversations. Three times a week, he works night shifts in a factory, not because he has to but because we all need to escape sometimes.

I hope YouTube people are too busy to visit normal people's houses just to get a signature. I hope they send the paperwork and I can forge Dad's scribble and have more time to wear him down.

But without a pause, Adrian says, "No problem. We'll see you tomorrow."

Shit.

Before he hangs up, he says, "We have high hopes for you, Jessica."

I'm glad someone does.

6

Some broken people look fine from the outside, but not my dad. He wears his heartbreak like a second skin, his eyes gray and heavy, his grief shouting over everything else.

"Hey," I say.

He nods and puts his lips together in his best attempt at a smile.

"I have something to ask."

He reaches for the remote and mutes the TV.

I take a deep breath, almost chicken out, then say, "I've applied for a show. It's called *The Eye*."

He sighs and says, "Okay."

"It's on YouTube. I'll be filming my life, and they need your permission."

He stares me down, because there's only so long I can look into his eyes before I want to cry.

"You'll be filming your life?"

I nod.

"And who will be watching?"

"I don't know. Whoever wants to."

"No."

He unmutes the TV, and the sound makes me jump, drowning out the reply I'm planning in my head.

But I say it anyway, a shortened version, a three-word battle cry. "It's for Mom."

He stares at me, and this time, I don't look away.

I don't care if I cry. I don't care if, when I look long enough, I see the dad he used to be, mixed with the sadness he fights so hard to contain. I stare until my eyes are burning and I see Dad's *no* crumble in his mouth.

He turns off the TV, breathes deeply, and says, "Tell me more."

7

If I concentrate, I can still hear Mom's laughter, and if I close my eyes, I can picture Dad's smile, the real one, the one that could win an argument with a single flash. If I really focus, I can go back to certain moments, ones that didn't feel special at the time but are now all I have.

Mom would leave notes around the house for Dad to find: tiny reminders of how much she loved him. Once, a slip of paper fell into my bowl along with my cereal, and when I asked Mom what it said, she whispered, "Your dad can read it to you when he finds it."

Then she dropped it back into the box, and when he came downstairs, we watched him find the note and smile.

The message was just one word: *Always*.

They wore their love like some people wear designer brands. They advertised it with every look, every whisper, every secret smile. People used to say they were made for each other, and Mom would grin and say they were made for me.

The bottom falls out of my world every time I think that.

Sometimes I imagine my life if Mom was the one left behind, and I feel guilty because I know things would be different.

She wouldn't have broken down like Dad did. She would have fought through her pain and lived on.

8

When they arrive, I lead Adrian and his colleague into the living room and pray that Dad hasn't changed his mind.

"Mr. Simmons," Adrian says, holding out his hand.

Dad takes it like a robot, does the same with the girl, and then looks at me.

"So," I say, "where do we sign?"

Adrian laughs. "Someone's eager!" Then he says, "You're very brave for doing this."

I'm not sure who he's talking to, so I smile, and Dad does his best impression of happy.

Adrian says, "This is a wonderful setting." He's walking around the living room, going over to touch things, then stopping at the last minute, nodding to himself, and pointing at random places.

The girl must know why, because whenever he points, she writes something on her iPad.

"This is my assistant, Lauren," Adrian says.

She looks about my age, and when she rolls her eyes, I smile and imagine her being Adrian's boss one day.

He has a slap-worthy grin on his face, and he's treating our living room like a movie set, but that's a small sacrifice if it means finding the Magpie Man.

When we sit down, I grip my hands together in my lap, hoping no one sees them shaking.

"We're here to explain the process," Adrian says, "and to ensure you're fully aware of the...all-encompassing nature of the show.

"This is about five young adults who have experienced something extraordinary. People with stories to tell. It's the first reality show of its kind truly for the online generation. The camera crew will start filming before Jessica wakes up. At least that's what the audience will think. We'll stage that part. Unless you're a heavy sleeper. There will also be a highlights package, available the following day. We'll edit Jessica's best moments and post sixty-minute videos on her channel every Tuesday morning."

Dad looks at me and says, "You agreed to this?"

I nod and think back to our conversation last night. He listened to what I had to say. He sat in silence as I explained why this could help us find answers.

"If I reach enough people, I might actually find a witness or a clue or something," I'd said. "We can do this. All we need is a platform."

He didn't reply for a long time, and when he did, it wasn't what I wanted to hear.

"I'll talk to them," he'd said. "But no promises."

Seeing Dad's concern, Adrian stands up and holds his arms out. "This is powerful...an inside look at the life of a grieving family that refuses to be broken. A girl fighting back, seeking justice for her mother."

I catch him sneak a glance at my parents' wedding photo above the fireplace and imagine how many times that will be shown on screen.

Adrian can't contain his excitement, and I realize I was always going to be chosen. My patched-up family and its missing piece are gold dust, and I suddenly feel better, because if that's how he feels, maybe the audience will too.

I'm sure Adrian thinks this is just about me telling my story, that wanting to catch my mother's killer is a great hook. But he doesn't know how serious I am...or what I'm prepared to do.

Dad is slowly reading the contract, taking in every word. He stops every few pages and asks a question, rarely looking happy with the answer but continuing on anyway.

"Which school principal in their right mind would agree to this?" he asks.

Adrian smiles and says, "Every school involved is being paid well for their participation."

"Would you let your daughter do this?" he asks.

Adrian doesn't reply for a while, like he's drafting the answer in his head, then he says, "If I had one, I'd be wary too."

"Then why should I say yes?"

"Because this is a chance to tell her story. Something good might come out of it. Mr. Simmons, this show might even help people."

Dad glances at me, and I wonder if he sees through Adrian the way I can. Finally, he lays the contract on the table and says, "We're going to need some time."

Adrian smiles, but it wobbles at the edges. "We don't have much of that."

Ignoring him, looking straight at me, Dad says, "There are some things we need to discuss."

Adrian and Lauren exchange a look, then stand. "There's a get-together on Saturday," Adrian says. "It's a chance to meet the other stars." He calls them that, not me.

Adrian looks at my dad and says, "I understand this is difficult. But we wouldn't have picked Jessica if we didn't think she'd be a hit."

Dad stares at him, and I see a flicker of his fight. "I said we need some time."

9

When they're gone, I stand in the doorway, watching Dad holding the photograph of Mom he keeps within reach.

It was taken before I was born, my mother looking at something off-camera, her lips slightly parted. She looks stunning, blissful, safe.

I remember her in a million different ways, depending on how I feel or who's telling the story or who took the picture. This is Dad's memory, but like all the others, I've adapted it and made it my own.

I wonder what he thinks as he stares at it: if he feels sad that she's not around to make these decisions for him, if he blames her absence for my actions. Maybe it soothes him, because he hates having strangers in the house. Or maybe it's just habit, the face he turns to whenever he's alone.

I clear my throat, and he slides the photo into the side of his chair and looks up.

"They'll watch you sleep?" he asks.

"It's faked. We let them in, and I pretend to wake up. It's not as bad as it sounds. And the cameras stop filming at midnight. I'll be in control."

Dad shakes his head, but I keep going.

"I have a chance to do something. We have a shot at justice."

Dad's shoulders sag, and he breathes deeply. "There's no such thing as justice."

He reaches for the remote, but before he can end this conversation, I say, "No! I'm not letting you ruin this."

He looks at me with genuine shock, because this isn't how we speak to each other anymore. We don't shout. We don't disagree. We used to, when he soaked up my anger like a sponge. But over the last few years, we've learned to live in a quiet kind of turmoil.

Dad doesn't deserve my drama, but today is different. If he doesn't sign the contract, another parent for another applicant will, and I'll lose my chance.

"There *is* such a thing as justice," I say. "We've never seen it, but it exists. And this show might be our only chance. It's been ten years, and he's still out there. He's still killing, and he won't stop unless something changes.

"Remember what Mom used to say, about making yourself the hero of your story? This is our story, and we need to try."

I see the tears forming in Dad's eyes, and I could stop, but I'm done stopping.

"We could have three months to remind everyone what happened to us. We can put our story everywhere, talk about it every single week, and ensure it stays newsworthy. And we could do what the police couldn't. There are clues out there, Dad. Someone knows something."

I go to him and pull the photograph from the chair cushion and hold it up.

"She wants justice," I say. "She *needs* it. We all do. Please."

I let the last word hang there, begging to be rescued, until finally, Dad takes the photo from me, stares at his favorite memory, and says, "Okay."

10

You have to murder at least three people to be called a serial killer. The Magpie Man got there when I was nine.

The police hired profilers to paint a picture, to make clues when there were none, and I read every word. I became an expert in the one thing I truly hated.

They say he's between twenty-five and fifty, with a job that allows him to travel. This was long after he added Sophie Cresswell and Georgina Carson to his list. The list that started with my mom.

They think he could be married, with a partner who is easily manipulated or away a lot. They say he's likely to be ambivalent when the murders are reported and that he may make strange comments in a bid to secretly claim them as his own.

He's a "charmer" who may coerce his victims into situations they cannot escape. Although that wasn't the case with Mom.

That alley was her shortcut. She didn't follow someone in. They followed her.

Most serial killers have below-average IQs, but not the Magpie Man. The profilers think he is smart, methodical, desperate not to be caught.

His first three murders were in Doveton, Chester, and Glasgow. He didn't leave a single clue. Just a body and a number carved into their skin. That's all he ever leaves, no matter how closely the police look, no matter how many security cameras they check and witness appeals they make. His crimes are usually nine months apart, and the most recent, the thirteenth, was in September. She was named Lucy Halpern, and they found her in a park. That was five months ago.

Some people online think he's done now, because of the number. They think monsters finish when they reach a point made famous by horror stories. But I don't believe that, because when you've killed that many people, you don't stop.

It is only a matter of time before he kills again.

11

"Are you excited?" Adrian asks, and I fake the biggest smile I can manage.

"More than you know."

It's Saturday. We're in an elegant restaurant in London, and I'm the first to arrive.

I hand Adrian the paperwork, and he smiles, checks that every dotted line has been signed, then passes it to Lauren.

When you're a kid, London is the place where all the best surprises are, like Hamleys and musicals and museums. But now, alone, it reminds me I'm not that kid anymore.

I didn't sleep last night, worrying about who the other "stars" are and if their hooks are better than mine.

Lauren taps on her iPad while Adrian does a terrible job trying to keep me calm.

"You're probably really stoked to meet the others," he says, and I wonder where he gets his words from.

"I guess," I say, even though I'm shitting myself, because this is not exactly my comfort zone. But then neither is having my life streamed online, so I suppose I should get used to feeling permanently anxious on top of everything else.

"I think it's great what you're doing," he says. "Trying to find him when no one else could."

"Do you think I will?" I ask, and he smiles.

"Well, let's hope so."

Adrian stays quiet after that, and I know he isn't taking me seriously. He's making a mistake underestimating me. But this isn't a fight worth picking.

Eventually, the others arrive: two girls and two boys.

"Welcome," Adrian says, ushering everyone into their seats.

I sneak quick glances at each of them, catching one girl's eye and blushing.

The silence is already awkward when Adrian says, "Let's introduce ourselves."

"Okay," says a boy with hair that covers his ears and what looks like a scar creeping out from between the curls. "My name's Lucas Newman. I'm sixteen, and I used to be on TV."

"You're the little kid, from that comedy," one of the girls says, and Lucas nods.

Everyone recognizes him except me, because ten years ago, Dad and I didn't do what normal people did.

When no one goes next, Adrian says, "Ella, how about you?"

The girl who caught my eye says, "Well, I'm Ella and I'm seventeen. I'm pregnant...except...I've never had sex. My dad thinks it's an immaculate conception. It was his idea for me to do this."

I stare at her, waiting for the punchline. But she looks

deadly serious, and I wonder if she has an angle like I do or if she actually believes what she's saying.

Ella sees me staring and smiles, but she doesn't look happy. She looks like my nan when no one's watching.

When Adrian asks the other boy to speak, he sighs and says, "My name's Ryan. I'm nineteen, and my brother did something terrible."

We all look at each other, now connected by our curiosity, until Ryan says, "He was one of the men who went into the museum. He shot everyone, then blew himself up."

I remember that day, the breaking news, the hashtags, but it surprises me when Ryan says it was three years ago.

"I'm sorry," he says, and Ella reaches out to touch his hand, but he pulls it away.

"I'm Jess," I say. "My mother was killed by the Magpie Man."

Ryan looks up at me and nods, and I feel it: a moment of shared tragedy.

He reminds me of my dad: the way sorrow clings to his face, pulling on his lips and hanging heaviest in his eyes.

"And finally," Adrian says, smiling at the other girl.

"I'm Sonia," she says.

That's it. Just a name and a shrug of the shoulders. I look at Adrian, expecting him to push her for more, but he grins and explains that I'm Monday, Ryan is Tuesday, Ella is Wednesday, Lucas is Thursday, and Sonia is Friday.

"What if no one watches?" Ella asks.

We all look at Adrian, because secretly we've all thought it, and he smiles and says, "They'll watch."

"How can you be sure?" I ask.

He says, "Wouldn't you?"

I guess he's right. I suppose to start with, everyone will try it, and it's up to us to keep things interesting.

I've watched enough vloggers and reality shows to know that interesting means different things to different people. We watch hours of strangers doing nothing, talking shit, breaking up and making up, conversations we all have that are somehow so much better when someone else is having them.

"People will have their favorites," Adrian says. "Just be yourselves. That's why we picked you."

And then, calm as you like, he pulls out the twist.

"We haven't been completely honest with you," he says, and I'm terrified this is all a joke, that there is no show and, more importantly, no chance for justice. Or maybe it's already started. Maybe we're being filmed, and this is some sort of challenge.

"There will be five shows...initially. But only one of you will be continuing on."

We look at one another, realizing for the first time that we're in competition.

Lucas probably thinks he has an advantage because he used to be famous, but who remembers what was on TV years ago? And there's something about Sonia I don't trust, because the rest of us have stories, so why would they pick her if she doesn't?

"How long do we have?" Ryan asks.

"A month, as promised," Adrian replies. "But the three-month run is not guaranteed just because your viewing figures are high. They have to be the highest."

I thought I would get the extension no problem, but if it's only reserved for one of us, I don't have any time to waste.

12

Whenever I get home after I'm supposed to, I wish for something that will never happen. I want Mom to be standing there with a scowl on her face and a lecture coming to the boil. I want her to yell at me, asking where the hell I've been.

I want dinner to be silent and horrible, because she's annoyed at me and I'm annoyed at her for being so angry. And I want Dad to make everything okay with a silly comment that makes us laugh, our apologies coming through the giggles we can't contain.

But that doesn't happen. It never has. Mom was murdered before I was old enough to truly piss her off. She left my life with holes I fill with made-up memories, and I hate it.

I wish we'd had the raging fights you see on TV, the stupid arguments about nothing. I wish I didn't have quite so many missing pieces—the conversations we never had, the feelings we never shared.

What hurts most is her absence, the complete lack of her touch and her voice and her smell. That's what they don't tell you when you lose someone, that they're gone in more ways than you can count.

———

I get home from the meeting with the others and go straight upstairs to my room, where I've been writing the script for my first episode.

I know it's supposed to be spontaneous, but I can't risk that.

There's a plan, and I need to stick to it, which means saying certain things early on to set it in motion.

The quicker I go viral, the sooner people are talking about me, the better chance we have of finding him.

How will the others prepare? Will they change their plans now that Adrian has pitted us against one another? Ryan and Ella might, Lucas probably thinks he doesn't have to, and I have no idea about Sonia.

When Dad knocks on the door, I jump. He mumbles an apology and says, "How was your day?" He's trying to care even though he hates that I'm doing this.

"Okay," I say.

I could give him more. I could tell him about the others, about the competition, about the food we ate at the restaurant and how we didn't pay a penny.

But I stick with "okay" because I need to focus. Then, as he turns to leave, I say, "Dad…"

He smiles his broken smile, and I say, "Thanks for saying yes."

He nods, glances quickly around my room, then leaves.

I have a month, hopefully three, to catch a serial killer, but no one will watch if they hate me. I need to be likable, watchable, someone the audience can connect with.

I need to be the perfect reality star, which, thankfully, is nothing like being the perfect person.

13

I live in Doveton, a place only famous for the town next door. People only stop here to ask how close they are to Harmony. They only come in to go out the other side.

Harmony has a beach and restaurants and hotels. It has sand sculptors and galleries and a six-screen movie theater. Doveton has a Pizza Hut.

Before Mom's murder, it was safe, boring, unnewsworthy. The day before she died, a man committed suicide in the cemetery—all the town's tragedy wrapped up in a single week— and in the years since then, it has gone back to its old routine.

I go to school at St. Anthony's. He's the patron saint of lost things, which is kind of appropriate.

I have friends, even if it sounds like I've spent the last ten years moping in my room. I've known Hanna and Emily since sixth grade, and no matter who else has come and gone, we've always stuck together. They're my second attempt at BFFs. My first, Bernie and Aisha, fell away from me in the aftermath of Mom's murder.

In the middle of your grief, when it's too raw for most people to handle, they disappear, slowly stepping back until you turn around one day and they're gone.

Bernie lived next door to me when we were kids. Aisha lived two blocks over. But they faded away long before we outgrew each other. I have higher hopes for Emily and Hanna.

They don't know about the show yet, and I'm not sure how they'll react when I tell them. Hanna will probably be disappointed in me, and Emily will be jealous. But when she realizes how much she's going to be on camera, she'll be fine.

Hanna thinks she'll live in Doveton forever. If you want to piss her off, ask why there's no second *h*. She saves her dirtiest look for people who question her parents' spelling.

They own the ice-cream parlor in Harmony, running it with a mixture of passion and exasperation. I love watching them work: Hanna's dad yelling in Hungarian and her mom grumbling in Hindi.

Emily can't wait to leave. Her mom's a teacher's aide who cries all the time because her husband divorced her, and Emily says it's no fun living at home anymore. While my mom died, her dad just moved out, but the way her mom looks, you would think it was the other way around.

There are things you never say to a grieving person, like, "Keep your chin up," or "I know how you feel." And what you never, ever say is, "Pull yourself together." But secretly, that's what I want to say to Emily's mom. Then I feel guilty because everyone has their own shit to deal with.

They are going to be my costars—my two best friends—and their parents will be extras if they want to be. I haven't asked them yet. I haven't asked anyone. I might be surrounded by blurry faces.

But knowing how desperate people are to be famous these days, I doubt it.

14

"Can you explain this?" Mrs. Bradley asks, holding out a letter she's waving too quickly for me to read.

I shrug, and she hands it to me, and I see it's from the production company, requesting permission to film every Monday for up to three months.

I start reading, but she snatches it back before I'm halfway through and says, "So you want to be a star, Jessica?"

Mrs. Bradley is the school principal at St. Anthony's. She's stiff and serious with a face like a warning sign. I've never seen her smile.

She spends most of her time in her office. When she does come into a classroom, the temperature drops.

"I thought it would be good to put on my personal statement," I say, and she sits down and gestures for me to do the same.

"You realize I'm going to have to send a letter to the parents of every child in the school if I agree to this?" she says. "We can't have anyone on film without their permission."

"I know."

"What does your father think?"

"He's cool with it."

"I'd like to meet with him," Mrs. Bradley says. "Why are you doing this, Jessica?"

She has the power to stop this before it's even started, and I'm annoyed at myself for not realizing it earlier, for not trying to sweet-talk her.

"You know about my mom," I say, and she nods. "She always wanted to be famous." This is a lie. Everything I'm about to say is. "She dreamed of being an actress, but when I came along, well, she put it off. And then..."

Never underestimate the power of a pause.

Mrs. Bradley sighs, and I see the sympathy that used to follow me everywhere, her nods now sincere, her lips pushed into an understanding half smile.

"I'm not talented in that way," I say. "I don't do drama. I can't sing. But I can do this."

I stare at her until she says, "You don't have to. Your mother would be proud of you anyway."

People say that a lot. Strangers think pride is a universal feeling in dead parents. But if Mom is looking down on me, she's probably a little disappointed. I haven't done anything since she was killed, but I can change that now.

The daughter of the Magpie Man's first victim is going online every week for a month, and if he's as messed up as I think, he'll want to see how I turned out. In some sick way, I'm as much his achievement as I am Mom and Dad's, so if you're talking about pride, the Magpie Man is most likely to feel it.

I am his fucked-up creation after all.

15

Every Tuesday and Thursday, Nan comes over to clean the house and make sure we're eating healthily. Dad used to love cooking but not now.

On Friday nights, my parents would go through their cookbooks, ensuring we always had two completely new meals every week. They filled our cupboards and our stomachs with things I'd never heard of that nearly always tasted great.

But Dad doesn't do that anymore. Mostly he lets the microwave do the cooking. He buys what you can take out of a package and eat a few minutes later.

Nan is careful not to make anything that reminds us of Mom. She leaves spinach out of the Bolognese sauce and chili out of everything. Every year, she makes my second-favorite birthday cake, not knowing that I buy carrot cake from the baker's at least once a week, remembering Mom's recipe with every bite.

Nan talks to Dad, but he only says so much before looking

weary. Sometimes I see the frustration she tries to hide, an argument bubbling below the surface. But if she tells Dad what she's thinking, she does it when I'm not around.

She's been looking after us ever since Mom died, because she didn't think we could look after ourselves. And whatever Dad thinks, I like it, because it means there's someone else in the house. She doesn't only clean the bathroom; she temporarily washes away the gloom.

Dad was angry when she rewrote his story of what happened to Mom. I heard them arguing the day after Nan told me what the Magpie Man had really done.

That's the problem with love: people show it in different ways. Dad protected me with lies, while Nan thought truth was the best medicine. I think it's probably a little of both.

When I get home, she boils the kettle like she always does, and although I've been dreading this conversation, I say, "I'm going to be on the internet, and you might be, too, if you want to be."

She looks confused, so I explain the show to her. I say I'll be a little like a celebrity for a while.

"A celebrity," she says, rolling the word around her tongue. "Are you sure that's a good idea?"

It's probably not, but what choice do I have? I'm not doing this for that kind of fame. If it happens anyway, I'll deal with it.

Thirteen times, the Magpie Man has struck, and thirteen times, he has left nothing behind but a body.

"It's something I have to do," I tell Nan, and because she always wants the best for me, she agrees not to have her face blurred out.

"I'll have to get my hair done," she says.

16

"You can't be serious," Hanna says, and Emily, at exactly the same time, screeches and hugs me, and these are my two best friends in a nutshell.

"I'm *very* serious," I say.

Hanna shakes her head. "I thought you hated vloggers."

"I don't *hate* them. Besides, this isn't vlogging."

"What is it then?"

"It's reality programming for the online generation."

That's a quote from the contract we had to sign.

Hanna makes a face, and Emily says, "Well, *I* think it's brilliant."

I've known her so long I can tell exactly what she's thinking as she zones out, daydreaming about what she should wear for the first episode and what this means for her Instagram account.

"What if I don't want to be involved?" Hanna says, and although she would never do that, I play along.

"Then you'll be a blurry face, but I care what you think."

She laughs, losing the disappointed-parent act. "What did your dad say?" she asks.

"He didn't say no. Well, he did. But I convinced him. Mrs. Bradley said yes...after a little bit of emotional blackmail."

Emily touches her hair, and I can see the cogs whirring as she figures out if it needs cutting before the big day.

"Why are you doing this?" Hanna asks, so I tell them everything.

17

I have to sign more paperwork, giving the production team permission to access my phone and my social media accounts. This means that every time I get a notification or a message, the producers will see it. They can log in to everything, read everything, and, if they want, share everything with the rest of the world. They can put my messages on the viewers' screens, filling in the blanks.

What this also means is that I'm going to have to tell everyone not to write anything they don't want the whole world to know.

It's all in the welcome pack, which explains what will happen when we go live and how much of my life will be public property. The only place cameras aren't allowed is the bathroom. Everywhere else is fair game.

Yesterday, Adrian's team turned our home into a studio. In every corner of every room, there are tiny cameras, and if you're quiet, you can hear them when they turn.

The letters from Mrs. Bradley have gone out, and people at school are looking at me differently.

"They're jealous," Emily says.

"Some of them," says Hanna. She still isn't completely on board, but she understands why I'm doing this, and when your mom was murdered, people tend not to argue.

Sometimes I catch her looking at me like she's trying to figure something out, like she knows this is out of character and is worried about my well-being. I'm used to those looks, although it's been a while since I saw one.

I'm not outgoing. I don't crave attention like some people at school—the ones who treat drama as their bread and butter. Maybe I would have if Mom was still around. Maybe I would have grown into a completely different person. Now I'm forcing myself to be someone else to get my story across.

Eventually, even when your mother was murdered, people stop shouting for you, and you have to shout for yourself.

Emily shows me her signed permission slip and says, "Tell them they can only film my good side," and I'm not entirely sure she's joking.

Two weeks from now, I'll be followed by a camera crew, and the weirdness of that is starting to sink in.

"My mom took some convincing," Emily says. "She's worried I'll get a stalker."

"If anyone's going to get a stalker, it will be Jess," Hanna says.

"No one's getting a stalker," I say, although the thought of it makes me feel cold inside.

I imagine quitting, calling Adrian and saying I've changed my mind. But I've been doing that all my life—hiding by doing nothing.

It's my turn to seek.

18

Ads for my channel start streaming online, and by the end of the week, my Instagram follower count has gone through the roof.

Below a picture of me, taken specially for the show, it says:

The Eye: Hunting the Magpie Man
Can she catch the killer? Subscribe here to find out.

This is actually happening. It's what I wanted, but the nerves come anyway. Every image of me on screen, every notification, stings in a way I can't describe.

I reach for Mom's bathrobe and search for her smell. It's long gone but it still helps.

"I'm doing this for you," I whisper, then I imagine how the others feel.

Ella, Ryan, Lucas, and Sonia have ads of their own. But this is a competition I have to win. Mom's story is too important to be lost after a month.

I google Ryan's brother, the one who went into that museum and shot twenty-seven people before blowing himself up. How do you deal with something like that, when someone you love turns out to be a monster?

I search Lucas's Wikipedia page and watch old clips of his show on YouTube. He looks like every other little kid on TV, and I wonder how much money he made and if once you have a taste of celebrity, you hate the taste of everything else.

Then I Facebook-stalk Ella, and there's no sign of a boyfriend, and I wonder which part is the lie—the pregnancy or the cause.

And finally I search for Sonia and can't find her anywhere. She doesn't have any social media accounts, and she's nowhere on Google, and I wonder why they chose her.

19

The night before we go live, there's a rehearsal, which seems strange to me, because isn't this supposed to be spontaneous?

But the director, Danny, who I have never met before, says, "We want your introduction to be perfect. We don't want anything going wrong in the very first scene."

He's older than me, but he still looks too young to be doing this. When I catch his eye, he stares a little too long, and I feel a blush rise in my stomach and crawl up my neck. Everything about him is neat and tidy—his hair, his clothes, his attitude.

While my panic is growing by the second, Danny radiates calm, and I can already see why they hired him. He's not impressed by me. He doesn't treat me like a "star." He sees me as something to move around a scene.

"What do you wear to bed?" Danny asks.

"I'm sorry?"

"When you go to sleep," he says, "what do you wear?"

For a second, I think about telling him where to go, but then I realize that for the next month, nothing is private. He isn't being creepy. He isn't coming on to me. He's doing his job.

I pull my pajamas from under my pillow and hold them out to him, wishing they were clean and matching.

"Cool. Put them on." He sees my face and says, "We need to replicate your wake-up experience."

After I've changed in the bathroom, Danny says, "Okay, pretend it's the morning."

I climb into bed, and he asks, "What side do you wake up on?"

"I don't know."

He makes a face. "What side do you fall asleep on?"

"My right," I say.

Danny nods. "We'll go with that. Lie on your right side and close your eyes...and...action!"

Danny clears his throat, then again, and I guess he's trying to tell me something. So I do what I think I do when I wake up, and when I open my eyes, I see Michael the cameraman across the room.

When I don't do anything, Danny waves his hands and mouths, "Go," but I just lie there until he says, "Cut!" Then, "You can't do that tomorrow. That's what this is for: to prepare you."

This is why they'll be here in the mornings. Even with cameras all over the house, they need to ensure the best possible start.

We do the scene again, and they're happier the second time. While Michael packs up, Danny speaks to me like I'm a real person and not a prop.

"You'll be fine," he says. "I promise."

"How do you know?" I ask.

He smiles and says, "I'd be more worried if you were taking this in stride."

Each of the five of us has a different director, and I wonder if I got lucky.

He is definitely nice to look at, and this quick change of character suggests he knows he's a little bit of an asshole at work and is trying to make up for it now.

They're about to leave when Dad appears in the hallway and says, "Could I have a word?"

He's looking at Danny and Michael, who exchange a glance, then follow him into the living room.

What now? If Dad is having second thoughts, he'd tell me first. At least I hope so. But he doesn't waste words these days, so whatever he has planned, it must be important.

Dad sits up, his back straight and his eyes focused, and I remember how big he used to seem to me.

He looks at me, swallows, then says, "I don't agree with this. But I've said yes because of what it means to Jess."

For a second, I think that's it, then he swallows again, breathes out, and says, "She's seventeen. I want you to remember that."

I can't help but smile, because he's trying to intimidate them. If I ever bring a boy home, I guess this is what will happen. I love it when my old dad shines through, even if this time, it's pretty embarrassing.

"You have nothing to worry about," Danny says. "We're good at our jobs. And we only want the best for Jessica."

"Do you have kids?" Dad asks.

"I have a daughter," Michael says. "She's almost six months."

That surprises me, because he doesn't look like a father. He seems a few years older than Danny, but a lot messier, like a hipster who's been living in the wild.

"And you?"

Danny shakes his head. "Maybe one day."

He looks awkward, and when I catch his eye, he makes a face, and I feel a flicker in my stomach and remind myself to wear clean pajamas tonight.

"We understand," Danny says. "You want to protect her. We won't do anything to jeopardize that."

"I hope not," Dad says, and although he's smiling, it sounds like a warning.

20

When they've gone, I look around my room at the cameras and the empty coffee cups, but I barely see them.

All I can focus on is the picture of me and Mom, taken the day I was born, seven years and fifty-two days before she died. She looks exhausted but also happy.

"I'm scared," I tell her. "What if this doesn't work?"

Wherever she is, wherever she isn't, I talk to her. Or I talk to myself and hope she's listening.

"I've made a choice," I whisper. "I'm sorry if that makes you angry. I'm sorry if you don't want me filling our house with cameras and strangers and putting Dad through all this again. But I've waited ten years. I've waited so long for them to catch him, and they haven't. I don't think they ever will... not unless something changes.

"I'm scared I'll mess it up, Mom. But I'm terrified of feeling this way for a lifetime. If we made the Magpie Man, maybe we can destroy him too."

I leave a gap for her to reply, with a sign or a coincidence, but she never does.

She only smiles from the picture by my bed, and that will have to be enough.

21

I don't open my eyes right away. I lie there, feeling increasingly uncomfortable, knowing there's a camera pointed at me and that out there, on phones and iPads and computer screens, I'm being watched instead of the morning news.

I can hear Danny breathing, and I imagine the moment right before Mom came face-to-face with the Magpie Man. When she sensed him but couldn't see him. When she knew her time was almost up.

I fight the urge to cry, trying to slow my heart by focusing on the memory of my mother for five, ten, fifteen seconds.

When I do open my eyes, I see the blinking red light on Michael's camera. Danny is sitting on my beanbag with a smile on his face.

His smile says: *It's showtime.* It says: *Action!* It says: *Welcome to the rest of your life.*

I lie in bed, stretching under the covers, trying to act as

normal as possible. I wonder if Lucas, Ella, Sonia, and Ryan are tuning in, seeing what I do well and what I mess up.

There are two ways to go now. I either get it right or I don't. I either start with a bang or I choke.

Danny is only a director in terms of camera angles and lighting. He's only there to capture whatever I do. There's no script except the one I've rehearsed in my head over and over again.

So with time already running out, I sit up, stare into the camera, and say, "Hi."

22

"My name is Jessica Simmons," I say, "and my mom was killed by the Magpie Man."

I don't have time to ease them in. I have to start strong.

"Ten years ago, on January twenty-second, my mom was killed in the alley near my house as she walked home from work. She was murdered by a man who was just getting started."

This speech has gone through more rewrites than I can count.

"I was seven when she died. When my dad told me, he took the horror away. He told me she was taken by someone who collected beautiful things, and that was where the name came from.

"My dad called him the Magpie Man, and I told my friends at school, and they told their parents. Somewhere along the line, the newspapers started putting it on their front pages, and suddenly, we'd made a monster."

I look at Danny, making sure this is okay, and he nods but doesn't smile.

"We didn't know he would become a serial killer. My mom was the first person he murdered. But there are thirteen now, and he won't stop. He will keep going until he's caught.

"He killed Lucy Halpern in September. I wish I didn't know her name. I wish I didn't know any of their names. It's been five months since he last struck. If he sticks to his pattern, we have around four months to catch him.

"I don't want to be famous. I don't want anything except justice. You can judge me any way you want. I don't care. This show isn't about me. It is about the thirteen women who are gone...and the one man who took them.

"Maybe you know something. Maybe you think you do. Maybe you have always suspected your dad or your brother or your neighbor. Maybe now you should tell someone."

I don't know if this is what they expected when they signed me up, but this is what they're getting. She was forgotten once, but she won't be forgotten again.

"If you're watching," I say, calming my breathing, steadying myself for the end, "if the monster who murdered my mother is watching this, you should know you didn't break me. You made me. And if no one else can stop you, I will."

23

I stand up and walk to the bathroom, because that is the only place I can break down.

There's no yelling "Cut!" Not until midnight. Until then, the cameras film everything, and I need to stay strong. But here I can quietly sob into a towel, the courage I felt during my speech crumbling.

Mom makes me strong. But if I remember too much, everything fractures.

"You're my star," she said once, sitting next to me on the top step as I cried about a play I didn't want to do.

"Don't worry about the other parents," she whispered. "Focus on me."

I did. I was fine. And three months later, she was dead.

When I've run out of tears, I shower, get dressed, and walk back out, ready for a new scene.

24

At school, Emily runs over and hugs me and says, "You were amazing," then she looks directly at the camera and smiles.

She has a new haircut and is wearing even more makeup than usual, and I don't recognize any of her clothes. She's taking her costar role very seriously.

Hanna doesn't pay attention to the camera. She reaches out and squeezes my hand, and I smile and nod. This is our silent sign that I'm okay.

All around us, people are stopping and staring—the ones the audience can see and the blurry faces. How it works is facial recognition. Once Mrs. Bradley had the permission slips, she gave the production company the school photos of everyone who was happy to be filmed. The cameras have been programmed to recognize those faces while all the others are automatically blurred out, so they are just school uniforms with smudges for heads.

The woman in the bakery, the guy in the fish shop, the supermarket cashiers and bus drivers and strangers in the street, because the camera doesn't have a record of their faces, they are all blurs.

A few tenth-grade girls are giggling and pointing at Danny and trying to catch his eye, but he pretends not to notice.

On the bus on the way to school, when the camera was nowhere near my hand, he squeezed it the way I always wished Dad would, just to pretend everything was all right. And suddenly, there was another feeling in the mix, one I wasn't prepared for. If I think about it too much, I start to panic, because I have a job to do, and there's no time for distractions.

Some people have their phones out, watching my livestream and trying to sneak their way into the shot. But most keep their distance.

During classes, it's clear a couple of teachers like that I have a camera crew with me and others not so much.

Mr. Collins, our English lit teacher, does his best to keep his back to us for the whole period, which I'm sure is against the rules of the Department of Education.

I don't blame him. I think teachers have the right to be blurred out just as much as their students, but Mrs. Bradley decided for them. I don't feel guilty, though, even if he gives me the evil eye as I leave, like it's my fault he's going to be observed once a week for at least a month and not only when the teacher evaluators visit the classroom.

I have two free periods today, and for the first one, Hanna and I make small talk while Danny and Michael sit in the corner. No one else speaks to us. A few kids hang around, hoping to be extras, but most avoid the room altogether, watching from the doorway or quickly making a detour to the other side of the eleventh-grade homeroom when they notice the camera.

Seniors get an entire upstairs area in the main building. However, our homeroom is an old portable hut that used to be two classrooms but is now full of secondhand sofas and a microwave. At least no one bothers us here.

Hanna clearly doesn't feel comfortable being filmed, but she's doing her best, and I'm grateful she hasn't left me.

For my second free period, with both Hanna and Emily in class, I pretend to read while Michael films what has to be one of the most boring hours in history.

Adrian told us to do what we always do. He said people would watch when they could and that our highlights the following morning will make up a large portion of our views. But I'm still worried I should be doing more.

In between classes and at lunch, younger students wait on the edges, getting close but not too close, and when I get home, I still have absolutely no idea who is watching this.

We get my ratings on Tuesdays, so soon I'll find out if this was a huge waste of time.

I worry that only four people watched long enough for it to count—Emily, Hanna, Dad, and Nan—then double it because Lucas, Ella, Sonia, and Ryan must have. But eight viewers doesn't justify anything.

If it's not a lot higher than that, I'll be ditched in less than a month.

25

I have dinner alone while Dad sits in the other room.

Michael focuses his camera on random objects while I eat, the empty can of soup on the counter, the overflowing trash can, the sad man in the living room.

Dad tries hard, but sometimes his efforts get lost in the storm. He has bad days and better days, and he finds it easier to pretend when there are fewer people watching.

When it's just the two of us, if we're lucky, the grief loses its grip. Those moments are rare, but with the world watching, it won't happen tonight.

Dad may not realize it yet, but he is going to be a star too. If *star* is the right word.

I've already seen Danny watching him, knowing he can get two for the price of one, the dead mom's daughter and the dead wife's husband. I don't blame him. It certainly makes for a better show than me eating a bowl of soup.

I haven't spoken directly to the camera since this morning. I don't want to overdo it. And I haven't checked my phone, scared that my social media feeds will kill my hopes of a good opening episode before the ratings have even come through. I wonder if the producers have been searching my notifications all day, choosing the best ones to put on screen.

After dinner, I lie on my bed, listening to Twenty One Pilots, and it's surprisingly easy to forget the camera is even there.

Danny and Michael have left. They sign off at six, leaving the tiny cameras in the corners of every room to do their job for them.

If I do go out, the contract says I have to wear two body cams they gave me. One is a head cam that films what I can see, and the other ties around my chest and points back at me like a selfie stick.

I watch the camera watching me. At least on TV shows, there are people to talk to. At least vloggers fill every second with noise. If I want to go viral, I need to keep talking and hope something clicks.

"Are you watching?" I ask. "Of course you're not."

I go back to staring, and then, because I'm only going to beat the other four if I try harder, I say, "Why did you do it? Why her?"

It's what I've always wanted to ask: of all the people out there, why did he choose my mom? Was she handpicked, or was it bad luck? Did he follow her for weeks, waiting for his moment? Or was she in the wrong place at the wrong time?

"I hate you," I whisper. "I've never met you, but I fucking hate you."

I hear the camera whirring, and I imagine someone in the studio zooming in on my face.

"Do you have a mother?" I ask. "Do you love her?"

No one answers. But for the first time, I can picture him watching.

It's the darkness outside. That's when your nightmares come alive.

"Do you like the name we gave you?" I ask. "The Magpie Man... It sounds so harmless...unless you know the truth."

I'm not afraid to say his name. I will shout it from the rooftops if I have to.

I listen to my breathing and imagine Dad in the other room, choosing between old movies and late-night, one-way conversations with his daughter.

"I love you, Dad," I say, just in case.

And then I get ready for bed and pull the covers over my face so no one can see me.

At midnight, the camera clicks off, and I finally fall asleep.

26

When I wake up, I don't open my eyes right away.

It's Tuesday, so no one is watching, but it still takes a moment to realize that even after only one day of filming. I feel relieved, then scared how quickly it went.

At school, the people who stayed in the background come a little closer without the camera, and some of them even talk to me.

"Hey," a freshman girl says. "Great show."

"I'm looking forward to the next one," someone shouts behind me, and when I turn, there's a group of tenth-grade boys who nod in unison.

When Hanna sees me, she says, "It wasn't completely awful."

She says it with a smile, but still Emily huffs and says, "That part when you said you loved your dad. It had me tearing up."

"You saw that?"

They both nod, and Hanna says, "Do you think he was watching?"

I assume she means Dad, so I say, "I don't know. He doesn't like me doing it."

"No," Hanna says. "*Him*. Do you think he heard what you said?"

"Probably not."

"I think he did," Emily says, and that scares me, because the thought of talking to the Magpie Man, even through a screen, makes me feel sick despite being exactly what I want.

We have English first, and Mr. Collins seems relieved that he can look at us today, but he still seems irritated with me.

This is nothing new. He's usually irritated with someone in the class.

Mr. Collins is tall and thin with thick black eyebrows that make it look like he's permanently angry. He likes us to remember our books and forget our sense of humor.

At lunch, I get a text from Danny that says: Viewing figures are in. You got just over 274,000. That's a great start!

I have to get Emily to confirm how many zeroes there are, because I keep counting three.

"It *is* three," she says. "Two hundred and seventy-four *thousand*."

I try to process the number but I can't. More than a quarter of a million people watched me for at least an hour yesterday. That's how the ratings are measured. Plenty more turned off after a few minutes, but 274,000 kept watching, and most of them subscribed.

This plan might work after all.

27

When I check Facebook, I have 807 friend requests, and on Instagram, I have over 9,000 new followers.

I have tons of messages, and it takes me all day to get to the most important one, the one from a man who says he knows exactly how I feel because his mom was killed by the Magpie Man. His name is Ross, he's twenty-five, and his mother, Sharon, was the fifth victim.

I feel nervous before I feel excited. I always hoped someone like me would watch, but that doesn't stop me being suspicious.

I check out his Facebook page. He has a husband. He looks happy. But then so do I if you ask me to smile for a camera.

When I'm not live, my messages are kept by the producers, used as a recap for the following Monday if they're juicy enough.

Hi, Jessica. I saw your speech and thought it was amazing. I'm sorry if this is strange, but if you ever

want to talk, I'm here. I won't bother you again. I just
wanted to reach out.

I don't reply right away. Instead, I stalk him, going further
and further back in his timeline until I see a gap big enough to
be the one when he was grieving.

It takes a certain type of person to update their status when
a parent has just been murdered, and Ross isn't one of them.
I'm grateful for that. It's another sign that he's a normal guy
thinking he's doing the right thing by contacting me.

It also means I'm ahead of schedule, because mine wasn't
the only family destroyed by the Magpie Man, and I need all
the help I can get.

28

"You should get the verified badge," Emily says. "I've already seen some fake accounts in your name and…"

"And what?"

"The Magpie Man has one now. A Twitter account, I mean." She hands me her phone.

The profile picture is a magpie, and the account has only tweeted once, but it already has more than a thousand followers.

"It's not really him," Hanna says, and while I know she's right, it still makes me shiver.

The first tweet says:

I'm watching you, Jessica.

I feel the tears come again and try to blink them away, but they slip out anyway.

When Hanna notices, she squeezes my hand. "There are some creepy people out there."

I take a few deep breaths, desperate to stay calm. It's only going to get worse. I knew that before I started. And if I can't handle this, I might as well quit now. There were always going to be disgusting people, creeps forcing their way into my story, because that's what they do. But it still feels overwhelming.

"I'm sure he'll be blocked," Hanna says, but even if he is, another will spring up in his place.

I think about deleting my Twitter account, but I'll have to check the contract, because it probably says I can't.

To change the subject, I tell them about Ross's friend request.

"Is he cute?" Emily asks. When I say he's gay, she says, "I refer you to my original question."

She smiles, and I can't help laughing, and then Hanna says, "Does he know anything?"

"I don't think so. I think he's just being nice."

Although I hope it's more than that. I hope eventually, if I can speak to everyone, I will find a pattern the police couldn't see.

29

If I'm going to beat the others, I need to keep up.

Tuesday—Ryan—passed me by, so I watch his highlights.

What the producers do is cut together our best scenes and turn our day into an hour: a neat and tidy roundup for people who didn't watch us live. The highlights are then added to our channel: sixty-minute videos you can click on whenever you want. Those, combined with the live stats, determine which of us gets three months rather than one.

Once you've done it yourself—talked to the world through a camera lens with no idea how many people are watching—it's interesting to see how others do it.

Ryan lives with his mother and older sister, and neither of them like what he's doing.

I watch them argue with him, his mother turning directly to the camera and saying, "This isn't right!"

While Dad's grief has seeped into his pores, Ryan's family's sadness has expanded, bursting out without warning. I wonder how he got them to sign the contract. Did he guilt-trip them like I did?

When Ryan's mother isn't shouting, she sits in the corners of shots, watching as he apologizes for his brother's actions.

Today—Wednesday—it's Ella. She is still pregnant and still claiming to be a virgin. She's in her living room with her parents and her brother, and she's holding her tummy, stroking a bump you can just about make out. I guess it's her version of product placement.

Ella is watching something—not herself—and her parents are laughing while her brother pushes his feet into Ella's face from the other end of the sofa. She swats them away, but they come again.

Sibling rivalry is a game I'll never play. The rules don't make sense to me. Maybe if Mom hadn't died, I would have a brother or sister. Maybe I was all she wanted.

Ella doesn't seem to be trying very hard.

Most of us are in this to promote something—justice or a miracle or our own brand.

Lucas, the former child actor, is on tomorrow, and I bet he won't waste time playing happy families. He wants to get his career back, and Ryan wants to say sorry for his brother, and Sonia...who knows what she wants?

Watching Ella and her family makes me go downstairs to be with Dad. He's at the table, fiddling with computer parts, and he shows me the smallest smile when I sit across from him. For a while, I watch him work.

He used to work in IT. Now he spends hours fixing things that anyone else would throw out.

"Did you watch me on Monday?"

Dad sighs but doesn't answer. Instead, he says, "I should have told you from the start that your mother was never coming back."

It catches me by surprise, and I don't know how to reply.

I know Dad was protecting me. He didn't mean to create a monster when he named the Magpie Man. But he did, and he lives with that every day.

"I thought I was doing the right thing," he says. "I'm sorry."

I see the effort it took for him to say that rise and fall behind his eyes. Then I kiss his cheek, and for a moment, I see my old dad.

He is still in there, buried deep but breaking through.

30

"My name is Lucas Newman," Lucas says. "You probably remember me from *The Wordsmiths*."

I don't.

"You're probably wondering what I've been up to since the show ended."

I'm not.

This is how Lucas introduces himself to his audience. He's expecting ready-made fans, guaranteed subscribers: women who were girls when they watched him when he was a kid in a comedy about a family of writers. I think he's playing this wrong.

I get bored and turn it off, checking the comments for anything that might mean something.

Every day, more people want to be my friend, more people want to follow me, and more people tell me how sorry they are about what happened to my mom. And every day, there are leads that quickly become dead ends.

Every day, strangers say they know who the Magpie Man is, but whenever I allow a message request, they ask for my number, ask what I'm wearing, ask me to send photos, and I'm back to square one.

Some comments accuse my dad, so I quickly scroll past those. Others mention random people, so I write a list and look for patterns. But the same name never comes up twice. And then there are the conspiracies—the ones that say she was having an affair and was killed by a dumped lover, the ones that say she's still alive, the ones that say I did it.

It used to upset me, but it's something I've grown up with— the idiots who think they've solved the crime.

I reread Ross's message, check his social media one last time for any obvious psycho signs, then reply.

> Thanks for contacting me. It's good to hear from someone who knows how it feels. I'm sorry for your loss.

If he's anything like me, he will hate that, but it's what you say, even if you hate hearing it. The guidebook for talking to grieving people is short and full of crap, but until someone writes a better one, it's all we've got.

I make myself some toast and do a slice for Dad, which may or may not be eaten by the time Nan comes over. Today, she will tidy the house and cook us dinner, and by next Tuesday, the place will be a shithole again.

I should notice before I open the front door, but I step out and close it behind me, then realize there are people standing there.

"Jessica," one of them says, "can we ask you a few questions?"

The woman has a notepad and pen, and next to her, a man takes my picture.

"What sort of questions?" I ask.

"We love the show," the woman says. "Do you think they'll ever find the person who did it?"

When it happened, there were camera crews and reporters everywhere. They left us alone once they realized Dad was never leaving the house again and Nan told them all to get lost. It's been a long time since anyone cared what was happening here.

"I hope so," I say.

I can feel the photographer capturing my face from every possible angle.

"Has anyone been in contact yet?" the woman asks. "I'm Sara, by the way. I'd love to tell your story."

She doesn't know about Ross. But she will on Monday. Everyone will see his message and my reply, and I wonder how long it will be before they're camping outside my front door, until they're fighting each other for a comment, not letting one reporter record every word. Hopefully, it won't be long.

"Who do you work for?" I ask.

Sara smiles. "The *Doveton Messenger*."

That's not enough. I need bigger papers, famous papers. I need to be on front pages that people pay for, home pages they check the moment they wake up.

"If you ever want to talk," she says.

I stop and look at her. "If I ever want to talk, you'll listen, right?"

She smiles and nods, and I say, "Thank you."

That seems to make her happy, and when I start walking, she doesn't follow me.

If she wants to help, she could start by putting the murders back on the front page. Every single newspaper could remind the world what he did, over and over, until he is caught.

31

If Danny had his way, this would happen on Monday, but the first time I meet Ross, I don't want anyone watching.

He lives close enough for us to meet in town.

Not all the victims shared the same zip code. Some were hundreds of miles away. That's why the Magpie Man wasn't called a serial killer at first, because nine months after Mom was murdered, his second victim was found in Chester, and the first thing they thought was copycat.

Then he went to Glasgow for number 3, and the message boards said it was a cult. They said it wasn't two people, it was hundreds, slowly adding to a body count that would never stop. I was terrified when I read that, imagining a group of murderers all over the country.

When Margaret McKenzie was killed in London and they found the number 4 carved into her chest, the police appointed a special detective who was as useless as everyone else. And then Sharon Custis was killed a few miles from Doveton, and they finally blamed him for all five.

Maybe that's why Ross contacted me—because we share more than a story.

I often think about the left behind: people like me whose lives are destroyed but who must keep living. The Magpie Man is responsible for a lot of those people, and I'm about to meet another one.

If something huge happens on the days I'm off-screen, I am supposed to film it myself with the minicams. But this is part of a bigger plan, and I can't spoil it. I want to gather up the left behind, and Ross is my first chance.

Because I'm not totally stupid—after what happened to Mom—I tell Hanna what I'm doing, and she comes with me.

Outside Starbucks, she says, "If it gets weird, just shout," then she walks in, orders her coffee, and sits down.

A few minutes later, I do the same, making sure she can see me.

We're twenty minutes early. My coffee will be finished or cold by the time Ross arrives. But this is how to be careful.

Every now and then, Hanna looks at me, then away. No smile, no wink, no sign we know each other. She's better at this kind of thing than Emily, who would make it blatantly obvious we were together. Hanna just sits reading, or pretending to read. She would make a great spy.

I keep checking the time, and almost exactly when we agreed, Ross arrives, looking as nervous as I feel.

He sees me and holds his hand up, then comes over without ordering. "Hi," he says.

"Hi."

"You want another?" He points at my empty cup, and when I shake my head, he walks to the counter.

He seems normal, just a guy meeting a girl in a coffee shop to compare murder stories.

It takes forever for him to get his coffee, and when he comes back, he sits across from me and sighs. "This is weird."

I smile. "It is. Thanks for coming."

"Thank *you*. I wasn't sure you would even reply to my message."

He doesn't know I was banking on him, or at least people like him, getting in touch.

Up close, you can see his hair is already going gray at the sides, and he keeps looking at me, then away. He rolls his wedding ring around his finger, only stopping when he drinks. In the moments when his hands aren't doing anything, they shake.

"So," I say. "What do you think of the show?"

Ross smiles and says, "I've only watched you. I'm not interested in the others."

I feel a flicker of hope, because if he feels that way, maybe others do too.

"When I found out you were doing it, I had to watch," he says. "I had to see what you were like."

"And?"

"The speech you made...I wasn't expecting that. It brought everything back. I want to help you."

"No one can figure it out," I say. "The police can't stop him."

Ross nods. "Tell me about it. You'd think there'd be a break-through by now. You'd think he would have slipped up...that someone would know something."

"I used to think he was a monster," I say. "Not like a bad man but an actual monster. That would explain why he was never caught."

In movies, monsters aren't caught by detectives. They are caught by reluctant heroes. They bite off more than they can chew.

When you're a kid and the Magpie Man keeps killing, your imagination eventually does the rest.

"You weren't the only one," Ross says. "I've thought so many different things through the years. It's good to find someone who understands."

"What happened to your mom?" I ask.

I already know. I've memorized every fact about every victim. But I need to hear him tell it, to make sure he is who he says he is.

"I was eighteen," Ross says, his voice cracking slightly. "Mom asked me to go buy some milk but I refused to. I was an asshole back then. So she went out instead. She went out to make sure *I* had milk for my cereal the next morning. She never came back."

I know what happened.

Sharon Custis—Ross's mom—was on her way back when she was strangled, the number 5 carved into her belly, the milk her son refused to buy lying next to her in the street.

"I was such a shit," Ross says. "Why didn't I just say yes?"

If he had, she might still be here. But it's not Ross's fault. He didn't kill anyone. He made a decision he can never take back, and that moment claws at him whenever he closes his eyes.

I didn't send my mom into that alley, but I think about it every day. I wonder if I was the reason she took a shortcut, if she was so desperate to see me that she tried to shave five minutes off her journey.

Ross has his head down, and I catch Hanna looking at me. She raises her eyebrows, and I quickly nod, letting her know everything is okay.

If I was a different person, I would reach out and touch Ross's arm or say words designed to help. But I know it's useless, the things people do because they have to do something, the words they say because they can't stand the silence.

For people like me and Ross, silence is better than bullshit. So I let him reminisce or regret, until he looks up, shakes his head, and says, "I'll do anything to help you, Jessica. We can't let him get away with this."

"That's good," I reply, "because there is something I'd like you to do."

He stares at me, and when I see his eyes tear up, I almost stop. But I don't, because I can't.

"Will you find the others for me?" I ask. "The families of the other victims…will you ask them to help?"

32

On Sunday, Danny calls and asks if we're all set for tomorrow.

"Anything happen I should know about?" he asks.

He knows I met Ross because he has access to my Facebook, so there's no point lying to him.

"Did you film it?" he asks. When I say no, he says, "Jess, you have to start taking this seriously."

"I *am* taking it seriously. That's why I'm doing this. It's about as serious as it could get."

"It doesn't seem that way," he says. "What if you only get four weeks? What if one of the others beats you in the ratings? What then?"

"They won't," I say, angry that he can't see what this means to me. "My story is important."

"Then prove it."

We're quiet for a while, then Danny says, "We can't confuse the audience. They need to know who everyone is. What if Ross suddenly turns up on-screen?"

"He won't," I lie. "He doesn't want to be famous."

I should be honest with Danny. I should tell him my plan comes in stages—first the introduction, then the search for clues, all tied into the hope that someone says something important.

Then the left behind. The others, like me, desperate for justice and ready to tell their own stories. It's easy to ignore one sad girl on the internet. But it's a lot harder to ignore an army of them. That's why I need Ross's help.

I should let Danny in on my plan so he gets off my back. But I'm scared it won't work. I'm terrified I've overthought it or underestimated people's apathy, and in four weeks, this will be finished before it really started.

"Okay," I say. "From now on, I'll film everything."

It's easier to say that than tell him about things that might never happen.

33

Throughout the day, they fill the viewers in by putting my messages on-screen, so they know who Ross is and what we said to each other online. They don't know what we said face-to-face. Not yet.

I told him not to send me any more messages and gave him Dad's cell phone number if he needed to get in touch.

Dad doesn't use it anymore. When he does have to call someone, he uses the house phone, but mostly it's the other way around—Nan calling to check in or one of Dad's old friends inviting him out, even though they already know the answer. I'm scared that eventually, even his best buddies will give up trying to get him back to the real world. But they haven't yet, and I think Hanna and Emily would be the same if it was me.

I found Dad's phone stuffed in the junk drawer, wrapped in a charger cord that thankfully still works. I'm relieved it wasn't hidden in the attic, buried in the piles we pull out every couple of years or in the one special box Dad asked me not to touch.

So now I have a second phone, one the producers don't know about. I feel guilty not telling Danny, but I have to be smart.

With the girls knowing not to send me anything except small-talk messages, I think I'm safe. But that's the first mistake, because you never are, not really.

The text is from an unknown number, and the moment I click on it, the studio sees it too.

I'll kill you like I killed your mother.

If you're watching me, you know exactly what I just read, because they will post it instantly. If you're not, it will be the headline in my recap.

I feel sick, and Emily can see something's wrong. "You okay, Jess?" she asks, but I can't speak.

She leads me to a seat, and I show her my phone.

"Shit," she says, passing it to Hanna.

"Who sent this?" Hanna asks.

I shake my head and say, "Unknown number."

They look at me, expecting more, but I want to throw up.

Since the show started, there have been weirdos and that stupid Magpie Man Twitter account but nothing like this.

"They have my number," I say. "It must be someone I know."

I look around the school, at all the strangers we call friends just long enough to get through the day. We swap our numbers with people we hardly speak to, and every couple of years, we delete names we don't recognize anymore.

It could be any of them, because if they don't have it, they can find someone who does.

There are plenty of people at school who will find this funny, and if I had to point a finger, it would be at the tenth-grade mean girls. They leave us alone because we're older than them. But they make up for it with their sneers.

Like everyone, they whisper when I pass, but their whispers are louder. They don't try to hide their bitchiness. They make it clear what they think of my show, my reasons, my life. Emily says they are jealous, although I doubt it.

My phone pings again.

You will be number 14.

"You need to show the police," Emily says. "This isn't funny."

She's right, about both, but the police couldn't solve the crime when they had a dead body, so what help will they be with a couple of texts?

As it turns out, I don't need to call the police. They're waiting for me when I get home.

34

When I open the front door, a man walks toward me, but it's not my dad.

Next to him, a woman stands and smiles. "Jessica," she says. "We're here about the texts."

Dad is sitting in his chair with a face like thunder. I imagine what they've told him and wonder if this is where he'll draw the line.

"We know you received a threatening message today," the policewoman says, and I wonder if this is how they solve crimes these days, watching online videos and waiting for something horrible to happen.

I nod and sit on the sofa. Behind me, Danny is whispering something to Michael, and I feel the camera zoom in on my face.

The policeman looks at them. "This is a private matter."

Danny shrugs and says, "It's Monday."

"You only know about it because of them," I tell the officers. "They have to stay."

The policeman looks annoyed but doesn't argue.

The woman does all the talking then. "Do you have any idea who might have sent them?" she asks.

I shake my head, wondering what this will do to my ratings.

"Could it have been the man you met on Saturday?"

"Ross? How..."

I look at Danny, who shrugs again, and I realize the police *are* paying attention, that the show is doing its job.

"It's not him," I say. "He doesn't have my number."

But what if it is? What if I'm not as good at spotting horrific people as I thought?

"Someone at school then? Do you have any..." She lets me fill in the blank.

"Enemies?" I say. "No, I don't think so."

"We are taking this very seriously," the policewoman says. "A threat has been made against your life. Has anything else strange happened recently?"

You mean apart from me agreeing to be filmed and conducting police interviews in front of the whole world?

"No," I say.

She hands me a card. Her name is Lorraine. "If you think of anything, please call me."

I nod, and they leave without saying goodbye to my father.

Whatever happened when it was just the three of them, he clearly didn't make a good impression.

When they are gone, I go back to the living room, hoping to

explain before Dad comes out fighting. But he's standing up, pointing for me to sit.

"It's nothing to worry about," I tell him.

I've waited a long time for my dad to laugh again but not like this. A single "Ha!" is followed by a shake of the head. Then he points again until I'm sitting, and it feels strange not looking down at him.

He starts pacing the room, and I wonder if I've pissed my dad off so much that he's finally going to shout over his grief. A part of me hopes I have. But when he talks, it's slow and quiet.

"I agreed to this," he says, "because you said it was for your mother."

"It is."

"Someone threatened you. Is that what you wanted?"

"It's a joke. It's probably someone at school."

"And if it's not?"

Dad's top lip twitches, and he won't look me in the eye.

"Please don't stop me from doing this," I say. "I'm on to something. I know I am. I just need time."

Dad sits in his chair, and I hope his fight has faded away. We limit our anger to short bursts or risk crying all evening. But he doesn't give in. He reaches for my hand, drawing circles in my palm like he did when I was a kid, and says, "Someone threatened my daughter today. What do you expect me to do? I lost her, Jess. I won't lose you as well."

"You're not going to," I say, my heart breaking for him like it has a thousand times since Mom died.

We sit in silence until Dad says, "I gave it a chance."

"We're nearly halfway through the four weeks. Can I at least have that? Please, Dad! I'll be careful."

He may do it in his own way, but he protects me, and that will never change.

Suddenly, he stares over my shoulder, at Michael filming everything and Danny standing by his side. Then he looks around our living room, a room that has barely changed in ten years except for the growing collection of Mom's photos that fill every surface.

"I don't want this for you," Dad says. Then, so quietly only I can hear, "Two more weeks. But if the police come back here, it's over."

35

"Are you okay?" Danny asks.

He's not supposed to speak on camera unless it's absolutely necessary. I guess this is one of those times. I can see the worry in his face.

I nod, and he says, "You're right—it's someone fooling around."

There's more than one way to go viral, and if my heartfelt introduction didn't do it, if my story still feels like old news, maybe the threat of something worse will actually help.

When his camera is turned off, just before they leave, Michael says, "I got some great footage of you and your dad."

That's the difference between him and Danny: Michael still treats me like a prop.

"Don't let them win," Danny whispers. "Whoever they are, they want a reaction."

"Just like you," I say. I meant it as a joke, but he doesn't laugh.

"We'll see you next week, Jess. And if you get any more messages, call the police."

"I will."

When they've gone, I go straight upstairs to my room and stare at the camera on the wall.

At midnight, I put a sock over it, just in case, then lie in bed, thinking about who might have sent the texts.

It probably is some idiot at school trying to be funny. After all, the real Magpie Man didn't text his victims first.

But people change. What if he really is watching?

36

The messages keep coming.

I see you

You look so helpless when you sleep

I can't wait to see what your insides look like

I try to ignore them, but each one reminds me of my mom lying there, helpless.

Lorraine calls and says the person is using a number-changing app, so it's not as easy to trace it and break down their door. She says the police are doing all they can to help.

I don't believe her but thank her anyway.

I feel sick whenever I get a new notification. My inbox is a twisted list of reminders of how much I've lost.

Danny messages me with this week's viewing figures.

A 159,000 increase. Good job.

Whoever's sending the texts, they're helping.

Back at school, Hanna says, "It's Ross. It has to be."

I've thought a lot about that, but it can't be him. I saw him. I heard him. He wants justice like I do. There's no reason for Ross to mess with me.

"He doesn't have my phone number. I gave him the number to this."

I pull out my dad's phone, and Emily grabs it and says, "This is old," stretching the "old" out far longer than she needs to.

Hanna frowns. "I told you to stop doing that."

She means keeping a phone in my bra, because her mom knows someone who got breast cancer and believes whatever is in a smartphone is bad for your boobs. But Dad's phone is ancient.

Emily hands it back to me and says, "Could he get it?"

"What?"

"The number...to your real phone. Could this Ross guy get it?"

"He wants to help," I say. "He has nothing to do with this."

I know I should be more suspicious of Ross. But if I admit that, I'm scared of what it meant for our first meeting. I connected with the family of another victim. That's what I need to be true.

"You should have protection," Hanna says. "They should have someone outside your house."

"It's just some loner trying to scare you," Emily says. "Change your number and don't tell anyone except us."

It's the most obvious solution, and I have thought about it, but I don't want to. Every message is another sign that this is working, that my face on a screen is doing something.

If I didn't know better, I would believe the nagging feeling that maybe it's the real Magpie Man contacting me because he thinks he can get away with it. But I do know better.

Know your enemy. That's rule number one if you want to beat them. This enemy wouldn't text. He wouldn't risk it. But my audience doesn't need to know that.

I don't have time to catch an impostor. I need to put all my efforts into the real thing.

37

"Hi," Ross says. "Are you okay?"

I'm calling on Dad's old phone, lying on my bed with the lights off and wondering if this was a good idea.

"I'm fine," I say, because it's what I always say. "I just wanted to talk."

"What's up?"

We could speak about the texts. We could discuss the show. But I need something different tonight.

"I miss her," I whisper. "Every single day."

Ross doesn't answer right away, but when he does, his voice sounds closer somehow.

"You always will," he says.

He doesn't add anything else, like, "That's a good thing," or, "She's always with you." He has heard it all before. That's why I called him.

"I feel empty," I say. "My dad gave in to it, and I don't even blame him anymore. It's so fucking hard to keep living."

"But we do it," Ross replies, and I smile into the darkness. "We do."

"You know the worst thing for me?" he says. "It's all the firsts you have without them. I came out without her. I graduated without her. I got married without her."

Ross was eighteen when his mother died, older than I am now. He had eleven more years with her, and it still wasn't enough. It wasn't even close.

"If this doesn't work, I don't know what I'll do," I whisper. "I'm tired of being the girl with the murdered mom."

"That won't change, Jess. But you can be more than that. You can be the woman with a soul mate, the woman with kids, the woman with a job she loves—whatever you want. A life worth living."

The tears come silently, but I don't wipe them away.

"I've made some progress connecting with the other families," he says. "Your show is making others want to talk. It shouldn't be long now."

I smile and imagine a time when this will be worth it, when I can look back on the show and be proud of our efforts. Whatever happens, it's already helping, because I've found some light in the darkness.

"Tell me about your mom," I say, and for the next hour, I listen to Ross remembering his life before it was broken, telling me stories that calm my fears.

38

After theology class, Mr. Humphries asks me to stay behind while he talks to Bernie.

During class, at opposite sides of the classroom, it's easy to forget we used to be best friends. But as I wait for our teacher to talk her through last week's homework, it feels awkward how we knew each other before we really knew ourselves.

Bernie smiles as she walks past, polite rather than friendly, and I hope she loves her new friends as much as I love Emily and Hanna.

"Jessica," Mr. Humphries says, pointing for me to sit down. "I won't keep you long."

If you graded St. Anthony's teachers from best to worst, he would get the best marks.

Mr. Humphries is my dad's age, but he dresses a lot sharper. The edges of his tattoos poke from his shirtsleeves, and we all have our theories what they are.

He never talks down to us or shouts for no reason. Some

teachers think loudness is their most important asset, but he knows it's fairness. If you've pissed him off, you know you deserve it.

"I wanted to talk to you about Mayfield Lodge," he says.

I nod, trying to stay calm even though I'd forgotten all about it.

Every March, the eleventh-grade theology class goes on a retreat, and when they come back, they're different. You can see it in their smiles and how they walk. They look lighter. And it freaks the rest of us out. This year, it's our turn.

"I've spoken to them," Mr. Humphries says. "They will not sanction any additional visitors."

Emily will be gutted if I don't go. So will I.

Mr. Humphries smiles. "I haven't finished yet. They still want you to come, Jess. And they understand that on the first day, you have certain responsibilities."

I think of the minicams sitting untouched on my desk at home.

"Provided you can film yourself, there won't be a problem. I thought I would warn you now so you can speak to the appropriate people."

It means that for one week, if Adrian and Danny agree, I will go solo.

"Thank you. I'll ask."

"If they say no, I'm afraid you won't be able to come. But you'll get a full refund."

Emily is waiting for me outside, and when I tell her, she says, "You'd better come. You're not leaving me on my own."

There are ten other people in our theology class, six girls and

four boys, but none of them are what you would call friends.
If I don't go, Emily will sulk her way through the whole week.

Before the show, I was looking forward to Mayfield Lodge.
Now I'm worried, because I forgot to mention it on my application form, and that will be the fourth week.

For four of us, it will be our last week, and I'm going to have to do it alone.

39

That night, I catch up on what I've missed from the others.

It's hard to keep up, and I worry my audience is feeling the same, wonder if their busy lives will get in the way and they'll stop watching.

I watch Sonia first. There are lots of theories about her. People have even started messaging me.

Have you met Sonia?

What is she hiding?

I'm scared of the answer, because if it's bigger than hunting a serial killer, I'm screwed. Her highlights don't really deserve that word. But her subscribers increase anyway.

"I'm sorry to all the families of the people my brother killed," Ryan says. "I know it doesn't mean much, but I truly am."

I watch a woman whose husband was shot hug Ryan in his living room. They sob in each other's arms, and I feel guilty for competing with him. In the background, his mother sits with her head in her hands.

Then Ella's father tells everyone that his daughter is pregnant despite never having had sex. He has a white strip under a black collar. No wonder he's pushing this as an immaculate conception.

Ella stands beside him, her eyes down and a bright red shame spot creeping up her neck. Her viewers are a mixture of those who believe her and those calling her a slut.

Lucas hasn't done anything you'd expect him to do, like sleep with a bunch of girls or say something controversial. I thought he would be my biggest challenge, but it's like he has given up.

When I call Danny, he says, "A one-hundred-and-fifty-nine-thousand increase from week one. You didn't think that was worth replying to?"

I smile to myself: there's no way they'll stop me going to Mayfield Lodge if my ratings keep going up.

"How does that compare with the others?"

Danny laughs. "You know I can't tell you that, Jess. But you're doing well."

I swallow my nerves and say, "Well enough?"

He laughs again, and for a moment, I think he's actually going to tell me, but instead, he says, "How's things...with the texts?"

"It's okay."

"What about the police?" he asks, and I shake my head even though he can't see me.

"They're as useful as they've ever been."

I hear him take a deep breath. "I know I'm your director, and I know I should be impartial. But just be careful. I don't want you getting hurt."

I close my eyes and smile, because his words sound comforting and electric at the same time.

And then I glance at Mom's photo, and as quick as that, the feeling is gone. To change the subject, I tell him about Mayfield Lodge.

"I can go but only if you don't."

He laughs. "I'll have to speak to Adrian. But I don't see a problem, provided you promise to use the cameras all day."

"I will."

"You should start getting used to them," he says. "I can give you another quick tutorial if you like."

Sometimes his words sound like flirting, but I can't be certain.

"Sure," I say, "I'd like that," because sometimes my words sound like flirting, too, at least to me.

I shouldn't be thinking like that. I need to stay focused, because my life isn't a love story.

If Mom were still alive, she might have prepared me for love. She might have made it magical. But all I know is that even when you find your soul mate, you are one terrible day from losing them.

Nan says that's no way for a seventeen-year-old to think. She says chances are there to be taken.

"How about Saturday?" Danny asks.

"I can't. We're having a girls' day out."

Once a month, Emily, Hanna, and I go to Harmony, for a shopping trip to an outlet place called the Waves. We have a sleepover, rotating between our houses, and because Dad doesn't have the energy to bother us, it's always best when it's here. When it's at Hanna's, her parents won't leave us alone. Her dad especially—he fills every silence at the dinner table and comes into her room without knocking and understands hints about as much as I understand Hungarian. He's as different from my dad as it's possible to be. The others find it annoying, how friendly he is. They wish he would leave us alone. But I like that Hanna's dad pays attention to us. It's a nice change. At Emily's, we feel guilty going to her room, so instead we watch movies in the living room with her mom.

So yes, everyone prefers coming to my house, because Dad leaves us alone. He never complains about the music being too loud. He never gets in the way.

"We can find a different time, then," Danny says, and it could be my imagination, but he sounds disappointed.

40

Almost every day, Sara the reporter stands outside my house, no one else, not even the photographer she was with the first time.

A quick look at the *Doveton Messenger* website told me she has only worked there since December. I would be her biggest story yet.

Last time, back when our story was national news, the newspapers printed whatever they wanted, making up lies when Dad and Nan refused to talk. This time, I want complete control: another chapter in the script I started on the first show.

"Hi," I say.

Sara looks shocked, swallows, and says, "Hello."

I've walked past her so many times that this has shaken her out of her routine. She doesn't start firing questions at me. She looks nervous, waiting for me to fill the silence.

The newspapers have the power to make anything real. They

were the ones who turned the Magpie Man from a character created by my dad to a name you couldn't escape. Now I need them to do the same to me, even if I have to start small, even if my first interview is with the *Messenger*.

When I start talking, she doesn't write in English. She makes squiggles that look like a foreign language, covering the page in nonsense only she can understand.

"He used to be a monster," I say, "but now he's hiding behind a phone. He's pathetic."

The police profilers say he's proud of his crimes. They say he sees himself as superior, because he has reached double digits, signaling his intent from his very first kill.

If I mock him, if I call him out, maybe he'll respond.

I finish with another plea for information, and when I'm done, Sara nods and clicks her tongue, smiling like she got exactly what she wanted.

"This is perfect," she says.

Hopefully, after it's published, others will follow: better papers, bigger platforms.

Maybe this time next week, the world will be back outside our door.

41

After our day shopping at the Waves, Hanna and Emily come back to my place.

"Hi, Mr. Simmons," Hanna says from the hall.

She always stands in the entranceway, as if our living room is off-limits, but Emily has other ideas.

She walks right in, sits next to Dad, and says, "How's it going?"

This is Emily's way of dealing with the grief that rests on my father like a layer of dust. She ignores it.

"Wanna see what I bought?" Emily asks.

"Why not?"

She smiles, pulling top after top from bag after bag and critiquing each one. But Dad lets her, and the grin that briefly flickers across his face tells me he enjoys these silly moments as much as Emily.

In my room, we order pizza, then argue for an hour about what movie to watch.

"So," Emily says with a sly smile on her face, "Danny."

"What about him?"

She raises an eyebrow and says, "Anything happen after all that filming?"

"No!" I say, and they both laugh.

"I think you would," Hanna says.

Emily adds, "I think we *all* would."

I make a face, and Emily goes, "What? He's cute."

"I prefer Michael," Hanna says.

Emily stares at her. "Are you serious?"

"I like that he doesn't try too hard."

"He doesn't try *at all*."

"They're in their twenties," I say.

"Ryan Gosling is, like, forty," Hanna says, and you can't argue with that kind of logic, so we sit quietly for a while, probably thinking about the same thing.

They want me to have a love interest. Adrian probably does too.

Maybe Danny is my director on purpose, because he's good-looking and because I'm a girl and, well, we all know what happens next.

But it won't happen this time. I hate stories where a pretty boy turns up and the girl is, like, *He literally defines my entire universe.* My life is defined by something bigger than that.

Hanna reaches for her shopping bag and pulls out the new top she bought, then points at the camera with the sock over it and says, "Are there any more of those?"

"Not in here," I say. "I only cover that one to make sure."

That's when my phone beeps and they both look at me, because if we are together, it's unlikely to be anything good.

I don't want to read it, but Emily nods, and I can see she's desperate to know what it says.

Are you having fun, girls? I'm outside. Come and play.

I drop the phone on my bed and walk to the window, feeling a chill rise up my back.

"What?" Hanna asks. "Is it him?"

"Turn the light off," I say.

"Why?"

"Turn it off and come here."

The room goes dark, and they stand on either side of me, looking outside.

"What is it?" Emily asks.

"He says he's watching."

I see Hanna shiver, and Emily reaches for the curtains and pulls them open.

"I can't see anyone," she says, and before I can stop her, she's reaching for my phone, reading the message, then putting her shoes on and walking to the door.

"Where are you going?" Hanna asks.

"To find out who's doing this. I'm going to stop him."

"What if it's—" Hanna says.

But Emily shouts, "It's not! It's not him. It's some weirdo who thinks this is funny."

She looks at me like she wants me to agree with her, but I don't know what to do.

Emily rushes out of my room, and from the top of the stairs, I watch her open the front door and walk outside. Only then, when she marches headfirst into the darkness, do I move.

Hanna looks terrified, and I lead her back to the window,

where we can see Emily staring down the street, and I tell Hanna to stay there.

"If you see anything, if you see anyone, call the police."

She nods, and I run outside, then freeze after three steps into the black.

It's not the color, it's the sound. The evening hums, and my head tightens until I realize I'm holding my breath.

I don't know what I'm doing. But I can't leave my friend to chase this weirdo on her own, so I step forward, looking right then left, until I see a shadow a few houses down. I swallow hard, then dart into the patches of light made from streetlights and glowing windows.

The shadow moves quicker, running away from me, and that's when I realize I might be chasing the wrong person.

"Emily," I whisper, then again, louder this time.

A dog whimpers a few streets over, a whine that sounds like a warning, and as I turn, I see someone too close to escape.

"Hey," Emily says, just as I say, "Shit!"

She laughs, sees my face, then goes serious. "Did you see anyone?"

I look behind me, trying to figure out what I saw, then grab Emily's arm and pull her back toward the house.

"What are you doing?" she yells.

"Come inside," I say, as quietly and calmly as I can.

But Emily shakes her head, takes a deep breath, and shouts, "Where are you, you prick? I'm here! I'm ready to play!"

I grab her arm again, but she pulls it away. I can see curtains twitching and porch lights coming on. Most of the neighbors weren't here when Mom was murdered, but they know our history.

A man steps out of a house on the other side of the road and asks if we're all right.

"We're fine," I say. "Thank you. She's...a little drunk."

The man nods but doesn't close his door, just watches us as Emily looks back and forth, searching for something that isn't there.

"Please," I say. "Don't do this now. The neighbors..."

But it's more than that. I'm desperate to get back indoors. The night plays tricks on us all the time, but sometimes it's not a trick, and the longer I stay here, the more anxious I feel.

Emily looks like she's about to shout again when she catches my eye and stops.

"It's not him, Jess. It's some kid messing around...or a lonely old man with nothing better to do."

That's what I thought too. But the feeling on the back of my neck, the slow suffocation of a silent street at night, means I'm not so sure now.

"Jessica?"

Over my shoulder, I see Dad walking toward us, his face a mixture of confusion and concern. He still has his slippers on, and I remember Mom chiding him for treading dirt into the house.

"Inside shoes...outside shoes," she would say, holding each in turn. But Mom's rules have been forgotten now.

"It's okay," I say, touching Emily's hand and leading her back to the house. "Everything's fine."

I say that even if everything isn't fine, even if I have the strangest feeling that someone was outside after all.

Before I close the front door, I stand our gnome back up and hope it was Emily who knocked it over, not someone else.

42

We don't sleep much that night. Emily checks the window every hour, while the glow of Hanna's phone doesn't fade until I finally drift off around three.

The next morning, Emily wants me to tell the police, and Hanna wants to confiscate my phone. But I say no to both and wonder if this will be our little secret or if someone was recording the whole thing, if a neighbor was filming us shouting in the street and it's already online, if even through a sock, on a day it shouldn't, the camera in my bedroom filmed every word.

But no one calls and no one visits, not the police nor Danny nor anyone else.

If someone really was outside, I should have filmed it. It's things like this that will help me get the full three months. I need to get used to strapping on the head cam quickly, instinctively, so I practice for half an hour, on then off, over and over, until I can do it with my eyes closed.

Everything important needs to be recorded. Every possible clue needs to be piled up until the police can't ignore them.

Someone knew we were having a sleepover. They knew we were in the house the moment I got that text.

I pick up my phone and type a message. I send it and wait.

OK then. Come get me if you're brave enough.

43

Sara's article was published today, so I go on the *Doveton Messenger* home page, and there it is, my words under the headline:

YOUTUBE STAR FIGHTS BACK AFTER MAGPIE MAN MESSAGES
Serial killer branded "pathetic" by daughter of first victim

She has published my comments word for word, and over my shoulder, I hear the camera in the corner of the room whirring more than normal.

It's trying to focus on the story I'm reading, showing my viewers what I can see. To help, I turn on the head cam and point it at the laptop, waiting a few seconds as it refocuses until the words are clear.

Now everyone who's watching me can read Sara's article.

Jessica Simmons, the daughter of the Magpie Man's first victim, has spoken exclusively to the *Messenger* about her new internet show and her quest to bring her mother's killer to justice. The residents of Doveton will never forget what happened on that terrible night, when a wife and mother was savagely murdered, but seventeen-year-old Jessica wants the whole world to remember.

The more people who are reminded of Mom's fate, the more who believe the texts really are coming from the man who killed her, the better my chance of catching him.

When I've finished the story, I read the comments, pointing the camera at the ones that stand out, showing my viewers the difference between useful and useless.

"I haven't spoken to you for a while," I say. "Not like this anyway. But we're running out of time. What did you like today? What did you love? What did you share just because everyone else had?

"We fill our feeds with stuff that doesn't mean anything. But tonight, if you want to, you can change that. Please share this. Please spread the message, because he's still out there, and he's getting ready to kill again."

I'm scared I sound desperate. Because I am. But what choice do I have?

I'm nearly at the end of my third show, and I can't let this go so soon.

44

I lie in bed, watching the red light on the camera, waiting for it to blink off so I can finally get to sleep.

Until midnight, until I know no one is watching, I can't sleep a wink.

My phone says 11:11, and I check my messages, but whoever is sending the threats hasn't replied to my taunt.

I close my eyes and try to relax, and then my window smashes, glass spraying all over the room. I jump up before I know what I'm doing, stepping on something sharp and holding back a scream. There's a brick wrapped in paper in the middle of the floor, and I hear the camera zoom in on it.

I try to pull the glass out of my foot but I can't. It's too deep. I hobble to the window and look outside. There's a man standing there, looking up at me, and I quickly grab the head cam and point it outside. He stays still, watching, a hood covering his face.

I try to fight off the terror, but my hands are shaking in the half-light. Someone was outside on Saturday night. But they aren't hiding anymore.

My stomach is knotted and my breath comes out fast and jagged, tightening my chest until I have to swallow and slowly exhale, then again, over and over until the panic calms just enough for me to move.

I hold the camera up so everyone can see, and surely, someone will come. Surely, the police are watching. Surely, Danny is on his way. Surely, Emily and Hanna can see this and are already calling 999 to report an emergency.

But all that happens is a neighbor's front light blinks on, then, a few seconds later, off again.

The man stands there until I hear a car, the headlights shattering the space between the night and the shape within it, his body suddenly clear. He looks up one last time, then slowly walks away, and I realize no one is coming.

If I want to find out if it's really him, I have to do it myself, and I have to do it now.

45

I reach down, grip the glass, and yank it out of my foot, the pain surging through my body. I wince at the sting, the throbbing of the cut matching my heartbeat. My breath feels sharp, my stomach tight with a mixture of nausea and panic, and I realize it's now or never. Tears are streaming down my face, but the adrenaline stops me from breaking.

I wrap tissues around my foot, trying not to focus on the blood quickly soaking through. I pull on today's clothes, fasten the camera around my head, and wince as I push my foot into my shoe. I go downstairs and unlock the front door, then stop.

In here, I'm safe, but out there…

I want Dad to be home. But the living room is dark, and my father is working the zombie shift.

He would hate me for doing this, but I have to. I grip the handle, feel it click as I push, then walk outside.

The car that pulled up is the man from two doors down,

and he smiles as I walk past while I do my best to look normal. I want to ask him for help, but something stops me. Would he believe me? Would he tell me to wait for the police—the sirens and the solemn sighs that always come too late?

No. The hooded man couldn't have gone far. I try to walk faster, but the pain in my foot sends jolts up my leg.

I wonder what this looks like on-screen, some blurry camera footage and me panting in the background.

I get to the end of my block and look both ways, and there it is: the alley where Mom was killed. If I was the real Magpie Man, if I had thrown a brick through someone's window and wanted to shut them up or scare them or whatever the hell this is, the alley would be the perfect ending.

I try to move, but my legs are frozen to the spot. My breathing cuts through the nighttime hush, and I don't trust the space around me.

I think about turning around…going home…running away. And then I step forward and stare into the darkness, the last streetlight for one minute and forty-two seconds buzzing above me.

This is the safety Mom never reached. She started at the opposite end but never made it out.

I step forward again, then again, and I feel the darkness start to cover me. A rush goes through my body, and my heart is pounding, and the silence gets louder until it's ringing in my ears. I hear breathing, a snap, a rustle that makes me shiver.

And then someone grabs my arm from behind.

46

"Don't be stupid!"

I spin around, wondering why I didn't bring a weapon, and a boy is standing there, still holding my arm.

I shake him off, my heart pounding. He looks nervous.

"Who are you?"

"Jamie," he says, holding his hand out, then putting it in his pocket when I ignore it.

"Was it you?" I ask, even though I know the answer.

This skinny, scared-looking kid is nothing like the shadow I saw.

"No!" he says. "I'm here to save you."

I laugh, then realize I'm standing with my back to the alley, so I start to walk away.

"I was watching," Jamie says. "I couldn't let you go in there."

I should say thank you. But I let the man escape, whoever

he is, and all I have is a busted window and a cut foot and a kid who thinks he's my hero.

"I wasn't going to come," he says. "I wanted to keep watching. But when I thought you might actually go in"—he points at the alley—"it seemed like a bad idea."

"It probably was," I say. "Thank you."

Jamie smiles. "No problem. Now can we go home? I'm not gonna lie. I'm shitting myself in case he's actually in there."

47

Jamie lives six houses away, and when we get to his house, he stops and says, "Are you going to call the police?"

I remember what Dad said, about pulling the plug if they come back. But Jamie looks worried when I don't answer, so I say, "Sure."

"So I'll see you around?"

"I guess. And thanks again. It's nice to know someone around here is watching."

"Every week," he says.

I see a man looking at us through the window, half his face covered by curtain.

Jamie turns and says, "My dad. He likes to spy."

I catch the man's eye, and he doesn't stop staring. He holds my gaze until I shiver and turn away. I'm used to people watching me, but not like this.

When I look back, he's still staring, and I wonder why I've never noticed him before. He lives at number forty-three, I say to myself, just in case.

"I go to St. Anthony's," Jamie says. "But I don't blame you for not knowing me."

He starts to blush, and we both pretend not to notice.

"What grade?"

"Tenth."

He looks too small to be only a year younger than me. We don't really pay attention to the grades below us anyway. Emily sometimes points out cute boys, but I doubt this kid has ever been in that category, and she usually focuses up rather than down.

I don't pretend I recognize him. Instead, I say, "Well, I guess I'll see you soon."

His face looks bright red under the streetlight, and he says, "I should probably walk you home."

I wouldn't have asked, but I'm glad he offered, because even the length of a few houses now feels too far.

He looks up at my head cam then away. Then he turns to his dad and holds up five fingers, and the curtain falls back into place.

We walk home, and he waits until I'm inside before he leaves.

Dad still isn't here, and that scares me, because I don't want to be alone.

Upstairs, I put the camera on my desk, then pull off my sneakers and limp to the bathroom. The blood is starting to clot, and I wash it and wrap it and put a fresh sock on, then go back to my room. I'm looking out my broken window when I hear the camera click off.

Only then do I pick up the brick and remove the paper to see a drawing of a magpie and the number 14.

48

I get a freezer bag from the kitchen and tuck the paper inside, sealing it shut and imagining what the police will think if I hand it over.

I scrub the blood from my carpet, then lie awake until Dad comes home. He must have seen the damage in the dark, because he walks into my room without knocking.

"What happened?"

"Nothing," I say, hiding my foot from him.

I wanted so much for him to come home, but now he's here, I want to be alone again. I want to feel him close but not too close, the way I'm used to, through the sound of the TV and the rumble of his snoring when he falls asleep.

He touches the window frame, stares outside, then turns back with a look I haven't seen before.

"Who did this?" he asks.

I wonder if this is the moment that changes him, the one

we will look back on and laugh about—the day a brick and a hidden bleeding foot forced my dad back to life.

He leans into the black, then shakes his head, and says, "What am I supposed to do?"

With his back to me, in the dark, his voice sounds more fragile than ever.

"I thought this was over."

"I'm sorry," I say. It's all I have, and I know it's not enough.

When he turns, I see a tear slip down my father's cheek before it soaks into his beard.

"Are you going to call the police?" I ask.

He should. It's the responsible thing to do. But he doesn't want them back here. He doesn't want the reminders they bring.

He looks outside one last time, shakes his head again, and says, "Sleep in my room tonight."

I expect Dad to go downstairs, but instead he sits in the chair next to his bed, and every time I open my eyes, he's watching me.

"It's okay," he whispers. "I'm here."

49

I check my foot in the bathroom and hope it will heal on its own. The last thing I need is a hospital visit. The cut looks smaller in the daylight, but I smear it with antiseptic cream to be safe.

Then I'm outside, standing where he stood, looking up at my bedroom. The neighbors are looking, too, and I want to ask why they didn't come out last night. They must have heard something. Night makes normal noises louder, so smashing glass must have sounded like a siren in a road like ours. But I ignore them like they ignored me.

If they don't want to be part of my story, because they're scared or careless or judgmental or whatever, who cares? At least there's one person in one house on my street who's willing to help.

I don't notice the reporters until one of them clears their throat. To my left, four people from four different papers are keeping their distance. This is not the kind of reporting I'm used to, but maybe they saw what happened last night and are hedging their bets.

They're being polite and hoping I'm open to talking.

"Hi," I say. "Who's first?"

50

The moment I walk up to the school entrance, people are asking if I'm okay, if they caught him, if they really have to wait a week for the next episode.

When Hanna sees me, she runs over and hugs me and says, "I'm so sorry, Jess. I wasn't watching. I only saw this morning."

I imagine the producers working through the night to make my highlights video available as early as possible, and when I check my channel, I see it already has over sixty thousand views.

I try to tell Hanna it's cool, but I feel my lip wobble and my eyes filling up, and she sees and says, "Come on."

She hurries me into the bathroom and stands with her back against the door, then watches as I completely break down.

Out of nowhere, I am sobbing, so hard my stomach hurts, and when someone tries to come in, Hanna pushes back and says, "Sorry. Closed for emergency repairs."

She could be talking about me. She hugs me as I cry into her shoulder.

"I'm sorry," I say.

"Don't apologize. It must have been terrifying."

"It was."

On my own, at home, it's easy to pretend everything's fine. I've been doing it most of my life. But it's not fine. Someone threw a brick through my window and left a note that hinted I was next on a list that started ten years ago.

And I did exactly what they tell you not to. I didn't run away from a stranger. I chased him into the darkness.

"That Jamie seems nice," Hanna says.

"He is," I mumble into her shoulder.

Then I step back and wipe my face and look in the mirror. I'm a mess.

Hanna stands behind me, the two of us looking at our reflections, and says, "I think it's gone too far, Jess."

I picture the man standing in the street, how he didn't care who saw, how he knew that it was the perfect time to announce himself to my world. I was alone with an audience of thousands.

He could have broken my window any night of the week. He could have done it before Danny and Michael left. He could have done it when I wasn't there.

But he didn't. He knew exactly when I was home alone, and that terrifies me.

What if a neighbor *had* come out? He wouldn't have escaped a street full of saviors.

But maybe he was being careful the night Emily and Hanna stayed over. Maybe he wanted to see if anyone on my road was watching, and once he knew they weren't, he hurled his latest warning through my window.

51

Usually when I get home, Nan is making a cup of tea, the kettle just boiled as if she can hear me from the end of the street. But not today. Today, she's yelling at my dad.

"...and you can't even be bothered to fix it! It should be boarded up at the very least. I'll do it if you won't."

"Hey," I say.

Nan turns and says, "Jessica. We didn't hear you come in."

"I'm not surprised. What's happening?"

Nan looks at my dad, who quickly glances at me before staring at the floor.

"Nothing, darling," she says. "I was talking to your father about the window."

She doesn't ask what happened. Even my nan—who doesn't have Wi-Fi and calls it the "interweb"—even she knows why there's broken glass all over my bedroom floor.

"I'll fix it now," Dad mumbles, and we watch him go into the garage and come back with some wood and a hammer.

Before Mom died, Dad loved building things. Not only computers but little bits of magic. Now the garage is full of pieces of wood, but when I was a kid, that wood was transformed into toys and castles and bookshelves and anything you could imagine.

Nan goes to the kitchen to make the tea, and when I follow, she asks if I'm okay. I nod and think about hugging her. But I'm worried I'll cry again, so I keep my distance.

"I'm fine," I lie.

If I think about it, I feel terrified, because he knows where I live, whoever he is.

I force myself to smile and say, "I won't let some idiot ruin my chi."

She hugs me. "Your mom would be proud of you."

Nan says that whenever *she* is proud of me but doesn't want to spell it out. It always makes me happy-sad, but you learn to live with that.

I don't cry, and when Dad starts hammering upstairs, I'm grateful that she can shout him into action. But she is his mother-in-law. She was there when they got married. She was the woman he was desperate to impress when he first fell in love with her daughter.

So I guess she has a power that I don't.

52

If you don't know the whole story, you would assume my dad is an asshole. But he's not, because when Mom first died, some people pointed the finger at him. A few pointed more than a finger.

This isn't the first time we've had a brick thrown through our window, because if enough people are interested in your story, some will make you the villain. That's what happened with Dad, when someone started saying he didn't look upset enough while he was appealing for witnesses. They questioned his lack of tears, forgetting that by then, he was all cried out.

Like all bullshit, most people ignored it. But not everyone, including some idiot who thought spraying insults on our garage door was a good use of his time, who thought throwing a brick through our living room window was a perfectly normal thing to do.

If you'd seen my dad back then, you'd recognize the look

in his eyes when he saw my bedroom window shattered. He thought he was the reason. He felt the finger pointing at him again, but he was too tired to fight.

I remember the day it happened, the knock on the door and the hushed voices.

Mom was working late, so Dad had picked me up from school. He was making dinner—a real meal, with vegetables and spices and three saucepans on the stove.

A policeman whispered his way into our living room. He said maybe it would be better if I wasn't around to hear this.

Dad told me to go upstairs and play, so I did, because I was seven. I played while they told my dad his wife had been murdered within screaming distance of our house. Except she didn't scream. She didn't get the chance.

And when I came down, Dad was sitting in the living room with the scariest look on his face. The bulbs behind his eyes had blown. He looked broken.

At some point, he threw the dinner away, and he cried when I said I was hungry.

These aren't memories. They are stains. I couldn't forget them if I wanted to.

But what I know with absolute certainty is that my dad had nothing to do with my mom's murder.

53

That night, Danny calls and says, "I'm sorry I wasn't there."

"It's not your fault," I reply. "He would have waited until you left anyway."

"What did the police say?"

I pause while I consider telling Danny the truth. But I don't want him or Adrian flipping out, so I say, "They're looking into it."

"Are you going to continue?"

For a minute, I think all he's worried about is losing my audience, but before I can answer, he says, "No one would blame you for leaving the show."

I'm not so sure about that, not when he tells me my subscribers have doubled in a week. But why would I stop when it's working? I only have one guaranteed week left, and I need to take advantage of that, not throw it away.

My story is back in the news, with more reporters waiting

outside every day, gobbling up the comments I toss them and reminding everyone what the Magpie Man did to Mom and twelve women since.

"You shouldn't have gone after him," Danny says.

"At least I wore my head cam," I joke.

He huffs and says, "Well, there is that."

I don't tell him about the drawing and the number. If he thinks I'm in real trouble, he could tell Adrian to pull the plug, and then I'd be back at square one.

"I keep thinking, what if you were my sister?" Danny says. "I wouldn't let her do this. It's too dangerous."

"You have a sister?"

"Yeah, she's just like you—headstrong, confident. She doesn't take no for an answer."

I feel disappointed and realize he doesn't know me at all. I was scared that doing the show would let people see how weak I am, how my entire life is balled up in one horrible moment and every day since then is me trying to pull free. But they think I'm some kind of hero. They think I'm a fighter.

And maybe I am sometimes. Maybe I should have gone into the alley after all.

"If you need to talk, remember we have professionals on hand," Danny says.

"You mean psychiatrists."

He laughs, just a quick air puff down the phone, and says, "Or you could talk to me."

"I'll bear that in mind."

"If it happens again, call nine-nine-nine *before* running after them."

"I will," I say, surprised the police haven't already paid a visit. Maybe they aren't the big fans I thought they were.

Dad has boarded up my window, and before she left, Nan said the window replacement people were coming tomorrow.

I go into Dad's room and look out, but the street is empty except for a cat that suddenly darts up the road.

On the wall above his bed, if you look close enough, you can see the paint strokes Mom left when they were decorating. *I love you*, she wrote, too thick to be completely covered, a blemish unless you know the truth.

I feel the cut in my foot lightly throbbing, but when I check, it seems to be healing.

I don't know what I expected after three weeks of being live, but it wasn't this.

Holding the photo of me and Mom, I say, "I'll try harder."

Then I take the drawing of the magpie out of my bag and cover the 4 so instead of 14, it says 1.

That is what I need to focus on.

She is all that matters.

54

When I get home from school the next day, my window has been replaced, and the wood Dad used to board it up is back in the garage. There's a letter by the door, and inside is a copy of Sara's article from the *Messenger*.

Over the story, in thick red pen, someone has written:

I'LL SHOW YOU HOW PATHETIC I AM.

I look back at the envelope, which has my name on it but no address. Whoever did this put it at my door.

I compare it to the drawing of the magpie and the number 14, but it is impossible to tell if they're from the same person.

In one interview, I called him a freak show. In another, I said he must be weak to always target women. Today, to one of the last tabloids to arrive at my door, I said the Magpie Man should do us all a favor and kill himself.

I wanted to bait him. I thought the best way to stop him being careful was to piss him off.

It looks like I have.

55

Danny texts to say the producers have agreed to let me go to Mayfield Lodge without him. But will the retreat still let me come if I bring psychos to the window?

If things don't work out, this will be my last show, and I suddenly realize how much I need Danny and Michael. They make this so much easier. Without them, I'm scared I'll mess it up.

After theology, I ask Mr. Humphries if he thinks it's a good idea, if someone like me is meant for something like Mayfield Lodge.

"What do you mean, Jess?"

"It's a spiritual place, right? It's a quiet place?"

"It is."

"I'm neither of those things."

He laughs and sits on the edge of his desk. "Maybe that's the point. Maybe you need a little more quiet."

This is one of the reasons he's my favorite—because he never acts like I'm a burden. Teachers are always saying how little time they have, but if you need him, Mr. Humphries is there to help.

"Aren't you scared, taking me on the trip?"

He smiles and says, "I've done the risk assessment."

I wonder if there's a whole new section all about me, but I don't ask.

I think back to all the previous students who went to Mayfield Lodge before us, how different they were when they returned. Will that be me in a week? And will I be better or worse?

It's not the ideal time, but I have to see for myself what all the fuss is about. Plus, it's the closest I've had to a vacation in years.

All the way to English, I'm reminiscing about the weekends Nan and I used to take together, and I almost walk into Mr. Collins at the door. I mumble an apology as I step past.

He's the complete opposite of Mr. Humphries. He never looks pleased to see us, rarely smiles, and watches the clock more than we do. Some teachers are clearly in the wrong job.

"Books out," Mr. Collins says. "Page thirty-two."

He talks in commands, saving full sentences for parent-teacher conferences.

As I pull the book from my bag, something comes with it, falling to the floor by my feet.

It's from a newspaper, an ad with half the page missing. But when I turn it over, I see my mom's face smiling back at me and next to it the full, gory details of her death.

56

I can't concentrate, Mr. Collins's words drifting past in a fog, the newspaper article covering the words I should be studying.

There she is: my beautiful mother. She smiles up at me, reminding me of everything I know and everything I don't. This isn't one of the latest stories. It's from ten years ago. This is how the world was told she had died.

I've never seen this clipping before. It's not mine. But it was in my bag, not buried at the bottom but slipped beside a book I only use three times a week. This morning, the book was on my desk at home. Whoever put the article there, they did it today. Whoever it was goes to St. Anthony's.

"Fuck," I whisper, and Mr. Collins stops talking and looks at me.

"Did you say something, Miss Simmons?"

A couple of people around me giggle until Mr. Collins shuts them down with a stare.

"No," I say. "I'm sorry."

He keeps staring for a few more seconds, then turns back to his book.

If this was someone else's class, I could excuse myself, but Mr. Collins is an asshole when it comes to things like that. You don't ask to use the bathroom. We learned that the hard way in sixth grade and again last September. Some teachers change when you're in high school and some don't.

Mr. Humphries says Mr. Collins is "old school," but that's a polite way of saying he's a dick.

I push my fingers to my temples, trying to calm the headache that has come hard and fast.

Who did this? And why?

I look around the classroom and suddenly don't trust anybody.

I read the story over and over again, and when class ends, I fold it and tuck it in my pocket, my fingers smudged gray.

Who keeps a newspaper for ten years? We keep what we want to remember. We hoard what we can't live without.

I feel sick and my head is racing, and when I stand up to leave, I feel dizzy and fall back into my seat. The classroom is empty except for me and Mr. Collins.

He starts talking to himself, then notices me and says, "Jessica. It's lunchtime."

I stare up at him, yet all I can see is my mother's face.

I think about going home and not coming back. But I need to show someone, so I head straight to the homeroom, where Emily and Hanna are waiting for me.

"Hey," Emily says. "We're—"

But Hanna touches her arm to stop her and says, "What is it, Jess?"

She's getting used to these moments. She knows the look that comes before drama.

I pull the clipping from my pocket and hand it to her. "Someone put that in my bag today."

Emily leans over, and Hanna shakes her head and says, "Are you sure?"

"Yes, I'm sure. It wasn't there this morning, and now it is."

They don't know what to say, and I don't blame them. Even Emily is speechless.

Hanna says, "It has to be the same guy, the one with the brick. He must go here."

I shake my head. "It was published years ago. Why would someone keep it all this time?"

"Maybe they found it?" Emily says. "My mom keeps all sorts of crap."

"Or eBay," Hanna says. "You can buy anything online. They're doing it to freak you out."

"Well, it's working."

None of us laugh. We sit in silence, staring at the black-and-white photo of my mom, the woman neither of my best friends will ever know.

57

I look closely at everyone, studying the rest of the school, waiting for a crack to show.

I need to stay focused on the Magpie Man, but I don't know what's real anymore. I don't know what is dangerous and what is harmless.

I think of the shape outside my window, the brick and the drawing, the letter left at the front door, and now the article. Is it all the same person? What is a clue, and what is someone messing around? I need to figure out who's playing with me. This is too much to ignore.

Whoever put that article in my bag, I don't think it's *him*. He wouldn't risk getting caught. He'd be changing the habit of a lifetime. The only people he ever got that close to are dead.

I stare across the courtyard at the sixth and seventh graders turning every moment into a game, laughing their way to class like they don't have a care in the world.

That's when I see Jamie, the boy who pulled me back from

the alley, and he catches my eye before I can look away and bounds over with the widest smile. By the time he reaches me, it has changed into an awkward grimace.

"Hey," he says.

"Hi."

He doesn't say anything else, just stares at me as if he expects something until I ask, "What're you up to?"

It's stupid. But it's all I've got. I can talk to Hanna and Emily for hours about nothing, but I can't say a single decent sentence to a boy, even one like Jamie. Well, that's not entirely true. I have to script it first.

"I'm off to French," Jamie says, and for a split second, it looks like he's going to speak some more.

Don't ask me how, but I can actually see the thought cross his mind before he shakes his head and looks disappointed with himself. I smile because I like how goofy he is, then blush because I barely know him.

"Has anything else happened?" he asks. "You know...like before?"

I touch my bag and almost show Jamie the newspaper article before changing my mind. I don't know him well enough to be that honest, even if he is the only person on my street paying attention.

"No," I say. "It's been quiet."

I feel my tears push on whatever holds them back, then I shrug and walk away.

When I turn, Jamie is still staring at me, and I have two thoughts, one after the other: *I should have showed him* and *What if he did it?*

58

It sounds like it's in my dreams, a faraway scratching that grows louder until I realize I'm awake. I hold my breath and focus on the noise, convinced someone is in my room, rustling in the shadows.

But it's not that close. It's near but somehow distant at the same time. And when I concentrate, I hear a tap against my window, then something slowly scraping along the glass. I clench my fists, my heart racing, then I slip out of bed and creep to my desk, feeling for the head cam in the dark.

The noise stops for a moment, then starts again, a thud followed by a scrape, like fists and fingernails.

I have practiced how to use the camera so many times, but my hands won't do what I want them to. They're shaking and sweating and useless.

"Come on," I whisper. "You can do this."

The record light flashes on, my room glowing red, and I stand by my window, daring myself to pull back the curtain.

I follow the noise scraping from left to right, and I don't want to see what's there. If it's really him, what does he want from me?

My breathing fills the room, frantic and jagged, and my nails have cut tiny half-moons into my palms. But it's now or never, so I grip the curtain, focus on my mother, and pull.

Something slips below the window, and when I look down, he's standing by our front door. He has a long branch in his hand, and seeing his shape in the darkness, my heart finds another gear, pulsing through my skull.

He drops the branch and steps back, holding one arm to his face and turning the other around and around like he's playing charades, like he wants me to film him.

"Who are you?" I whisper, holding the camera up.

This is not going out live. Whatever I film, Danny will edit it and put it out as additional highlights.

He stands there, staring up at me, every part of him covered except his eyes, and I slowly reach for my phone, ready to dial 999. That's when I notice a shape behind him, slowly moving forward, getting closer step by careful step.

It's Jamie, and he has a hammer in his hand.

"What are you doing?" I whisper.

He's going to get hurt, and I can't handle this. I feel sick and helpless, and before I can do anything, he swings and smashes the man on the shoulder.

The man yells and turns, and Jamie swings again, hitting the man in the chest, and he stumbles back, looks both ways, then starts running.

Jamie pauses for a moment, as if he has realized how stupid

he's being, then he runs after the man, and I pull on a hoodie and my shoes and follow them, because sometimes I can be just as stupid.

I see them down the street, and Jamie tackles the man from behind, pulling him to the ground. He's holding the hammer above his head, saying something I can't hear while I run toward them, yelling Jamie's name.

He stares up at me and looks both happy and confused at the same time.

"I caught him," he says.

The man still has his face covered, but you can tell from his eyes that he's shitting himself.

Jamie looks down and says, "You are sick, you know that?"

Then he pulls off the man's hood and his hat and the scarf covering the bottom half of his face, and I can't believe my eyes.

"What the fuck?" I say.

And the man who smashed my window, the man standing like a shadow in the middle of my street, says, "I'm sorry, Jessica. You were never supposed to find out."

59

Michael the cameraman, the man I let into my bedroom every Monday morning, lies there, staring up at us, and says, "Could you lower the hammer?"

Jamie looks at me, and for a second, I imagine what would happen if he hit Michael in the face. But I reach out and touch his arm until it falls to his side, the hammer clanking on the pavement.

"It's okay," I say. "I know him."

Jamie stares at me with his mouth open, and I shake my head, unsure what to do next.

"Whose idea was it?" I say at last.

Michael doesn't answer. He stares at me in panic, his head turning left and right like he's looking for a way out.

"Whose idea was it?" I say again, louder this time, and Michael's eyes shoot back to me.

"It was mine," he whispers.

"Does Danny know?"

I don't think I want to hear the answer, but when Michael says, "No," I feel a wave of relief.

"He has no idea," Michael says. "I'm sorry, Jess. If this gets out, I'm fucked."

"Then you're fucked," Jamie says.

He looks hyper, bouncing from one foot to the other, but I turn back to Michael and ask, "Why?"

"I wanted the three months," he says. "We needed some peril."

"So you made it up? It was you all along?"

"I'm sorry."

His voice cracks, and for a moment, I think he's going to cry, but he shakes his head and whispers, "Our month is almost up. I wanted to make sure you got more time. I wanted the best possible show. And when the real Magpie Man didn't come…I thought I'd make it exciting."

"Did you send the texts?"

He nods.

"What's wrong with you? You scared the shit out of me. This isn't a game. It's my life."

He opens his mouth to answer, then stops. He sits with his head down.

"I wasn't even live today. Why bother when no one's watching?"

"Authenticity," Michael says. "It would have been too obvious if I'd only done it on Mondays. Someone would have thought we were faking it. I was relying on you filming. You're getting good at it."

I stare at the sky and wonder what the hell to do next.

My own cameraman betrayed me. We tried to make something real, and it was as fake as everything else.

"What now?" Jamie says, then turns to Michael. "Don't even think about pressing charges for the hammer thing. I thought you were a murderer."

Michael stares at me and says, "What are you going to do?"

I think about his baby daughter and wonder how he could do this, how he could scare me, how he could get my hopes up that I was really closing in on a monster.

If this gets out, that my cameraman fixed entire scenes, the show is over. No one will trust me anymore.

"You owe my dad for the window," I say, and then I grab Jamie's arm and pull him away.

"That's it?" Jamie asks.

"That's it. I need to get away from here. I have to think."

"What about him?"

I look at Michael slowly getting to his feet and say, "Where did you get the article?"

"What?"

"The story about my mom that you put in my bag... Where did you get it?"

"I don't know what you're talking about."

He looks genuinely confused. But then he is a good actor.

"You're lying," I say.

He shakes his head. "I promise you, Jessica. I sent the texts and I threw the brick. But that's all."

60

I phone Danny as soon as I wake up, and he mutters something into the phone, clears his throat, and tries again.

"Hey," I say. "I need to see you."

"Are you okay? Did something happen?"

"Yes. Are you free today?"

"Are *you* free today? Don't you have school?"

"This is more important than school," I tell him, and he agrees to come right away. When I get in his car, I hand him the camera. "Your friend is a freak."

"What?"

I lean over and push Play, and Danny watches Jamie creep up on Michael, chase him down the street, and unmask him.

"What the hell?" Danny says as I search for the slightest suggestion that he's pretending. He looks even more shocked than I was when I found out.

"Michael told me everything. He planned it to get better ratings."

Danny goes quiet for a while, then says, "Jess, I had no idea."

I don't answer, just stare at him until he asks, "What do you want to do?"

"What?"

"It's your show. I'd understand if you don't trust us anymore."

"No, I...I still trust *you*."

"We can get another cameraman," Danny says.

I laugh. "What's the point? It'll be over in a week. I actually thought it might have been *him*. How could I be so stupid?"

"You're not stupid," Danny says. "How about just you and me? We can film everything between us."

"What about Michael?"

"One word to Adrian and he'll be fired."

It's hard to be angry with Danny, but that doesn't mean I'm not.

I know it's foolish to think the Magpie Man was texting me, taunting me, standing outside my window. But now I don't have anything, not even the uncertainty.

I almost tell Danny about the newspaper article, because Michael seemed genuinely clueless when I mentioned it. But if it turns out to be as harmless as everything else, that's a thought too far.

"I'll see you when you're back from your retreat," Danny says. "It won't be our last show. I believe in you."

He can believe all he wants, but I have been chasing the wrong shadows and messaging the wrong monsters.

Even if I get the extension, I'm back to square one.

61

Emily is standing by the bus. She smiles and says, "Are you ready to see what all the fuss is about?"

The rest of the school gives us the evil eye as they walk past, because we're escaping for a week, our normal clothes and suitcases more offensive than if we were giving them the finger.

Emily is doing her best not to pay attention to my head cam, although her eyes keep shooting up, then back to my face.

When I woke up this morning, there was no one in my bedroom filming me, and I missed it. The thought of this being my last show is strange, and Emily's doing a terrible job of distracting me. It was weird how quickly I got used to Michael following me around, and now he's gone.

Now, I'm responsible for making this good enough.

"You'll be fine," Emily says, because sometimes she does notice what's happening, and I hope she's right.

Before we get on the bus, Mr. Collins barges over and starts handing out homework to the English lit students missing this week's class. We don't argue, because that would only make it worse. He would probably come back with twice as much.

As well as working at St. Anthony's, Mr. Collins tutors fifth graders for their standardized tests, and I wonder if he's nicer to them or if all teachers have one way of teaching no matter who they're talking to.

"Are you joining us?" Mr. Humphries asks.

Mr. Collins huffs. "I'll actually be working this week."

Mr. Humphries smiles like it's a joke, but you can see he's offended, and when Mr. Collins leaves, Emily whispers, "Prick."

Mr. Humphries grins until he catches me looking, then clears his throat and says, "Right, let's go."

I'm not quite awake enough for maximum Emily, so I put my headphones on and stare out the window until Jamie strolls past, sees me, and waves.

We didn't talk much after he caught Michael. I said, "Thank you," and he said, "Just doing my job."

It was a strange thing to say, but much stranger things happened that night.

Only now, seeing him watch the bus pull away, does a thought strike me like lightning.

I wasn't live. It wasn't Monday. So how did Jamie know Michael was outside my window? And why the hell did he have a hammer?

62

We drive through huge iron gates and down a gravel path, and then someone gasps and Emily says, "This is, like, my ideal wedding venue."

From outside, it's red and big and not what I pictured when I thought *monastery*. It looks like the luxury houses from boring TV shows—the definition of "grand."

We've seen pictures online and on the PowerPoint Mr. Humphries showed us in class, but they didn't look like this.

At the front doors, a guy stands, arms crossed and smiling, and when we get out, he says, "Welcome to Mayfield Lodge. My name is Tim."

Mr. Humphries shakes his hand, then stares up at the house and smiles. He looks happier than he ever does at school.

Behind me, Jennifer Erswell is giggling, saying what she would like to do to this Tim guy, and Emily makes a face, because she secretly hates her.

"Okay," Mr. Humphries says. "Hand over your phones."

There's a collective "*What?*" but he looks serious and says, "House rules. If I'd told you to leave them at home, you'd have sneaked them in."

Tim holds out a box, and one by one, we give him our phones while Mr. Humphries watches.

When we're done, Tim grins and says, "Grab your bags, and we'll show you to your rooms."

Inside, there are dark-brown beams stretched high across the ceiling and a floor glistening with polish.

"It's fucking awesome," someone mutters.

Mr. Humphries turns and says, "There will be none of that here. Have some respect."

Along one wall, a line of people stand smiling at us, and one at a time, they step forward and take our hands.

The girl in between me and Emily says, "Hello. I'm Saffron. Follow me."

Emily gives me a look, and I shrug, and then we're being led down a hallway and up the stairs.

I know I'm being quiet, but I'm still thinking about Jamie and the hammer. Luckily, Emily talks enough for both of us.

At the end of the hallway, Saffron says, "Here you are."

The room is basic, two beds and a sink and a desk, and Emily claims the bed by the window, then turns to Saffron and says, "I like this place."

She smiles and shows us the bathrooms and the fire exit. The showers are just holes in the floor surrounded by thin plastic curtains.

"So...do you live here?" Emily asks.

"For now," says Saffron.

Then she shows us the dining hall, which is like a converted barn with an alcove for the kitchen. The chairs have high backs, and the tables are shiny and already laid with silverware glistening under two enormous chandeliers.

"I like what you've done with the place," Emily says, and Saffron smiles and walks away.

"She's weird," I say.

Emily nods. "She is. But this place..."

She leaves a gap that we both fill with our own adjectives but only in our heads, and then the hall starts to fill up with the rest of the class, and everyone is smiling.

When Mr. Humphries walks past, he says, "What do you think, girls?"

Emily says, "It'll do."

He laughs and collects his food from the kitchen, and we copy him.

The tables are long, like in medieval feasts, which means Emily and I can't sit on our own. Instead, we have to sit with Ali Ballard and Pav Kaur and the Slovakian girl, Maya, who only joined junior year and looks over twenty.

"Isn't it amazing?" Ali asks, and we nod and do our best to ignore her.

Our group is three big, and that's how we like it. Without Hanna, it's the two of us, and we have no intention of faking friendships just because we're somewhere else. Even here, away from school, away from my family and the Magpie Man and everything I know, nothing has changed. Not really.

At the next table, Jennifer Erswell says, "Isn't this place orgasmic?"

Everything she says is sexual, even though we think she's never actually done it. I don't care either way. You don't scratch an itch like Jennifer. You let her talk and do your best to ignore her, or she'll latch on and never let go.

I look around at all the cliques forced to mingle, at Saffron and the other volunteers, at Mr. Humphries sitting with a woman who looks like a hippie and an old man with thin gray hair. I figure he's at least eighty, and as I stare, his eyes quickly dart from his food to my face, and I look away.

When I glance back, he's still staring at me, not smiling like the others, his face flat and emotionless, and when Emily sees what I'm doing, she nudges me and says, "I think he likes you."

But I don't think he does. He doesn't seem happy to see me at all.

The four boys in our class, Harrison, Yinka, Austin, and Sam, are squashed at one end of Jennifer's table, doing their best to leave a gap. They have a whole wing of the monastery to themselves—a room each while we're sharing in twos. They're nice enough, but I don't think they like being outnumbered.

Only then do I remember that all this is being livestreamed. My audience can see everything I can, and I wonder if it matters anymore.

I touch the camera wrapped around my head and try to recall when I got so comfortable wearing it.

We put our lives out there in all sorts of ways—on Instagram and Facebook and Twitter and Snapchat—but it's always edited. We handpick our best moments and hope the world gives a shit.

But this isn't a highlights reel. This is just a Monday. Not your average one maybe, but not cut up and stuck back together to make it more interesting.

I hope Danny is pleased with my first attempt at directing, even if it's our final show.

63

That evening, we hang out in a huge living room with comfy sofas, all chatting about our first day. The volunteers stand around the edges, but only Emily and I notice.

"Are they guarding us?" she asks.

"They freak me out," I say. "Do you think they're being weird?"

"They look drugged up," Emily says, and I know what she means.

They have a dozy kind of happiness on their faces, smiling like drunk people laughing at jokes inside their own heads.

Mr. Humphries is standing by a bookcase, and the woman he ate dinner with claps, and everyone quiets down.

"We hope you've enjoyed your first day," she says. "My name is Andrea, and I would like you to act like kangaroos."

We stare at one another, wondering if we misheard, but then she claps again and shouts, "Get up! Come on! This is not a drill. I want to see those kangaroos."

She's bouncing on the spot, and next to her, Mr. Humphries

is smiling like this is totally normal. When she rubs her nose on his shoulder, he laughs.

"Get up!" Andrea shouts. "Get up, get up, get up!"

I stare at Emily, who glances at my head cam, then back at the bouncing foolish person.

I check that the red light is still on, because whatever this is, Danny won't want me to miss it.

Pav whispers something to Ali, and Andrea swings around and says, "You! You are my first kangaroo."

Pav shakes her head and looks down, but the woman jumps forward and sticks her head under Pav's chin and nudges it, then sniffs her face.

"Is that fear I can smell?" Andrea asks, but Pav doesn't answer, and everyone is doing their best not to make eye contact while still watching to see what happens next.

Then Andrea grabs Pav's hand and pulls her up. Holding both arms, she starts pulling her up and down, whispering, "Boing, boing, boing," getting louder until she's shouting it, "BOING! BOING! BOING!"

And when she lets go, Pav keeps bouncing.

Then Andrea is making her way around the room, saying, "You're no fun. You're no fun. You're no fun," tapping each of us on the head as she goes.

The volunteers step forward and lift us up and make us bounce, and Saffron says, "Don't be scared."

Pav is still doing it, laughing now, and following Andrea around the room.

Emily shrugs and says, "Why not?" and she jumps, and I try it, just once, and feel awkward for stopping.

It feels like the first few moments of dancing when you know everyone is watching. And then it feels like the next few hours, when you don't care.

Before we realize it, we're bouncing all over the place, and I'm laughing, crashing into walls and sofas and people. After the last few weeks, it feels like a weight has been lifted. It feels like I'm floating.

And then Andrea yells, "Stop!" and we do, and I'm clinging to Jennifer's shoulders, and we're both gasping and giggling and smiling at each other.

"Okay," Andrea says. "Stop where you are and talk to whoever is next to you. Stop acting like kangaroos and start acting like people."

64

"That was clever," Jennifer says.

We're all sitting down again, everyone talking to someone they used to do their best to ignore.

I look over at Emily, who is chatting with the Slovakian girl, Maya, and they are laughing like they've been friends for years.

Mr. Humphries is talking to Yinka, Andrea to Pav, everyone to someone outside their clique.

"I can't believe we did that," I say, then I catch Jennifer looking at my head cam. "Can they see you?"

What I mean is did her parents sign the permission slip to unblur her face?

She nods. "I've watched some of it. I saw what happened to your window."

That's all anyone wants to talk about now, and I hope it's not what I'm remembered for.

"What do you think of this place?" I ask, trying to change the subject.

Jennifer looks around and smiles. "It's magical."

I think back to dinner when she called it "orgasmic" but don't mention that.

She seems different now, and if Emily's right and she is pretending, I wish she'd drop the act. I like this version of Jennifer a lot more.

Later, Andrea tells us to mingle, and by the end of the night, I've spoken to practically everyone here. Even the boys, who rarely say anything in class, can't stop talking. Forgetting to act cool, they are just normal.

When we go to our rooms, I push my bed in front of the door, because there's no lock, and Emily says, "I don't think you need to do that here."

I know what she means, but I do it anyway. Then we talk until Emily's whispers turn to snores.

At midnight, I turn the camera off and put it back in my suitcase.

I thought the first day here would be the hardest, because the world was watching, but no one seemed to care.

We all let go and acted like kangaroos and talked honestly, and if we were that open with a camera in our face, I can't wait for the rest of the week.

65

After breakfast, Mr. Humphries asks us to line up outside. When he starts reading our names, two at a time, my stomach flips.

"Jess," he says. "You're with Bernie today."

We exchange looks, then stare at the ground, and I wonder if she feels as awkward as I do.

Bernie, my old best friend, one-third of a group we assumed was more special than it turned out to be.

I hope I never think of Emily and Hanna like that—as a moment in time, a hobby we grew out of.

I haven't really spoken to Bernie since we were kids. We were inseparable when she lived next door. Then her mom remarried and they moved to Harmony. Although it was only a bus ride away, she changed schools, and by the time we arrived at St. Anthony's, we were strangers.

I guess we were drifting apart even before she moved, when

Bernie was kept away from the girl with the murdered mom as if tragedy were contagious. So basically this pairing could have been better.

"This is a spirit walk," Andrea says. "Be as open and honest as you wish. But try to enjoy it."

I look at Emily, who's been paired with Yinka, and she nods at Bernie and mouths, "Awkward."

The way every friendship group has been split, you know Mr. Humphries fixed it. But after last night, I shouldn't have been surprised.

Mayfield Lodge is surrounded by countryside, and every five minutes, they send another pair through the gates, one going right, the next left, then right again.

"If you bump into another pair, just keep walking," Andrea says. "This is a two-person exercise."

"What should we talk about?" Austin asks.

Andrea smiles. "Everything. Off you go," she tells us, and Bernie starts walking without looking at me.

Emily laughs and I roll my eyes, then follow.

Everywhere, there are cows and sheep and huge green fields. It feels like Harmony, only there's no sea breeze and no sound of the waves, only the gentle buzz of insects and birds singing.

For a long time, we don't say anything. We look the other way and pretend this isn't weird. Our conversations ran out a long time ago. But not talking is making me feel sick, so I say a few things in my head, then one out loud.

"I'm glad I came," I say.

Bernie looks at me. "Me too."

"I wasn't going to," I say, and Bernie nods.

"Me neither." Then she turns her head back to the cows in the field, and I think that's the end of it.

But still looking away, she says, "I wish it was like this all the time."

There are no animals on my side of the road, just green, but that is where I look and what I talk to.

"What did you think of the kangaroo thing?" I ask.

Bernie says, "Probably the same as you."

I look at her then, and she's already looking at me, the faintest impression of a smile on her face.

She's prettier than when we were friends. Her hair looks better, but her smile hasn't changed, and suddenly, I miss her.

"God knows what they've got planned for tonight," she says.

I laugh and realize this couldn't have happened yesterday. With a camera pointed at her face, Bernie wouldn't have said a word.

She knew me when I had a mom, and being alone with her now, for the first time in forever, I want to cry. By the time I got to middle school, I was old news.

When you're a kid and it's your first day at a new school, a part of you wants to shout how your mom was murdered, to get it out of the way.

Nan said I should find out who my friends were first. She said it's easy to be liked for the wrong reasons. That's why I waited to tell Hanna and Emily about the Magpie Man. But Bernie knew so much earlier, and that should mean more than it does.

Ten years later, forced together by the flick of a teacher's pen, she says, "How's your dad?"

"He's okay," I lie.

I don't tell her that what he's doing right now, any now, is sitting, staring, remembering a life that feels impossible.

"I always liked him," Bernie says. "I miss my dad so much. I don't see him anymore."

Her parents got divorced when we were babies, but he still picked her up on weekends. He'd wait outside and she would run to him, and they'd do whatever dads and daughters do when they only have a day to do it.

I remember once he argued with her mom's new boyfriend, Bernie's mom begging them not to, while we watched from a window, and after that, he stopped ringing the bell.

Families break in all sorts of ways, and I should feel sorry for her, but I don't. She was one of the first examples of how people drift away after death, our playdates going from weekly to rarely to never, because whose parents want their kids hanging out in a house of grief?

She stays quiet for a while, then she says, "My mom barely talks to me anymore. My sister's the princess, and I'm...I'm something else."

Bernie didn't have a sister when I knew her, but ten years is a long time, and I guess her mom's second marriage is going better than her first.

"I'm sure she loves you," I say, and Bernie gives the slightest nod, then a shake and a sigh.

"All she wants to know is what I'm going to do next," she says. "It's like she's forcing me out of the house. I have no idea what I'm going to do. I'm sixteen!"

"I don't know either."

"But you have an excuse!" Bernie says. Then, "Sorry. I just mean no one will pressure you to do anything. Your dad won't force you to apply for college if you don't want to."

We haven't had that talk yet, because I don't think college is for me. I'm scared of starting another new life, far away from the only people who get me. And I'm scared of leaving Dad on his own.

If things were different, if Bernie were still my best friend, I'd tell her the truth. I would explain how the eleventh-grade career day terrified me, how the thought of college placement tests and personal statements makes me feel sick.

That is all that matters at St. Anthony's. They don't care about the kids who aren't interested in degrees. When they handed out questionnaires asking where we saw ourselves in five years, there wasn't a box marked *Secured justice for dead mom*.

"I'll probably look after my dad," I say. "He's kind of useless."

It's supposed to be a joke, because I would rather laugh about it than admit I'd be useless without him too.

But Bernie looks serious and says, "That's not fair. You know what I'd give to have my dad back?"

Like Emily's mom, she doesn't understand that death is different from divorce. She thinks all loss is measured the same, even the kind you can fix.

"No offense, Bernie, but you have no idea what I've been through. I'm allowed to joke about my dad."

She's facing the field again, and for a long time, she doesn't speak, until she says, "And I can still miss mine."

"You can...but don't think it's the same thing. My mom died. She's never coming back. If your dad decides to give a shit, he could see you next week."

I think that's the end of the conversation, and I hope they don't ask us to go over it when we get back, because I don't think this is what they were hoping for.

It's not until we are about to walk through the gate that Bernie, still with her face away from me, says, "Fuck you, Jess."

66

That night, after dinner, they take us down a new hallway we haven't seen before.

At the end, a ladder leads into the ceiling, and we climb until we're sitting side by side in a loft space bigger than we imagined. Andrea sits in the middle with her eyes closed, a small table in front of her and a candle flickering in the darkness.

How quickly none of this feels weird—that is the power of Mayfield Lodge.

When my eyes get used to the darkness, I can make out framed pictures along the walls, group after group of smiling school kids.

When we are settled, Andrea clears her throat and says, "Welcome to the prayer room. Anyone who does not wish to pray outwardly may, of course, keep their reflections to themselves. But please, if you have anything to share with the group, do so. There are no strangers here. Not anymore."

I look over at Bernie, but she has her head down, and I wonder if she hates me or just what I said. Things escalated quickly, and I feel guilty for not being honest and for using the dead mom card when it had nothing to do with that.

Next to me, Emily squeezes my hand, and I squeeze back. Then Andrea lifts the candle and passes it to Saffron, and we listen to her pray.

"Please watch over our new visitors," she says. "Let us learn from one another and end the week better than we started it."

She probably says the same thing every time, but when she passes the candle to Mr. Humphries, I forget everything else and listen to him whisper into the darkness.

"We had a son," he says. "His name was Oliver. We lost him to cancer."

This isn't like any prayer I've ever heard. Mr. Humphries isn't asking for something. He's telling his story the way I told mine, and I hate myself for not knowing sooner. But then most heartbreak doesn't make it on to the news.

There are sniffles in the darkness, and when I feel a tear creeping down my cheek, I realize I'm not crying for myself. I'm crying for my teacher and his lost son.

When I get the candle, I don't speak out loud. I talk to the ghost in my head. I tell my mom how much I miss her, how sorry I am, how I will always love her and keep her memory alive.

Before I pass the candle to Emily, I make a promise to do this more often. Because she was with me, right there in the patterns the candle made. My mother: the trick of the light.

67

There's no bouncing around like kangaroos today. Back in the living room, we all feel super chill.

Only Mr. Humphries gets to feel this over and over. The rest of us get a single, temporary hit. But when you've heard what he said in the prayer room, it's no surprise he keeps coming back.

When Emily goes to the bathroom, the old man I saw talking to Mr. Humphries on the first night walks over and introduces himself.

"I'm Reg," he says.

He has a smile on his face this time, and it suits him better than the grumpy look he had yesterday at dinner. Whatever reason he had for staring me out, he seems to have forgotten.

"What did you think of the prayer room?" he asks.

"I may need some time to do it justice."

He smiles and says, "I understand."

"Are you a volunteer like Saffron?"

"No. Have you seen the RV?"

I nod.

"That's my home. I visited twelve years ago and never left."

"They let you stay here?"

"They do."

I watch Emily come back, see Reg, and then walk over to Eloise.

If this had happened last week, she would have given me a dirty look, because there was no one else to talk to. But since the kangaroos and the spirit walk and the prayer room, we are one big happy family.

I wonder if Reg knows who I am, but I like the idea that he doesn't. When everyone else knows your history, it's fun being a stranger for a while.

"I liked the photos in the prayer room of all the other schools," I say.

Reg tilts his head, and I say, "If we don't act so uptight, if we make new friends and think about stuff that actually matters, maybe we can be another picture on that wall."

"I think your place is already reserved," he says.

I don't have any granddads. My mom's father died before I was born, and my dad's dad passed away when I was three. But if I did, I would want them to be like Reg.

I feel different here...lighter. And I wonder if this is what closure feels like.

I always thought justice came first. But sitting here, surrounded by smiling faces and feeling waves of genuine happiness for the first time in a decade, I can imagine one without the other.

68

"I have something to tell you," I whisper, and when Emily grunts, I say, "Michael sent the texts. He was the one standing outside my window. It wasn't the Magpie Man. It was all a lie."

When she doesn't reply, I assume she's asleep, but then she says, "Fucker."

"And Jamie had a hammer."

"What?"

"That tenth-grade kid, the one who pulled me back from the alley. He crept up on Michael with a hammer. That's how we caught him."

The duvet rustles, and when the lamp flashes on, Emily is sitting up with eyes too wide for this time of night.

"I shouldn't have said anything."

"Fuck that. Tell me everything."

"Michael sent the messages and smashed my window, because

he wanted to make a better show. He didn't think I could do it, so he wrote a different script. But it means I wasn't even close to catching the killer. Everything that happened was fake."

"So what now?" Emily asks.

"I don't know. Danny thinks we can still get the full three months, but it's pointless anyway."

"It's not pointless. You've got people talking. They are thinking about you, Jess. So what if Michael was faking it? It's not over."

Emily swaps beds and pulls me into a hug, and I don't bother pulling away.

"How hard did Jamie hit him?" she asks.

"Hard."

We sit in silence for a while until she says, "He's saved you twice."

"I guess," I say, and it's not until Emily makes a face that I realize I'm grinning from ear to ear.

69

We all sit in the living room in silence, our goodbyes said, our tears cried, the feelings we have in the real world already coming back hard.

Living here would be so much better, so much easier, but for how long? Eventually, wherever you are, your history catches up.

Andrea claps, and as we're preparing to be kangaroos, she asks us to sit in a circle, and one by one, the volunteers pick someone at random to talk about.

When it's Reg's turn, he looks me in the eye and says, "I think Jessica is incredibly brave. I hope she realizes that."

This is how they prepare us for home, by pumping up our egos, and I guess there are worse ways to say goodbye.

Afterward, they turn up the music and let us hang out, and whenever I check the clock, it's an hour later than I thought it was.

I watch Jennifer move from person to person, whispering in their ears, and when she gets to me, she says, "We're having a party in my room tonight. Keep it on the down-low."

I laugh because she sounds ridiculous, and she smiles and says, "We have plenty to drink."

She leaves before I can reply, spreading the message to the rest of the room. She looks so suspicious, but Mr. Humphries and Andrea are talking quietly in the corner, and the other volunteers aren't paying attention.

When they turn the music down and tell us to leave, I start to make my way back to our room when Emily stops me and says, "Where are you going?"

"To bed."

"Or..."

"Or nothing. I'm tired."

Emily leans in so close her breath tickles my neck. "Jennifer... is having...a party."

I shrug, and she sighs and says, "One drink."

When I don't say anything, she says, "Please," then starts pulling my arm until I let her win.

She smiles with all her teeth and dances down the hallway, singing, "Boing! Boing!"

A lot has changed since those first reluctant bounces at the start of the week, and I'm going to miss this place more than I ever thought I would.

When Emily knocks on Jennifer's door, we hear whispers inside, then something slides across the floor, and Pav pokes her head out. When she sees us, she grins and lets us in, and the room is jammed with our entire class.

"We didn't think you were coming," Pav says, quickly closing the door and sliding a chair under the handle.

The boys are here too—everyone is—and on the desk by the window, there are about ten bottles of vodka and Bacardi and whiskey and something bright blue.

When Jennifer sees where I'm looking, she says, "Compliments of Maya."

I guess that's one perk of looking like you're over twenty: you never get IDed.

"Help yourself," Pav says, and Emily grabs a plastic cup and makes a vodka and Coke.

"Not for me," I say.

No one laughs or calls me a prude; they do their own thing, quietly talking and giggling and trying desperately to make this night last forever.

Mom didn't drink either. When her friends talked about it, they made it sound bigger than it was, like she didn't drink *anything*.

On the evenings they came over, you'd think my mother had given up breathing. But when they left, wobbly-legged and shouting, she would give me an extra kiss and whisper an extra good night, and I secretly promised to copy her.

Bernie and Eloise are chatting in the corner, and I think about going over and apologizing, because I don't want our argument to be a memory I keep from this place. But Emily distracts me, and the next time I look, Bernie has gone.

Even with the window open, the room is boiling, and after a while, more people start to leave.

The happiness is turning to sorrow, Ali silently sobbing into

Sam's shoulder, and at some unknown point, we stop wanting to be together and start wanting to be alone.

A few people head outside, and from the window, I watch Emily drift across the grass. She stops at a tree and starts climbing. Halfway up, she sits and stares away from us, into the huge black everything else.

Back home, she likes to sit in the tree in the woods behind her garden. She says it's nice being off the ground for a while. She says things look better closer to the sky.

There's another movement in the darkness, and I see Mr. Humphries pacing in the courtyard. He's talking to himself, and I wonder how he feels about going home.

When Austin and Yinka come around the corner, laughing, Mr. Humphries steps back until he's swallowed by the shadows.

Walking the hallway, I expect to bump into people but I don't. Everyone has found a solitary somewhere. Everyone is dealing with this in their own way.

I need to talk to someone, but Emily would be annoyed if I joined her in the tree, so instead I go to Bernie's room. Maybe, hopefully, I can make things right.

I listen at her door and hear rustling inside. I knock and no one answers, but there's murmuring, so I go in, and Bernie is lying on the bed, her limbs crooked like a doll thrown from a stroller. There's an empty vodka bottle on the bedside table.

I shake her and shout her name, but she doesn't respond. A pool of vomit is lying crusty on the bed, and thin yellow strands hang from her mouth.

"Bernie!" I shout. "Bernie! Wake up!" But she doesn't.

I go into the hall and scream, and when no one comes, I run to the living room to tell Andrea what's happened. Then she's leaning over Bernie, wiping the vomit from her mouth, and someone touches me—Mr. Humphries—and he pulls me into the hall and whispers how everything will be okay.

Over his shoulder, I see Reg, moving so fast, and the tears stinging my face make him shimmer.

"Move!" he says.

The hallway is filling with people, everyone asking what happened.

I say things, make noises at least, and then I'm fighting my way back into the room.

Reg is leaning over her. He's breathing into her mouth, then pushing hard on her chest. He does it over and over again until the screams have turned to whimpers, until our hopes have turned to fears, until we know she must be dead.

70

Reg doesn't stop until the paramedics arrive.

They order us into the hallway, and Mr. Humphries tells us to go to our rooms, but we don't. Instead, we wait silently in the living room while an ambulance rushes Bernie to the hospital.

We sit in the same place where we acted like kangaroos, where we laughed and danced, and some of us cry while others wonder if we should.

This is not how we want to remember Mayfield Lodge, but you don't get to pick your defining memories.

When Mr. Humphries comes in, Eloise runs to him and says, "Is she awake?"

"They're doing all they can," he replies, and the whole room shivers.

"I can't believe she'd do that," Harrison says.

Eloise shouts, "She didn't! She wouldn't!" But her voice

cracks, because it happened. No one saw it, but Bernie must have taken the bottle back to her room and drunk every last drop.

I haven't really known her for a long time, so I don't know what drama she has going on and if it's enough to justify drinking herself to death. But I keep thinking back to our spirit walk, wondering if what I said about her dad was enough to flick a switch.

I came here thinking my story was the only one worth telling, but everyone has something to say, and I was stupid for not listening sooner.

71

Reg answers the RV door and leads me inside.

"I think she was dead," I say, "until you saved her."

"I didn't do anything," he mumbles. "It was the paramedics."

I didn't sleep last night. Emily and I stared at different parts of the same ceiling, our words abandoning us.

This place was supposed to heal us. It was supposed to make us see things differently. But all I see is Bernie's lifeless body; all I feel is the panic of being powerless. And yet I don't want to leave.

No one talks about the show here. No one feels sorry for me or stands behind me, hoping to be on-camera. No one throws bricks through my window or slips horrible memories in my bag or makes Magpie Man memes.

Here, I am just Jess. I'm allowed to be quiet. I'm allowed to laugh without feeling guilty. I'm allowed to be the girl I might have been if Mom were still alive. Here, I feel closer to her than I have in years.

I've felt lost and scared for a decade. And it took coming here to realize my broken life isn't unique.

Mr. Humphries has spent years without the son he assumed would outlive him.

Bernie misses her dad enough to down a bottle of vodka and not care about the consequences.

I used to dream about the day they caught the Magpie Man.

I didn't know what would happen, but it had to be better than this. It had to be better than waking up every morning and feeling that terrible hole open all over again.

Mayfield has taught me to fill the hole with something else, with memories and prayers and new beginnings. But I'm scared to go back now, to my quiet house and my heartbroken dad and a show that didn't work.

I might already be canceled, or they may want me for another two months, and I don't know what's worse.

"I want to stay," I whisper.

Reg chuckles and says, "This isn't the place for you, Jessica. It's time to leave."

"And then what?"

"And then you live, like your mother would want you to. You can't grieve forever."

"You know who I am?"

"Of course. I know how brave you are," Reg says. "And I know your mother would be incredibly proud."

"You don't know anything about my family."

"I know how desperate you are to catch that man. And I know you've lost yourself in the chase. You need to move on. Your mother would want that."

"No offense, Reg, but that's bullshit."

My fists clench, and I'm shaking, because he can't speak for my mom.

He sighs, and there's that look again, the one he gave me on the first night. All his friendly-old-man vibes disappear, replaced by a look I recognize after all. He looks like my dad. He has the same sorrow stains. Only he's better at hiding them.

"I don't claim to know what you've gone through," Reg says, "but I do know loss. And I know that nothing good can come from drowning in it."

If I close my eyes slightly, if I concentrate hard enough, I can imagine my dad looking like Reg when he's old.

I watch a tear forming in the corner of his eye, but he blinks, and it's gone, then he touches my hand, his skin hard and rough.

"My wife passed away a year after we were married," he says. "I waited a lifetime to meet her, and she was taken from me in no time at all. She was sixty-three when she walked down the aisle, and she was still the most beautiful woman in the room."

Another tear forms, and this time, it slips out, falling into the cracks on his face before he wipes it away.

"She was ill the day I met her. But she didn't tell me. She wanted a love affair, and I gave it to her. And then I watched her die."

"I'm sorry," I whisper, but Reg shakes his head.

"We had a little while."

He sits in silence, staring over my shoulder at something only he can see.

When he comes back, he blinks away whatever memory he was recalling and says, "I meant no offense. But you are focusing on the wrong thing. Go home and forget about the Magpie Man. Focus on your mother. Remember the memories you were lucky enough to share."

I think about Reg's dead wife, Bernie's divorced parents, and all the other lives broken this way or that. I assumed that when you're dealt a hand as bad as mine, nothing else compares. But maybe Reg is right.

I need to start living.

72

The bus drops us back at school, and we all walk off in different directions. Some to the parents waiting with smiles on their faces, others to the back seats of cars already revving their engines, a few, like Emily, to the houses within walking distance, and me to the bus stop where I wait twenty minutes, then head home.

But first I knock on Jamie's door, and when he answers, I try to ignore his smile and say, "I have to ask you something."

"Okay."

"How did you know Michael was outside my house that night, and why did you have a hammer?"

It's a question I should have asked right away, but Jamie grins like he was expecting it and says, "I keep an eye out."

I flash back to the night we met, his dad's face half hidden by a curtain, and wonder if the whole family are snoops.

But like he can read my mind, Jamie says, "When I saw

him walk past, I grabbed the hammer from under the sink, just in case. I didn't want him to hurt you. I see your dad drive past sometimes, leaving for work, so I keep watch. I'm sorry if that's weird."

It is a little. But it's also cute, and I'm getting used to the idea of having a hero.

"Okay," I say, leaving before the blush reaches my cheeks.

I walk the final few steps slowly, imagining life after Mayfield, and as I lift my key, the front door opens, and Nan is there, smiling.

I'm not expecting her. This isn't one of her days. But I am so glad she's here.

I drop my suitcase and fall into her arms and cry, and she doesn't ask what's wrong. She just holds me the way only some people can: the way family should.

She hugs me long after I've finished sobbing, stroking my hair and whispering shushing noises into my ear.

When I step back, she says, "We've missed you."

"I've missed you too," I say.

I hear the floorboards creak, then Dad is at the bottom of the stairs. He has had a haircut, and when he holds his arms out, I let them close around me.

I expect to cry even harder, but instead, I feel warm and safe and glad to be home.

Dad's hugs come with small print. No matter how good they feel, they remind me of what we've lost. But they're worth it.

Then I tell them about Mayfield Lodge, and Dad doesn't take his eyes off me the whole time. Whenever I look back, he holds his smiles longer than usual.

I wonder if something happened while I was away. If Nan told him he had to try harder. If, like me, he had a realization this week—that life is too short to waste, no matter the cards you are dealt.

When I tell them about Bernie, Nan says, "We know, dear. The school phoned."

I don't say I might have been responsible. I'm trying to drown out that thought.

"You used to play together all the time," Dad says, and then he drifts off, and I wonder what moment he's revisiting.

I think about telling him what Bernie said on our spirit walk, how she had always liked him. But for some reason, I think it will make him sad.

Instead, I let Nan ask the questions, answering with a smile, all the while wondering how to tell them we may not need justice after all, not if Reg was right, and celebrating Mom is better than drowning in her loss.

Will they be angry with me? Or will they be relieved, because Dad didn't want me to do it in the first place and Nan must be realizing it's not as harmless as I made out?

73

When I charge my phone, I'm not prepared for what I see.

My notifications are ridiculous, and my subscribers have jumped from five hundred thousand to over a million.

"What's going on?" I whisper, and as if he heard me, Danny calls.

"Tell me you've been watching."

"Watching what?"

"The others."

When I don't answer, he says, "You got the full three months, Jess. They made sure."

"Who did?"

Danny laughs. "You have some catching up to do. Watch the highlights. Then you'll understand."

He hangs up before I can answer, so I click on Ella's channel, and her face fills the screen.

"I'm done with this," she says. "I only did it because my dad forced me to. I don't want you to watch me anymore.

I want you to watch Jessica Simmons. We have to catch the Magpie Man."

I can't believe what I'm seeing. She's sabotaging her ratings… for me. But why?

When I click on Lucas's latest episode, he says, "Fuck fame. It's time for justice. Don't worry about me. Do something important. Help catch a killer."

I'm scared to click on Ryan's, because I already know what he's going to do, and I can't process it.

When I finally do, he says, "I'm sorry for the terrible things my brother did. But he's gone now. The Magpie Man is still out there."

Tears tickle my cheeks, but I don't wipe them away.

I'm too busy watching Ryan stare into the camera and say, "I don't want anyone else to die."

I start sobbing. If Dad and Nan hear me through the floorboards, they don't intrude. Part of me wants them to. But another part needs to do this alone.

When I go to Sonia's channel, she smiles and says, "I know a lot of you have been waiting for the twist. I've read your theories about why they chose me. But you're wrong. I don't have a hook like the others. I was chosen as a test. Would people watch to see what happens next…even if nothing does?

"Could someone"—she makes air quotes—"'ordinary' win this thing by keeping you guessing? But I don't want to. I don't *have* to. I've spoken to the others, and we've agreed. You should be watching Jessica Simmons. We all should."

When Sonia is finished, I reach for Mom's picture and cry even harder.

I was thinking of quitting, but what now? I feel so full. I want to let out all the sadness and fear and anger. I want to scream until I'm empty. But some storms are secrets, so I close my eyes, calm mine as best I can, then unpack my suitcase.

It's almost empty when I see it. I already know what it is before I reach inside. This time, it's scrunched up, buried deep rather than gently tucked beside a book, but as I unfold it, I see that same photograph of my mother, in color this time, and the same story with different words.

It's another article, written a few days after her murder.

I go to my desk and find the other clipping, then lay them next to each other on the carpet.

I can't look away from her face. She looks so happy. She has no idea what's coming.

The sickness rises in my stomach, knotting it, then continuing anyway until I run to the bathroom and throw up.

Michael was telling the truth. He only did so much.

Whoever is giving me these articles was with me at Mayfield Lodge.

74

Danny finds out about Bernie five minutes after we walk up to the school entrance.

"Mr. Humphries has been fired," Emily says dramatically.

Hanna says, "Suspended. He has been suspended."

But surely, eventually, it will be the same thing.

I'm not sure if we should be talking about this on-camera, but Danny doesn't stop us.

Emily has already filled Hanna in on everything, but Hanna still makes a face when Ali, Pav, and Jennifer join us in the yard and start talking like we've been doing this for years.

"Has anyone heard if Bernie's okay?" Pav asks, and we all shrug.

I guess Bernie didn't tell anyone about our disagreement before she did it. If she had, they'd be blaming me, and I feel guilty.

We look for Eloise, because if anyone knows what's going on, she does, but there's no sign of her.

"It feels weird being back," Jennifer says.

Emily sighs. "I bet the other classes that went to Mayfield Lodge felt better, though."

In past years, students came back from Mayfield with happy thoughts and epiphanies. We came back with a horror story.

While everyone else talks, I watch them, looking for the slightest slip of the masks they wear, trying to figure out who put the article in my suitcase.

I was so close to quitting. This close to admitting, live, that I was giving up the search. But Sonia staged a coup. How can I give up after that?

Plus, Michael wasn't at Mayfield Lodge. He isn't the one giving me the articles. My list of suspects is limited, and I know them all.

I think of Jennifer's transformation from sex-obsessed to best-friend material, Pav's stint as a kangaroo, and Eloise's friendship with Bernie, and how any of them could have done it.

I think of Yinka, Sam, Austin, and Harrison, the only four boys in a class dominated by girls, and wonder if they are hiding in plain sight.

What if Maya planted it before offering a ton of alcohol as the perfect cover?

It could be any of them, but for once, my drama has been swallowed by someone else's. Bernie is today's headline, and if one of them is taunting me, they have the perfect story to hide behind.

When it's just the three of us, Hanna turns to Emily and says, "Since when are you friends with Jennifer Erswell?"

Emily shrugs. "Since now. She's all right."

"All she talks about is sex."

Emily and I laugh, and I can tell Hanna's annoyed. She hates private jokes when she doesn't know the punchline. But it feels good to laugh and mean it.

"She's actually really nice," I say. "Em was right. She makes up all the stuff about sex. But when you get to know her, she kind of admits that."

Hanna sighs and shakes her head. "I knew that place would make you weird, but I didn't think this would happen."

"What?" Emily asks. "You didn't think we'd make friends with people?"

"Other people," Hanna says. "It's always just the three of us."

This could turn into an argument, but it's kind of cute how jealous she is.

Before Hanna can get angry, I gather them in for a group hug and say, "It will always be us."

They smile and pull me in closer.

Over my shoulder, I see Danny recording every word.

Two months is a long time if we use it right. I can do this. And then I can live the kind of life I saw at Mayfield.

I think of Ella, Sonia, Lucas, and Ryan and feel so grateful. We all applied for a reason, but in the end, was fifteen minutes of fame enough for them? Even Ryan, who could only say sorry so many times.

"Why did they do it?" I ask Danny.

"Because your story matters." He smiles, and I can't help absorbing it, only for a moment, before I think of the newspaper articles and who is responsible.

"What now?" he asks, and I take a deep breath.

"Now we finish this."

75

I sit at my desk with the head cam pointing at my face, my laptop screen in front of me like a live-action mirror. My viewers can see exactly what I can, and I almost chicken out. But this is the next phase.

I have two more months to finish this, and for a second time, I need to start strong.

In the notepad where I wrote the script for my first show, this is the second bullet point on the third page.

Makeup tutorial...with a twist

This would have come sooner, but Michael's texts got in the way. Now I'm making up for lost time.

Applying the foundation, I say, "We all hide behind something."

In between the blusher and the powder, I say, "We all

wear masks of our own making, even around the people we love."

After the eyeshadow, I say, "We get so used to pretending that we forget who we really are."

While I add the eyeliner, then the mascara, I say, "I know you're watching. I know you're out there somewhere, desperate to see how I turned out. Well, here I am. On display for the whole world to see."

As I apply the lipstick, I glance down at the comments under my live feed, appearing then disappearing under the weight of so much hate, so much perversion, the few nice words quickly swallowed by everything else.

How many people watch me because they like me? And how many are here for different reasons?

For the finishing touch, I hold up my perfume, showing the name, then spray.

Only then do I unwrap the towel from around my head and show whoever is watching the finished product, my rusty-colored hair turned black.

I knew the twist, and even I'm shocked at the outcome, unable to speak for a moment, unable to do anything except stare at the picture I've painted over myself.

When I tear my eyes away from what I've done, I look at the image off-camera, at the photograph of my mother.

I look just like her.

I want to cry, and I imagine the makeup I've carefully applied washed away. But I fight back the tears and hold Mom's photo next to my face, my own twisted version of before and after.

I take three deep breaths, my eyes slipping to the comments, then back to the screen.

"I am her," I say. "And I'm still here."

Most of the makeup is mom's, but not the perfume. The makeup was cleared away years ago, packed neatly and tightly in a box and hidden in a drawer under the bed. When I discovered the makeup box, it felt like buried treasure. Now it feels like I'm wearing an extra layer of grief.

If the Magpie Man is watching, he will recognize this face. I want to remind him of the life he took and show him she is in me, in everything I'm doing to find him.

Mom's perfume has been used up over time, not-so-secretly sprayed on the pillow on her side of the bed every night for years. If Dad bought more, he has kept it hidden.

That's why I used my own for the final flourish.

And that's how I know the comment is real, the one that flashes up and is quickly pushed off the page, forcing me to chase it, scrolling down until I can be sure of what it said, until I know for certain that the Magpie Man is watching.

Most of the comments are threats or jokes or rants, but this one's a fact. Two words. One warning.

Wrong perfume.

76

It turns out Mr. Humphries hasn't been suspended, because the next day, everyone who went on the trip has to meet in an empty classroom, and he's there with Mrs. Bradley.

I'm relieved, because he didn't do anything wrong. *We* did. We had the party. Maya bought the alcohol. And Bernie grabbed a whole bottle before she left. Mr. Humphries had nothing to do with it.

I should be in English this morning, but Mr. Collins is away at an educator conference.

"What happened last week is regretful, and we should all be thankful that Bernadette is okay," Mrs. Bradley says.

You can hear the collective sigh of relief, and a few of us start mumbling until the principal says, "That's not to say it is the end of the matter. Who brought the alcohol to Mayfield Lodge?"

We all keep our eyes focused straight ahead, staring at

something that won't stare back. But I can still feel both teachers' eyes burning into my face, my back hot and sticky, the collective guilt of the room weighing heavily on us all.

One person in here is guiltier than most. I just need to figure out who that is.

There are only twelve people in our theology class, and with Bernie gone, that leaves me to watch the four boys, Eloise, Pav, Ali, Jennifer, and Maya.

"We will be conducting a thorough investigation," Mrs. Bradley says. "This is not acceptable behavior. You brought the school into disrepute and put a student's life at risk."

We sit in silence, desperate for this to be over.

"I expect to know the full details of that night by the end of today," she says, turning to Mr. Humphries, who steps forward and clears his throat.

I've never seen him nervous before, but he can hardly get his words out.

"If anyone needs to talk, the school counselor will be in all week," he says, "and my door is always open." He pauses for a moment, then catches the principal's eye and says, "Needless to say, I feel let down by all of you."

I don't think it's a coincidence that this is happening today, twenty-four hours after we came back to school, a day when they don't have a camera in their faces. Mrs. Bradley doesn't want this conversation online.

I don't stand up when they tell us we can go. I hold Emily's hand, silently telling her to stay with me, while the rest of the class leaves.

I watch them one by one, looking for the slightest clue,

because one of them must have left the article. And if they did, what does that mean if I finally have the Magpie Man's attention?

When it's just me and Emily, she turns and says, "What is it?"

I take the newspaper clipping out of my bag and show her. "That was in my suitcase when I came home from Mayfield Lodge."

Emily looks confused, then her eyes go wide, and she says, "So it was one of them?"

"It must have been. The first time, it happened at school, so it couldn't have been anyone who worked at the retreat."

"There was no lock on our bedroom door," Emily says. "That's fucking creepy."

I hadn't thought of that. Anyone could have snuck in at any time.

"What are we going to do?" Emily asks, and I like that she says "we."

Most days, I feel alone, even when I'm surrounded by people, and that has only increased since coming home.

I think back to Mayfield, to the suitcase I left open by my bed, to the door I only blocked on the first night, because by the second, I trusted everyone.

But that's the mistake: trusting people before they have earned it.

77

I watch my bag constantly, looking for hands that get too close, for someone giving themselves away.

I unzip my bag and let it hang loose at my side, my phone inside, pointing up, recording the ceiling. I wander the hallways, looking in the opposite direction, hoping someone makes their move and I catch their face on-camera. But, when I check, all I have is an empty bag and a rustled recording.

At lunch, I sit with Emily and Hanna, watching people walk through the cafeteria while they talk over me.

"I totally did not see it coming," Emily says. "I was watching, thinking what the fuck are you doing? And then you whipped the towel off and, bam, hair-dye twist."

I smile but don't reply, because I have too much to think about.

My head cam caught the perfume comment. But no one is talking about it because they don't know it's important. They were too busy looking at my face and my hair to worry about a couple of random words.

At least my friends are taking the news clippings seriously.

"If it was someone who went to Mayfield, we have ten suspects," Hanna says.

But Emily shakes her head. "It's not Jennifer or Ali or Pav or..."

"You can't rule people out because you suddenly like them," Hanna says. She still hasn't forgiven us for making new friends. She stares at her hands, then mumbles, "I wish I'd been there." And there it is, the real reason she's angry.

Emily laughs and pulls her into a hug. "We wish you'd been there too."

But if one of my theology classmates is doing this, what happened at Mayfield is a lie.

We're not friends. I'm part of some sick game, and they're happy to make me suffer.

78

Ten classmates, ten lockers. The challenge is to break into all of them.

Except it might not be much of a challenge, because when we were given our locker combinations, they weren't impossible-to-remember sequences. They were our birthdays, just the month and the day. We could have changed them if we'd wanted to, but most of us didn't bother.

Half an hour on Facebook gives me everything I need, and when school ends, I wait in the computer lab, watching the lazy teachers leave early and the good ones stay until it's dark.

Twice, the custodian tries to kick me out, and twice, I say something about last-minute studying. And now I'm standing by Jennifer's locker, setting the code to 1217, and feeling it click open.

Whoever is leaving the articles must be keeping them somewhere, so why not here?

Jennifer's locker is full of crap, old books the librarian has probably forgotten about, and gym clothes at least three years old, but no newspaper clippings.

I hear a noise behind me and freeze. A door slams down the hallway, someone shouts a goodbye, then silence.

It's weird being in an empty school. The hallways are usually jammed, the volume on maximum, but tonight, it feels like a cemetery.

I don't want to be here longer than I have to, so I move to Pav's locker, check my phone for her birthday, and then search.

Yinka's stinks of muddy soccer cleats, Maya's is covered in family photos, but one after another, I see nothing but normal.

Before I go, I look at the graduates' display, the faces of last year's seniors staring back at me. They are scattered across the country now.

I've walked past this display lots of times, but tonight, in the quiet, their smiles look sinister, as if they know something I don't.

Footsteps echo down the hallway, and I hold my breath. They're louder than before. They aren't going home. They're coming toward me.

I push my back against the lockers, but there's nowhere to hide. I move one step forward, then another, desperate not to make a sound. Being caught here after dark isn't something I want to explain. But they're faster than I am. They are racing around the corner while I shuffle.

I move back to the closest locker—Eloise's—unlock my phone, and search for her birthday in my notes.

"Who's that?" someone says behind me, and when I turn, Mr. Collins is standing there.

"Hi, sir," I say, swallowing the panic in my throat.

"Why are you here so late?"

"I forgot something," I say, gesturing to the locker.

When he doesn't move, I quickly glance at my phone, then enter the code, and feel a wave of relief when it opens.

Staring into Eloise's locker, I say, "Well, have a good night."

Mr. Collins tilts his head, but I push the door so he can't see the photo of Eloise and Bernie or the textbooks for the classes I don't take.

"You shouldn't be here," he says. "You could get locked in."

"It won't happen again," I say.

I close the locker without taking anything and hope he doesn't notice. But the way he looks at me, I'm not so sure.

When I get home, Dad gasps and stares at my head, and I touch my hair and say, "Sorry. I...I'm trying something new."

I left before he was up this morning, and I guess he hasn't watched yesterday's highlights yet, because he walks slowly toward me and whispers, "You look just like her."

"Is that okay? I can change it."

Dad shakes his head but doesn't reply, and I feel guilty for reminding him of Mom, even though her face is all over the house.

When Nan sees me, she makes a strange noise, then pulls me into a hug, and all evening, I catch both of them sneaking glances at me.

A few times, they look at each other, and something silent passes between them, and before Nan leaves, she hugs me extra tight and says, "I love you, darling. She would be so proud."

79

Five of us go to the hospital: me, Emily, Jennifer, Pav, and Ali.

Eloise has been going on her own, handing out tiny pieces of information as if Bernie's incident is too precious to share. I think she resents us, because before Mayfield, it was just the two of them. And maybe it would have gone back to that if things had been different.

I flash back to the moment I saw Bernie's body on the bed, how scared I was, how I forgot my own problems, because suddenly, they weren't the biggest in the room.

Mayfield was supposed to change us but not like this. We were supposed to come back smiling. But when I think of it, I see the bigger picture: how everyone is cracked and only the luckiest hold themselves together.

When we arrive, the nurse shakes her head and says, "Two at a time."

"How about three?" Emily asks.

The nurse huffs and says, "Two...at...a...time."

Emily makes a face behind her back, and Pav laughs and says, "How are we going to do this?"

"You and Emily go first," I say, "then Ali and Jennifer. I'll go on my own."

Emily looks confused and is about to argue when I say, "I found her. I'd like to talk to her alone."

Before Mayfield, she would never have agreed to go with Pav, but Emily nods and says, "Okay."

When they are gone, Ali and Jennifer make small talk while I watch the nurses moving from room to room.

I imagine what would have happened if Mom had made it to the hospital, if someone had found her alive and she'd been rushed in while doctors spoke in frantic codes like on TV. But there was nothing to resuscitate, nothing to help, only a body to pick apart for clues that weren't there.

I wonder why I think these things. Do I have a choice, or is it who I am? Am I destined to think bad thoughts for the rest of my life?

Emily touches my shoulder, shaking me out of my daydream, before I even notice she's back. "You okay?" she says.

I nod, watching as Ali and Jennifer go in.

I'm not sure if I want to go by myself anymore. I'm scared Bernie will say she only got drunk to forget what I told her—that her sadness was worthless compared to mine. But it's either that or I leave without saying anything, and that feels worse.

"How is she?" I ask Emily.

"Okay, I think. I expected her to be at death's door, to be honest."

I don't reply. I stare down the hallway and see Bernie's parents walking toward me.

Her mom is short and slim. She used to jog past our window every evening, and I remember watching her stretch in her front yard and wondering why she bothered.

She's smiling, and when she gets closer, she says, "Jessica. I'm so glad you came."

I stand up and let her hug me, then wait for her to fill the silence.

"Have you seen her yet?" she asks.

I shake my head. "It's two at a time."

Bernie's stepdad grins and says, "Don't listen to them. We're always sneaking in extras."

He has a beard now, thicker than the hair on his head, and I feel awkward for not knowing him better.

I nod, and when I don't reply, he says, "We heard you were the one who found her."

I nod again, because I know what's coming, and I don't want it.

"Thank you," he says. "For everything you've done."

I feel guilty, because I didn't do anything good. I told her she was pathetic for missing her dad, I flicked a switch she couldn't flick back, and when I found her, all I could do was scream.

Reg helped her, and Andrea, and the paramedics. I just watched it happen.

"You're welcome," I say, because it's better than the silence, and Bernie's mom touches my shoulder and gives me that look, the one that says she feels sorry for me, even though it's her daughter in the hospital.

When Ali and Jennifer come out, everyone looks at me, and I start to blush, swallowing the sickness as I reluctantly walk into the room. And there she is, sitting up straight and surrounded by presents. I wish I'd thought of that, but it's just another thing to feel guilty for.

I sit in the plastic seat next to Bernie's bed and say, "Hi."

"Hey."

I'm beginning to think leaving was the better option.

"How are you?"

"I'm all right," she says, although her eyes tell a different story. "It's nice to see you."

I hope that's true, even after what I said on our spirit walk.

"Was it my fault?" When Bernie asks what I mean, I say, "We argued. You swore at me."

She shakes her head but doesn't reply.

"I thought you were happy," I say.

"Not really," Bernie whispers. She fills every silence with a sigh, her eyes digging deep into my own, looking for something that scares me.

"I thought you were dead," I say at last, and she nods, as if she expected to be, as if she wanted to be.

"I'm so sorry, Jess. I didn't mean to scare you. I just... I wanted it to end."

"Wanted *what* to end?"

"This..."

When your mom has been ripped out of your life with no explanation, when your tiny broken family is all you have left, it's hard to have sympathy for people who give up. But the way Bernie looks, I can't help feeling sorry for her.

I touch her hand, and she squeezes it. I sit in silence, waiting for her to talk, because honestly, what could I possibly say to make her feel better?

"That place," she says, "it was so amazing, and everyone was so happy. And you know what I felt? Nothing. Just empty."

She looks pale and worn down by whatever invisible issues are eating away at her.

I understand what she meant now, when she said she wished every day could be like it was at Mayfield.

She takes a deep breath, then says, "They keep asking why I did it."

"Why did you?"

"I couldn't stop myself. I can't remember the last time I was happy."

I want to say it will be okay, but I hate it when people tell me that. It's lazy and it's wrong.

We lie to sad people because we think it will make them feel better. But sad people see through lies. You can only trick happy people with bullshit.

"They keep telling me things will get better," Bernie says. "They keep talking about the future. But when I think about it, all I see is nothing. Miles and miles of nothing."

I'm not used to being the shoulder to cry on.

I guess even now, ten years after Mom died, people don't burden me with their problems just in case. But Bernie doesn't care about hurting my feelings or adding to my worry pile, and in a weird way, I'm grateful for that.

"I didn't want to go home," she says. "I fucking hate it

there. So I got drunk, and then I kept drinking, and when I finished the bottle, I went to sleep, and now I'm here."

"I'm sorry," I whisper.

"What for?"

"For not being your friend anymore."

Bernie smiles and says, "We could change that."

I smile and sit with her, stroking her hand and listening to her talk, hoping it makes a difference.

80

A body has been found in a park in London, and police are appealing for witnesses.

If you've been through this yourself, you know the details are sketchy because the detectives are holding things back.

When the police first want the public's help, they keep it vague. They say where the crime happened and roughly what time. They say whether the victim was a man or a woman. The real clues come out later, when no one has come forward and the investigation stalls.

Serial killers are not serial killers until they start collecting bodies. It's their habits that give them their names.

The Magpie Man was no one when he killed my mom, but now he's a monster you warn kids about. He last killed in September, so if the usual nine-month gap is intentional, he has struck two months early.

I think it's him. Don't ask me how. I can feel it.

I go online and try to find more information, but everywhere is saying the same thing.

I don't know how this woman died. I don't know if it's a clue or a coincidence.

When they found my mother, the bottom of her mouth was swollen black, her tongue crushed between her teeth, her hyoid bone and windpipe and larynx all broken.

When your mom was strangled to death, you eventually look up the specifics and wish you hadn't.

In the nightmares I had when I finally realized she was gone, I could see fine crescent echoes of fingernails on her smudged and caved-in neck. But the truth is there were no fingernail marks, because the Magpie Man was careful not to leave DNA, only fabric from the kind of cheap black gloves you can buy at any store.

After he strangled her, he carved the number 1 into her chest. Then he went home.

He has done it twelve more times since then.

What if the thing the newsreader isn't telling us, that the police aren't revealing, is that the monster has killed again?

81

He carved the number 14 into her chest. The news leaks online, and by the end of the day, it's everywhere.

My notifications intensify, and my face is all over the news because of the show. I've learned to avoid the comment sections.

Danny texts, asking if I'm okay, and I type at least twenty different replies before settling on: Not really.

Hanna and Emily come over, and although I don't want to leave the house, they won't take no for an answer.

Outside, Sara has been joined by an army of professional shouters and expert elbow shovers, all of them desperate for a comment from the girl who woke up a nightmare.

Emily's mom is waiting in the car, and she smiles at me in the mirror but doesn't speak. They've planned this, and I'm grateful for my friends.

We drive to Harmony, and Hanna bangs on the window of the ice-cream parlor until her dad waves his arms from inside.

"I'm coming!" he yells. Then, almost in a whisper, he says, "Hello, Jessica."

I'm not used to him being quiet. But sympathy changes people.

We sit by the window, and Hanna's mom brings us three giant hot chocolates, rubbing my shoulder as she leaves.

My two best friends smile at me, but I can't smile back. When I try, it cracks at the edges and makes me want to cry.

He usually kills every nine months, but not this time. Is it my fault that he has struck early? Is he rattled or happy to play the game?

Hanna picks up my phone and says, "This is a weapon of mass destruction. You'll make yourself paranoid reading all the hate on here."

"Is it really that bad?"

Hanna exchanges a look with Emily. "Yes, Jess. It is fucking terrible. They're saying it's your fault."

"I didn't want him to kill again," I whisper.

I wanted the whole world to remember how dangerous he is, to be watching for the slightest clue from the people they love or the people they have always suspected. I wanted my story to be everywhere you looked. But I didn't want this.

The world can change its mind in an instant. They can feel sorry for you one minute and hate you the next.

He killed. Him. Not me. But I called him pathetic. I called him weak. I called him out, and he responded as only he could.

"I wanted justice," I whisper, and Hanna squeezes my hand, then swaps a look with Emily that I can't interpret.

"What?" I ask. When they look confused, I say, "Do you think this is my fault?"

Together, too quickly, they say, "No," and, "Of course not," and I desperately hope they're not lying.

I couldn't blame them. I tried so hard to get Mom back into the headlines. I got the full three months, but am I any closer to catching him?

All I have is a mess of possible clues that are probably nothing, and if he has killed again because of me, that's terrifying. Whatever they're saying in the comments, they are right to point the finger at me.

I think about the family of the latest woman to die. Her name has been released now: Lorna Banks, twenty-eight, from Chiswick. She was a lawyer with a two-year-old son and a fiancé.

Those are the details that matter in a story like this. Just as my mom was a wife with a seven-year-old daughter when she died.

My phone rings, and Emily says, "Don't answer that. Or say, 'No comment.'"

But when I look at the caller ID, I smile and click green.

82

"How are you, darling?" Nan asks.

"It's not about me," I say. "It's happened again. Another family is broken because of that asshole."

It's not how I expected to reply. But I'm angry. And Nan understands that anger in a way that Emily and Hanna never will.

"Maybe I should stop. I don't want anyone else getting hurt."

I wanted justice for thirteen families, not heartbreak for another.

"He would have killed again, Jessica. You're not to blame." Nan's voice is quiet down the phone, and I hate myself for doing this to her.

I feel sick, my head and my heart pounding, the image of Lorna Banks's smiling face replacing Bernie's body in my mind. It's on the front page of every newspaper, at the beginning of every television report: a photo taken at a better time, one she never imagined would be the one she was remembered for.

Mom's newspaper photo was taken on her wedding day. Her eyes are sparkling, watching something or someone unseen, her smile wide, her veil caught on the wind.

That is the image printed in the newspaper reports still haunting me. Nan chose it, and I wonder who chose Lorna's. I wonder if her fiancé will be as broken as Dad is or if one day, he'll move on. I wonder what her two-year-old will become.

And that is when I realize I can't stop, because when that boy is my age, I want him to know his mother's murderer was caught, not still out there somewhere.

"I think I'm losing it," I whisper.

"Stay strong, darling," Nan says. "We're in this together."

83

I almost don't call, but what choice do I have?

When the policewoman, Lorraine, answers her phone, I say, "I have some clues."

"Okay."

"There was a comment on one of my videos. It said 'wrong perfume.'"

I realize how stupid this sounds, but I'm scared I should have told the police sooner.

"I'm not sure I understand, Jessica."

"He knows what perfume my mother wore. I think he's watching me."

"Or maybe it was a lucky guess."

"There's more," I say. "I've been getting these articles... newspaper clippings. I've had two now. I think they're from someone at school."

I hear Lorraine sigh down the phone and hate her for not taking me seriously.

"It's connected," I say. "I don't know how, but I think it can help us catch him."

"We appreciate what you're trying to do," she says. "But I'm sure you've seen the news. Everyone is working twenty-four-seven to find him."

"Are you?"

Lorraine doesn't reply right away. And when she does, she ignores my question and says, "The texts, the articles, this comment...it was all to be expected. There are some cruel people out there."

There are, except some are a lot crueler than others.

84

Another Monday morning: just me and Danny in my bedroom, me slowly opening my eyes and him with a serious look on his face.

I thought about doing another piece directly to the camera, reaching out to the family of Lorna Banks and apologizing for their loss. But Danny advised me not to. He said that after some of the online comments, I should avoid the word *sorry* in case it looked like I was taking the blame.

I know Nan was right. The Magpie Man would have killed again, with or without me. But right now, it's hard to separate that. Especially when I know he's watching.

The day passes quietly, nothing new, nothing exciting. Without Michael standing outside my window, my life is pretty boring, at least for an audience, and I understand why he did it. He wanted to make the best possible show. He wanted to make something everyone talks about the next day.

I wanted that too. We just went about it in different ways.

The news has an update on Lorna Banks. A reporter standing in the rain says police now believe she was killed by the serial killer known as the Magpie Man.

My mom's picture flashes on the screen, then other people's moms and wives and sisters.

I feel the camera in the corner of the living room close in on me as the reporter gives details of their deaths. Then it turns to Dad, who doesn't react when he sees his dead wife's photograph.

Every night since they found Lorna Banks's body, I put the news on at six o'clock. Today, I rushed Danny out of the house so I wouldn't miss it.

Dad doesn't complain. He waits until I'm done, then changes the channel.

Computer parts sit untouched on the dining table—one broken thing refusing to fix another.

He has shrunk further into himself since the latest murder. He only talks when he has to, and his words come out small and cracked.

We avoid saying the obvious. Dad may have named him, but he won't say that name anymore.

I'm desperate for a clue. But he left nothing behind. No DNA, no security camera footage, no witnesses.

No hope.

85

At exactly 10:00 p.m., I unlock the front door and leave, cameras fastened to my head and waist. Dad has left for work, so there's no one to talk me out of it.

I think back to the night I almost chased Michael into the alley, how it felt to stand on the edge of something terrible.

What I'm about to do should get me more front pages and more coverage. But it's more than that, because I know he's watching. He commented on the perfume, and he killed two months early, so what if I am getting to him after all? And what if I can use myself as bait?

Lorna Banks didn't deserve to die. If he comes for anyone else, it should be me.

When I walk past Jamie's house, he runs out and shouts, "Jess! What are you doing?" Like always, he is watching. I wish tonight he had other things to do.

"Don't worry," I say. "Go back inside and watch."

"Why?"

"Just go home. I'm fine. I need to do this." When he keeps walking, I say, "Stop trying to save me. I don't need saving."

Jamie looks genuinely upset and says, "I'm only trying to help."

"Then go and watch me like everyone else. Let me entertain you."

I don't mean to sound like a bitch, or maybe I do. Either way, I want him gone, because I'm running out of ways to make a difference.

He shakes his head, opens his mouth to say something, then walks away.

I feel sick, the adrenaline that got me out of the house replaced with a dread I can't shake.

But I need to do this.

86

It is just an alley. It is only a shortcut home. But not for me. Not anymore.

I listen to the buzz of the streetlight, the distant whir of cars too far away to help, and I step forward. And this time, I keep moving, one foot in front of the other, again and again, each crack of leaves and twigs and litter louder than the last.

When I'm halfway through, I stop and wait. I need my breathing to slow and my heart to follow before I can speak.

The longer I stand here, the tighter the darkness grips me until the sense of someone at my back forces me to talk to remind me they are out there, watching, waiting.

My words come out as a whisper, so I start over, louder this time, even though talking in the darkness only increases the terror.

I want to whisper, I want to shrink, but I need them to hear me. I need to stand tall.

"I didn't want anyone else to die," I say. "I wanted to catch you, not make you kill again."

Every noise sounds like a warning, and I imagine Mom standing here instead of me, hurrying but not fast enough, the moment she knew she should have gone the long way around.

"You're scum, you know that? All you do is destroy. And before everyone starts telling me I'm taunting you, making you murder, that's not what this is. I'm here, right now. I'm ready. If you want to hurt anyone, hurt me. I'm used to it."

I don't know how much my audience can see. I don't know if the tiny flashlight on the camera pointing up at me is enough to make me anything more than a shadow. But I do know I don't want anyone else to die.

"Are you scared of coming for me?" I ask. "You know where I live. You know where I am right now. What are you waiting for?"

I feel my phone vibrate in my pocket, and when I look down, I see it's Danny. He will try to talk me out of this. He'll say I'm going too far.

So I click red, ignoring every call and text that comes over the next twenty minutes from Danny and Hanna and Emily as I stand silently in the alley, waiting for the Magpie Man.

I think of Jamie watching at home, how he pulled me back when there was nothing to fear. He was a hero when I didn't need one. Now all I want is a monster.

But nothing happens. No one comes.

I get used to the noises the night makes.

The hum of the alley softens, the sense of someone close fades, replaced by sadness, as I realize this is all for show.

I'm doing it for my audience. I'm doing it to get them off my back.

I wanted him to come, but I knew deep down that he wouldn't. Why would he walk into a trap I'm not even trying to hide? But that doesn't mean he's not watching, and it doesn't mean he's not tempted. He knows I'm here. He knows I'm waiting.

I walk to the end of the alley, the side I rarely see, and step into the street. I'm about to turn and walk back, giving my audience one last look at the journey Mom started but never finished, when I hear a different noise, one that tells me not everyone is watching this at home.

87

"*Jess-i-ca*," someone sings. "*We're watching you.*"

I hear a giggle, a shush, the sounds of bitches warming up. And then I see them.

The girls dance toward me while the boys swagger. When they get close, one of the boys reaches for my body cam, and I step back.

"Let's have a look," he says.

I don't reply, just start backing toward the alley that is suddenly my only escape. But the other boy jumps behind me and yanks the head cam off, then points it at me and says, "Smile."

The girls laugh, and the boy with the camera points it at them until one says, "Not at us, you prick."

That's when I recognize her. She's in tenth grade; they both are. They belong to the group that think they're better than us, the mean girls whose whispers travel the length of a hallway. But I don't know the boys, and that scares me.

The one with the camera points it back at me, and the girls start singing again, "*Jess-i-ca. Jess-i-ca.*"

And then, "*One for sorrow, two for joy.*"

That's when the other boy leans in, so close I can smell his breath, and says, "Three for the girl with a dead mom."

The body cam is still pointing up at me, recording my reaction, my audience seeing the tears as they fall and hearing the laughter that follows.

"She's crying," one of the boys says. "I thought you were supposed to be some kind of badass, chasing after a serial killer. If he found you, he'd ruin you."

I try to grab the camera, but he jumps back and laughs.

"Fuck you," I say, stepping forward and making fists.

That's when I hear movement from the alley, pounding footsteps and heavy breathing.

The four of them exchange looks, throw the camera on the ground, and run.

88

When Jamie gets to me, I'm pulling off the body cam, hiding from my audience just long enough to break down.

"I told you not to," he says.

I turn and say, "I didn't ask you to come." But if he hadn't, they would still be here.

As I pick up the head cam, Jamie says, "Are you okay?"

He should have started with that. But if he had, the tears would have come harder, faster. Because I'm not okay.

I went into the alley to call the Magpie Man out and say that if he wants to kill anyone, it should be me. Instead, everyone saw me for what I am: weak, scared, alone.

"I don't know what to do," I say, and Jamie reaches for my hand, then stops. But I wish he hadn't. "I'm losing myself," I say. "I had a plan. I had a script to follow. But I don't know what's important anymore."

"We should go," he says, and as we step into the alley, I hold his hand and don't let go until I'm home.

89

I don't go to school. I can't. When the doorbell rings, Dad ignores it, because everyone goes away eventually.

Nan used to hate how he would never answer the door or pick up the phone. She made us come up with an emergency ring, just in case.

I was eleven when Nan told me that if I was ever in trouble, I should ring three times, hang up, ring twice, hang up, then ring three times more. She told Dad that was the special ring, and if he heard it, he had to get out of his chair.

It upset me, having to teach my father how to act in an emergency, but those first few years were the hardest, and he has come a long way since.

I get tired of the noise so I open the door, ready to yell in a reporter's face. I thought they'd all left, the latest murder taking them to a different doorstep. But I guess not.

A woman is standing there, holding a picture of me. "Is this you?" she shouts.

"What?"

"Is. This. You?"

I nod, and she straightens her back, breathes out, and then lets rip.

"Do you know what you've done? Do you have any idea? You think life is some kind of game? Because it's not. It's real. You can sit behind your screen and say whatever you want, because no one can hurt you from there. You can tempt someone out of the shadows, and you know what? When they come, they won't come for you. They'll come for someone else, someone who doesn't deserve it.

"My daughter didn't deserve it. She was a mother. She was getting married. You robbed her of that. And for what? Justice? There's no justice. You didn't do anything good. You got someone killed."

She isn't shouting anymore. She's whispering. And then I realize who she is—Lorna Banks's mother.

This is how Dad was when it first happened. When you can't get to the person worthy of your blame, you blame anyone.

"I'm sorry," I say, and her eyes go wide.

"*Sorry?* You're *sorry?* If you'd kept quiet, this wouldn't have happened. I had no idea who you were. I didn't know what you were doing until it was too late."

Tears paint mascara tracks down her blotchy cheeks, and she looks both ways, then back at me.

For a second, I think she's going to hit me, but she shakes her head and says, "You have no idea."

I want to tell her I have the exact idea, because what gives her the right to own heartache?

I still wake up sometimes after dreaming of Mom, and for a fraction of a second, I think she's there before the truth tears the morning in two. I still stare at her picture and will her back to life. I still miss her so much.

Lorna Banks's mom opens her mouth to speak again, but before she does, my dad walks into the hallway and says, "You should come in."

90

She hesitates, then steps inside and waits.

"It's okay," Dad says.

She looks deflated, tiny, broken. It's as if she pumped herself full of anger, and now, emptied of it and standing silently in our hallway, she has halved in size.

"Cup of tea?" I say, and she stares at me, confused.

This clearly isn't how she thought things would go. But when I woke up this morning, I didn't expect to have the mother of the Magpie Man's fourteenth victim in my house.

She nods and follows me into the kitchen, watches me boil the kettle, make three cups, then hand one to her.

"This is..." I pause.

"Frances," she says.

"This is Frances, and this is my dad."

"Hello," he says, then, pointing to the living room, "Have a seat."

"I'm sorry about Lorna," I say, but she isn't listening.

She's too busy staring at my dad, her eyes flitting from his odd socks to his stained shirt to the beard that creeps out rather than down like an out-of-control bush. It used to be red, but now there are only small flecks of orange wrapped in gray.

He must look a mess to her. But Dad's face, his sorrow, the same rumpled clothes he wears over and over again, I've grown so used to them, I don't notice anymore.

Frances looks around our living room until her eyes catch mine.

"We know what you're going through," I say. "I'm sorry about what happened, but we've been going through it for years."

She opens her mouth to speak, then closes it again, her eyes focusing on my parents' wedding photo. She stares at it for a long time, and when I look over at Dad, he is staring too—at the day he smiled the most genuine smile of his life.

"I'm sorry," Frances whispers. "I just...I don't know what to do."

She looks at my dad, hoping for something he doesn't have the energy to give.

"When I found out what you were doing..."

She doesn't finish the sentence, but I know what she means. When she found out what I was doing, she had someone to blame. She saw me challenging the Magpie Man, tempting him out of the shadows. In her mind, I opened the door to her own personal hell.

"I didn't think it through," I say, "and I'm so sorry for that."

Lorna's mom looks at me and pushes her lips together in the shape of a smile. Then she looks at my dad and says, "I understand why you did it."

She finishes her tea, stands, and walks over to him. Then she leans down and kisses his cheek, and he can't hide the shock on his face.

I wonder if there's anything left inside him still to break, because he looks sad for her.

For so long, he has only looked sad for himself. But the way he stares at Frances, I know he's sorry for *her* pain.

"Does it get easier?" she asks.

Dad sighs and says, "It settles. But it never stops hurting."

She looks around the room one last time and says, "I can't help but wonder..."

Again she leaves the sentence half spoken, and I wonder if Lorna was the end to all her thoughts and she has lost the ability to complete them now, if Mom would have been the same if I'd been the one taken that day.

"If you ever need to talk," I say, "you obviously know where I am."

I smile, and she tries to.

Then, as if she has just realized something, she says, "I'd like that," so we swap numbers.

I give her the one to my secret second phone, like I did with Ross, because if she ever has something to say, I doubt she'll want the whole world knowing.

When she's gone, Dad calls to me from the living room and says, "We should talk."

91

"How much can I ignore before I'm the one to blame?" Dad asks.

I sit next to him and hold his hand, wondering what Frances's surprise visit has done to him.

"I saw you go in the alley," he says. "I watched it this morning. I saw what those kids did to you."

"I'm sorry."

"Are you? Really? I know this is important to you, and I've tried to let you work through this yourself, but you keep doing reckless things. You're not making it easy for me, Jess."

"I know. But it's not easy for me either. You think I wanted to do this?"

I point to my hair, and Dad stares into his lap and nods.

"I didn't want to go into the alley. I had no choice. People are blaming me for Lorna's death, and I thought...I don't know...I thought if I made myself the target, it would force his hand. If I showed I wasn't scared of him, maybe he would come for me. And then we could catch him."

Dad starts pacing, then crouches next to me and says, "It's my job to keep you safe...and I'm failing."

This is it. This is my dad belatedly putting his foot down.

But before he can, I say, "I'm the one failing. We can do this differently. We can do it safely."

Then I tell him what Ross and I have been planning.

He listens without interrupting, nodding in all the right places, and when I'm done, he says, "Okay." Then, "Why did you give that woman my phone number?"

"I didn't think you used it anymore. You never answered it when it was on."

I guess that's the end of the conversation, but as I leave, he says, "Don't delete the messages."

It's a weird thing to say, but his voice sounds different, kinder, like it was when he used to whisper me to sleep, talking me out of whatever nightmare I'd had before I realized they weren't nightmares at all.

I go upstairs, and when I check the phone, there are more missed calls and messages from Ross, and I make a promise to keep it with me from now on. I quickly read through them, then listen to a voicemail he left last night.

"What's the point of a secret phone if you never answer it?" he says. "Anyway, I have some news. Call me when you can."

I should phone him right away, but I keep thinking about what Dad said, so I click on the old texts, and what I find makes my heart stop.

Can you get some chopped tomatoes on the way home? xxx

I love you, gorgeous xxx

Don't forget it's Jess's play on Wednesday.

They are messages from Mom. I can't see Dad's replies.

Before smartphones, you couldn't read your texts like it was the story of your life. Everything was a moment in time, and there was only enough space to save the best. Except Dad didn't know he should be saving them. That one day, too soon, the texts would stop.

I wonder how many times he read them before he stopped charging the phone.

I try to imagine Mom speaking the words out loud. Her voice, like everything else, has faded over time. But it feels like I've found a secret. It feels like she has come back to me, just when I need her most.

Her phone was never found, taken by whoever killed her, destroyed before it could be tracked. But at least now I have a glimpse of the moments she and Dad shared when they were apart.

When I call Ross, he says, "Finally. I'm almost done. We should be ready in another week or so."

I hope this part of the plan goes better than the last. I hope when I go back to school that Monday's show is already old news, even if that's too much to wish for.

"I owe you," I tell Ross, and then I call Frances Banks.

"Hello?"

"Hi," I say. "You probably didn't expect to hear from me so soon."

There is silence, then, "Jessica?"

"Look, I totally understand if you don't want to, but we're doing something. With your help, we can catch him."

92

Their names are Becca and Taryn, the girls who cornered me at the wrong end of the alley, the ones who laughed while the boys did their dirty work.

When I see them walking toward me, I sneak into the bathroom, but when the door swings open, I know they've followed, and I wait for the song to start again, planning what to do if they hit me.

Becca reaches into her bag, and when she pulls her hand out, I flinch. She pushes something into my chest and says, "You're sick."

"What?"

"Don't think I won't show the police."

I have no idea what she's talking about until she lets whatever she's holding fall to the floor, and I see it and step back and cry out.

"Where did you get that?" I ask.

The girls look at each other, a silent message passing between them, then Becca says, "Don't act dumb."

"I've never seen that before." If I had, I would remember.

On the ground, between us, a Polaroid picture of a body none of us want to look at, a reminder that this is not a game. I force myself to look harder, but it's not my mom.

The woman in the photo has blond hair. That's all I can make out before I have to look away again.

"How do you know where I live?" Becca asks.

When I don't answer, Taryn says, "I bet it was you. I bet you killed those women."

"I was seven," I say, and for a second, I almost laugh, because how stupid can she be?

But the image on the floor means laughing isn't an option.

"When did you get it?" I ask.

"Yesterday," Becca says. "It was under the front door. There's something on the back. I know it was you."

I pick it up and turn it over. In small black capitals, it says, ONE FOR SORROW.

The song they were taunting me with. Now someone is singing it back to them.

"Have you shown anyone else?" I ask.

Becca grins and says, "Not yet. But I will."

"I need to give this to the police," I say, thinking of Lorraine, imagining how she'll react to an actual clue.

But Becca snatches it back and says, "*I'm* showing the police. And I'm telling them it was you."

"It wasn't," I whisper, but whatever they think, I don't care as long as they tell the right people.

The Magpie Man took it. He has kept it for years. If anything has his DNA on, it's this.

"I'll come with you," I say.

"What?"

"I'll come with you. To the police station. Call them now."

The girls look at each other. Whatever they expected when they cornered me, it wasn't this.

Behind them, the door opens, and a sixth grader sees us, turns, and walks out again.

"Maybe it wasn't her," Taryn says.

Becca shivers. "Or maybe she's playing us."

But I already have my phone out, dialing the number on Lorraine's card that's still in my purse.

When she hears me leaving a message, Becca throws the photo back on the floor, and they leave in silence. Without their boyfriends, they're as scared as I am.

But my fear is just getting started, because the Magpie Man knows where she lives. He walked right up to her door and left that.

I think back to the warning written across Sara's article— *I'll show you how pathetic I am*—and realize there is more to come.

93

I hand Lorraine the photo without saying a word, and her face changes so quickly, so completely, that I know I've done the right thing.

"Where did you get this?" she asks, so I tell her everything.

"I'll need to speak to the other girls."

"I only know their first names," I say. "You'll have to talk to Mrs. Bradley."

I can't help smiling at the thought of the police turning up on Becca's doorstep. She will have to explain that night in the alley, the song she sang, the fact that the Magpie Man was listening.

Is he angry that someone else is taunting me? Does he want me all to himself? And how did he know Becca's address? He must live close by, and he must be up early, before people leave for school, or late, when everyone else is asleep. You wouldn't risk leaving something like that in daylight.

He responded to my makeup video, he killed two months early, and now this. Is he rattled? Is what I'm doing working after all?

He did this to mess with the girls who messed with me, and that is both exciting and terrifying.

94

"It's bold," Danny says when I tell him the plan. "I might need extra cameras."

"But we can do it?"

"Of course we can. It's brilliant."

"One other thing," I say. "Do we have a budget?"

Danny laughs. "How much are we talking?"

"Enough to make a statement."

Then I call Ross, and we figure out specifics. It's hard not to tell Emily or Hanna, but the best shocks catch everyone by surprise, and I want theirs to be genuine. We need to do this now. We need to go to the next level before the Magpie Man strikes again.

The woman in the photograph was Sandra Stoneham, number 12 on his list.

The police haven't found any DNA, but they know more than they used to. They know he keeps pictures of his victims.

Now they are calling him a collector, the search narrowing to people with a passion for Polaroid cameras, for those who see beauty in horror.

I've thought of Mom's Polaroid so many times, wondering if I'll ever see it, wondering if I want to. But seeing Sandra Stoneham's body and the message that went with it, I know it's time for the next part of the plan.

I've got his attention. Now I need to catch him.

95

On Sunday night, Ross calls and tells me everyone is ready. He asks how I'm feeling, and with a wave of nausea creeping up my throat, I pretend I'm absolutely fine.

I can't sleep. But I must have dozed off, because when my alarm wakes me at 6:00 a.m., I jump up in a panic like I've missed the whole thing.

"Okay," I whisper. "It's showtime."

I should eat breakfast, because it's going to be a busy morning, but the thought makes my stomach turn. I'm too anxious about what we're going to do to think about cereal. Instead, I shower, get dressed, and wait for the doorbell to ring.

I pause for a second before opening it, worried what I might see, then I turn and pull, and Ross is standing there with a huge smile on his face.

"We're here," he says, and I can't believe my eyes.

There must be at least thirty people, and when Ross catches me staring, he says, "Forty-three," and then, "I've been busy."

I smile and step aside, letting stranger after stranger into my house. Only they aren't strangers.

I recognize so many of their faces from newspaper clippings and television reports, from social media appeals and my own dusty dreams. These are the left behind, the parents and grandparents and brothers and sisters and children of the Magpie Man's victims.

Don't ask me how, but Ross got them all to agree. He found me...and then he found everyone else.

Last in, hanging back, is Frances Banks.

"I'm glad you came," I say, and she nods.

"I had to."

96

Dad is in the bathroom when everyone arrives, and as they fill up the living room and kitchen, I quickly realize we haven't thought this through.

"How big is your backyard?" Ross asks.

"Big enough."

He nods and gets everyone's attention, then looks at me like he's expecting something. If they want an inspirational speech, they came to the wrong place.

Instead, I say, "This way," leading them out the back where they stand around, looking awkwardly at one another.

"What time does Danny get here?" Ross asks.

"Usually seven, but I told him to be early today."

Ross nods and says, "You should say something."

"Now?"

"Yes. They came because of you."

"They came because of *you*," I say.

Ross laughs. "Just talk to them."

That wave of sickness I've been feeling since yesterday is now a tsunami.

"Hey," I say. "Erm, look, thank you for coming."

A few of them smile, but most stare with blank faces.

Then I see Frances and think of her grandson, Lorna's son, who will never see his mother again, and it triggers something in me.

"I started doing this for my mom," I say. "I wanted justice, because she has never come close to getting that. I thought I could go live once a week and remind everyone what he did, and somehow, someone would realize who he was or finally give him up, and we would end this. But all I did was attract horrible people and stalkers. And then I met Ross. He listened to my idea and thought it was a good one. And he somehow got you all together. And I'm so grateful for that."

I catch Frances's eye, then look away and say, "I am so, so sorry for what he did, to all of you. If I could have caught him when I was seven, I would have. He took my mother. He stole her for no reason, and I hate him for that."

Everyone is nodding now, then they look past me, at something over my shoulder, and when I turn, Dad is there. He looks both happy and nervous, but there's also a look of understanding—because he recognizes them too.

"Everyone, this is my dad. Dad, this is everyone."

97

Danny looks at his watch, then he nods at me, his fingers counting down five...four...three...two...one. The red light on the camera flashes on, and we are live.

"I haven't done this for a while," I say, "but today is different. There is someone out there lying to you. There's someone out there who pretends they're like everyone else, and then, when you're not looking, they murder people.

"One of you knows him. One of you is sitting next to him right now. And he's acting completely normal, because that's how he gets away with it.

"One of you is being lied to by the person you love, and if you look hard enough, you will realize that. Because there's no such thing as the perfect lie, and there is no such thing as the perfect crime.

"You think because my mom was killed a decade ago... because the same man killed thirteen other people without being caught...you think because he hasn't left a clue at the crime scene that he hasn't left a clue anywhere? Of course he has. You just have to look for it.

"That's all we're asking...that you look, really look, at the person sitting next to you, and you find that clue. Because he can't do this again. We've suffered enough."

The camera moves slowly away from my face, panning back until you can see the army standing behind me. We all stare into the camera, burning our faces into the eyes of everyone watching, all forty-five of us, my dad included.

"We're the families of the fourteen women he murdered. When the police say he never leaves anything behind, not a clue or a security camera image or a strand of DNA, they're wrong. We are what he left behind."

The camera stays on us for thirty long seconds, then the screen goes blank, the live feed shutting down. Danny said Adrian agreed, because it made a better show.

It gives us time to set up for the next shot, which is me talking to the father of Sophie Cresswell, the girl who was killed nine months after my mom.

For the whole day, I talk to the families of the Magpie Man's victims, their grief more visible the closer we get to the end.

When I talk to the husband and the sister of Sandra Stoneham, I feel guilty for seeing the photograph of her body and wonder if the police have shown them. Would they look if they had the choice? Would I?

When it's my turn to speak, Dad rests his hand on my arm and says, "May I?"

"I didn't think you'd want to," I say.

"Neither did I," he whispers.

Dad takes my seat, and when I move away, he holds my hand and says, "Let's do this together."

Danny adjusts the camera and gives the signal.

Dad breathes out, straightens his shoulders, and says, "I don't know what to say. But I have to say something. My daughter is braver than I'll ever be. She's so strong. And her mom would be so proud. But she can't tell her. Because she's gone."

I squeeze Dad's fingers, and he looks up at me, then back at the camera, and says, "I didn't want her to do this show. How wrong I was."

By the time Frances speaks, there's a rawness that will only be eroded by time, a bitterness, an anger, a frustration that comes out in rants, then sobs, then finally a numb acceptance.

Afterward, we pose for a picture we hope will accompany the headlines on tonight's news.

I used to think it was enough to remind the world of what *I've* been through, to keep the image of *my* mother in the public consciousness. But I was wrong. We needed to come together and remind the world exactly how evil that monster is. We needed to show him that we're not going to stand for it anymore.

When we've all told our stories, I lock myself in the bathroom, the only place the cameras can't go, and I cry, harder and longer than I have in years.

My audience has a distraction, my backyard full of grieving extras, but then Danny knocks on the door and asks if I'm all right.

"Just a minute!" I call, looking in the mirror, then pulling one top off to reveal another underneath.

I feel the tears come again but fight them back, then I take a deep breath and open the bathroom door. Danny is there with the camera, and when he sees me, he smiles.

I'm wearing a T-shirt that simply reads ALIVE. This is what the budget went on: fifty plain white tees that I've written on.

I walk back into the backyard, feeling the nerves stretching in my stomach and crawling up my throat.

In my hand is a box stuffed with the bright red tops, the bright red word telling him he hasn't won. He killed her. He killed them all. But we remain, and we are stronger than we have been for years.

When the others see me, some smile, some stare, some don't even notice I've changed. But Dad notices, squinting like he's looking directly at the sun, like he can't quite believe his eyes.

I should have warned him. But in its own way, this is part of the plan, and as if Danny can read my mind, he points the camera at my dad.

When I see him swallow his sadness, blinking away whatever this makes him feel, I know I've done the right thing.

Laying the box on the grass, I step back and watch as Dad reaches inside and pulls a T-shirt over his head. Then everyone copies, until we are all wearing the same defiant message.

I grip Dad's hand and squeeze, and the hand that used to hold me so tight, that used to carry me around like I was the most precious thing in the world, squeezes back.

"We're coming for you," I say into the camera.

For a moment, I'm worried the others think I have gone too far. I'm scared they think I've made it all about myself again.

But one by one, they move until they're standing behind us, and I know he'll see this. It will be everywhere.

He will see the girl he didn't break, standing next to the man whose soul he shattered and the army of everyone else, all of us together, all of us alive.

98

That evening, as Danny and I sit in the kitchen, he says, "Today was a good day."

Everyone else has gone, even Ross, who hung back to celebrate what felt like a success.

Dad is still outside, sitting alone on the bench Mom made him buy. He said we didn't need it. He said the lawn chairs were more comfortable. But now he's sitting on the rusty metal, staring into the distance.

Danny is behind the camera, and when I don't respond, he says, "What do you think, Jess?"

I shake myself out of my daydream, smile at my invisible audience, and say, "I hope we made a difference."

Danny doesn't leave at six. Instead, we watch the news together, and as they announce the headlines, I see my face on the screen, along with Dad's and Ross's and everyone else's.

I laugh. I can't help it. I start giggling, and Danny is zooming in on me, but I don't care.

We have reminded the whole country how monstrous the monster is. Not someone you should try to copy. Not someone you set up fake profiles in honor of. Someone you catch. Someone you stop.

On TV, the reporter says, "In a powerful show of support and expressing anger at what they perceive as failed justice, the victims of the serial killer known as the Magpie Man came together today to remind the world of his crimes. Through the heartbreaking recollections of their loved ones, the families of the fourteen known victims brought the horror back into the public consciousness on the weekly YouTube show *The Eye: Hunting the Magpie Man*."

The reporter tells the viewers who I am, shows a few clips, including one of Ross talking about his mother, then says that if anyone has any information, they should call the police.

I used to think it was a wasted plea, but if what we did works, maybe this time, someone *will* have a clue.

The last image is all of us wearing the T-shirts, silently shouting the same one-word message.

When the story is over, I turn to the camera, look past it into Danny's eyes, and say, "Today was a good day."

99

"So?" Emily says.

"Two weeks' community service, and I lose my free periods for a month."

That's my punishment for missing school to film the left behind.

Mrs. Bradley was pissed off, but she can only do so much. She knows suspending me will make her look horrible.

St. Anthony's community service means mentoring the younger kids or helping in the library or joining an after-school club. It means "reinforcing school spirit."

"That's not too bad," Hanna says. But she would say that, because she actually volunteered to coach field hockey.

"I still can't believe Ross got them all to agree," Emily says. "Was it strange having them at your house?"

I think about how special it was, seeing all the left behind come together, hearing them speak and watching them listen.

We were powerful, because we're still here, and we always will be.

"I can't really explain it," I say, "but it made me feel...stronger, I guess. We understood what everyone is going through."

"Are you going to see them again?" Hanna asks, and I imagine us forming some kind of support group, resurrecting our dead mothers and sisters and daughters once a week with tea and cookies. I don't say it out loud, but I like that idea.

Being with other people whose sorrow matched mine, it made me feel closer to Mom. And it made me realize that talking can help if the right people are listening.

"Did you see my dad?"

I don't tell them I was proud of him. I'd rather keep that to myself.

They both nod and smile, and Hanna says, "It was amazing. I can't remember the last time I saw him standing up."

She looks guilty, like it's a joke she shouldn't have made, so I laugh and say, "Me neither."

"And those T-shirts," Emily says. "Your mom would be proud."

She looks away, the slightest blush creeping into her cheeks, but she shouldn't feel embarrassed for saying it. I think she's right.

"So," Hanna says, "what are you going to do for your community service?"

I think for a minute, then say, "I'll let Mrs. Bradley decide for me."

I don't have any skills or passions. All I've ever wanted is to catch the Magpie Man. But since Mayfield, I've been thinking differently. I've been wondering what comes next. Like Reg said, I need to move on, but to what?

It's a thought for another day, for a moment when I've achieved a different set of goals. My exams, my future, they won't mean anything if he's still out there.

That's what I'm thinking when I see a crowd in the courtyard, and through a gap, I spot Bernie.

She is faking a smile, the kind sad people recognize but everyone else mistakes for the real thing. When she catches my eye, she has a different kind of smile, one with meaning, and I smile back, then feel embarrassed and stare at the floor.

I'm about to walk away when she calls my name, then runs over, hugs me, and whispers, "Thank you" in my ear.

She doesn't let go for a long time, just snuggles into my shoulder, and if this wasn't in the courtyard, I might enjoy it.

"Welcome back," I say at last.

"Meet me at lunch," she says. "Under the tree."

100

We were best friends...and then we weren't.

Our friendship faded over time, the grief I felt hardening until no one could break through. By the time it softened, she was long gone. I used to blame Bernie for disappearing, but it wasn't her fault. She was only a kid doing what her parents said.

When it first happened, she hugged me, because it was all she could do. And I never appreciated that. I got older and bitter and remembered her wrong. She wasn't the best friend who ditched me.

I'm thinking all this as we sit under the tree until Bernie says, "I have to go to therapy now. Every Saturday, Mom and I have to talk about what happened."

"What's that like?"

"Shit."

We smile at each other, and Bernie takes a deep breath and

says, "I should have thanked you at the hospital. You saved my life."

"I didn't do anything."

"You found me."

I look into her eyes and try to remember what she was like when we were kids.

Before Mayfield, this wouldn't have happened, but I know better now.

"Do you remember my mom?" I ask.

Bernie smiles and says, "Of course. She was beautiful."

"I'm sorry if I was upset with you when we were kids. I wish we'd stayed in touch."

Bernie's face drops. "Me too. It wasn't your fault. My mom was so desperate for a new life. When she married my stepdad, she forgot all about Doveton."

We are quiet for a while, then Bernie says, "Remember that sleepover, with the pillow fort?"

It had started in my bedroom, the two of us under my duvet propped up with an umbrella. But it didn't stop there. Mom followed us inside, said it wasn't big enough, and pulled her duvet in too.

Then we were in the hallway, our silliness expanding as Dad brought the bedding from the spare room, then the sheets from the linen closet, all propped up by the wood he kept in the garage. We crawled from room to room, giggling in the glow from our flashlight, until we fell asleep.

The next morning, we found Mom and Dad cuddled up in a different part of the fort, and neither of us wanted to wake them.

I love Hanna and Emily, but we don't have stories like that.

I started this without knowing where it would end. All I wanted was justice. But life is bigger than a single thought, no matter how much it consumes you.

Closure isn't only finding the Magpie Man. It's finding who I was and who I want to be.

"What's your therapist like?" I ask.

Bernie says, "She's a counselor."

"What's the difference?"

"I don't know."

I know what grief feels like. I know how dark it gets when there's no way past it.

Maybe I don't need to forget what happened to Mom to move on. Maybe I can use it to help other people.

"What are you thinking about?" Bernie asks, and I shake myself out of my daydream.

"The future."

101

The messages and comments come thick and fast, mainly from psychos, idiots, and trolls.

There are some from people who genuinely want to help, from people who saw the left behind standing side by side and felt compelled to contact me. That's what they say, that something "compelled" them to send me a DM or a tweet that tells me nothing I don't already know.

> Did the bus have a security camera? Maybe some-
> one followed her?

> Could it have been an ex-boyfriend? When did your
> mom and dad get together?

I wonder how many more have contacted the phone number given out on the news. I think about calling Lorraine, but if they had an actual lead, she wouldn't tell me.

I spend two hours reading the messages, quickly deciding which to delete and which to keep. And just as I'm about to log off, a new one arrives.

> Hey, my name is Clara. I might know something that could help you.

That's it. Short, sweet, and vague as hell.

Nasty people can't hide their nastiness in their writing. Idiots can't wait to get to the punchline, and trolls are angry and full of swears. Perverts quickly shift from pleasantries to demands.

But this girl is different. She knows something, or at least she thinks she might, so I set up a new account, one only I have access to, then reply.

> Hey. It's Jessica Simmons. Thanks for contacting me. I'd love to hear what you have to say.

No demands, no suggestion of a meeting that might scare her off.

I stare at my screen for ten, fifteen, twenty minutes, feeling increasingly anxious until she replies.

> I'm probably being stupid.

Twenty minutes to write four words.

At first, I feel angry, then I wonder if this is a catfish situation, and then once I realize there's no choice, I reply.

Maybe it's nothing. But you wrote to me for a reason, and I would really like your help.

Another fifteen-minute wait until she says:

OK.

102

Her name is Clara. That's the only information I have about her. This girl is a mystery, and I've got enough of those to solve already. She won't meet face-to-face, and I don't blame her.

She wanted to do this online, but I want to hear her voice. I need to hear the gaps between her sentences and when she takes a breath and how she says every single word.

I sent her my other number, and now, almost twenty-four hours after her first message, Dad's phone starts to vibrate.

"Hey," I say.

"Hey."

"Thanks for calling."

She doesn't reply, so I say, "Do you watch the show?"

"Yes."

She sounds young.

I wait for her to say something else, and when she doesn't, I say, "I know you're worried. But anything you think might help us catch him could be the clue we're looking for."

Still nothing, which makes me trust her, because she's genuinely scared or nervous or both.

"I got a lot of messages after the last show," I say. "Yours was the only one I responded to."

She makes a noise, an intake of breath, then says, "I shouldn't."

"You can tell me anything, Clara. It's just me and you, and I'd rather hear what you have to say."

She sighs and clears her throat. "I saw you on the news. There was a man talking about his mom."

"That was Ross. His mother was killed by the Magpie Man."

Another intake of breath and then, "Why do you call him that?"

"My dad called him that. The newspapers found out, and now everyone says it. Like Jack the Ripper." I hear what sounds like crying and say, "I'm sorry. I really appreciate you messaging me."

She's quiet for a while, blows her nose, then says, "It was so sad, seeing all those people together. It made my mom cry."

I feel glad that it did its job and wonder how many others were brought to tears by the sight of forty-five people staring blankly into a camera, their stories recounted one by one from Dad's to Frances Banks's, from my mother to Lorna and the twelve in between.

"She held me really tight," Clara says, "like she does whenever something sad happens. She doesn't know what I saw. No one does."

I hear quiet sobbing, and I whisper, "It's okay."

Whatever she thinks she knows, it's big, and my heart races because maybe we finally have a witness.

I don't want to scare her away, so I sit listening to her cry until she says, "Are you still there?"

"Yes."

"I know his real name," Clara says.

"What is it?" I ask, but she doesn't reply.

I leave a gap for her to fill, first with sniffs and whimpers, then a whispered, "I'm sorry."

"Don't be," I say. "Where do you live?"

"Close."

"Close to what? Close to me?"

I shouldn't be forcing information out of her. I should be patient. But I need to know.

"Can you tell me who you're talking about?" I ask.

"I wrote it down," she whispers. "I wrote it all down and was going to send it to you...but I couldn't."

"That's okay."

I can feel my heart pounding, and I'm desperately trying not to push her too hard.

"Are you talking about the Magpie Man? Do you know his name?"

The phone goes dead, and when I call back, she doesn't answer. After at least twenty attempts, it goes straight to voicemail.

"Call me back," I say. "Please."

But she doesn't phone or reply to my messages.

Whatever she knows, she is too scared to say it out loud.

103

I usually don't pay attention to the younger students, but today, I'm watching closely.

I watch every girl who passes me, looking for any suggestion that one of them is Clara. But when they see me, they either smile or make a face and scuttle away, freaked out by the weird eleventh grader staring at them.

You can tell the ones who watch my show and the ones who don't. The ones who smile at me think they're making friends with a celebrity. The others think I'm picking a fight.

"What are you doing?" Hanna asks, and I tell her about Clara.

"That's exciting," she says.

I shrug. "Not really. I don't know anything about her, and she's not answering my calls. She's disappeared."

Hanna watches me staring around the courtyard. "I know an easier way."

I look at her until she smiles and says, "SIRK."

I don't get it at first, but then I do, because the teachers have this program on their computers—Student Information Record Keeper, or SIRK—to record us and keep all our information in one place.

It literally knows everything about everyone at the school, and if Clara goes here, she'll be in it.

The problem is teachers rarely leave their laptops unguarded. And when they do, they lock them.

If I want to see if Clara goes to St. Anthony's, I need to break a pretty big rule.

104

When I tell Emily my plan, she scowls and says, "No fucking way."

"Why not?"

"If you get caught, we'll both be in serious trouble. There's some really confidential information on there."

On my page, under special notes, it says, MOTHER IS DECEASED. It's a warning to new teachers to watch what they say. I saw it once, over a teacher's shoulder in sixth grade, and I hated it. Three words, all in capitals—a reminder that never loses its sting.

"Imagine what it says about everyone else," Emily says. "Humphries will go ballistic if he catches you."

"He won't catch me."

Emily shakes her head and says, "I love you, Jess. But I'm not getting expelled for you."

"I think you're overreacting."

"I think *you're* overreacting. Some girl says she knows the Magpie Man and then disappears. It's probably the same person leaving the articles. Or it's those tenth graders messing with you again."

"I don't think so."

"Well, that's up to you. But this is too risky."

She stares at me, doing her best impression of someone responsible, and I say, "Fine. I'll do it on my own."

I start walking away, even when I think this isn't working, until I hear her catch up and groan.

"If we get caught, I'm blaming you for everything."

105

Theology hasn't been the same since Mayfield Lodge.

We should be sharing private jokes about the place, going off on tangents as we reminisce about Andrea and Saffron and Reg, laughing about the kangaroos, and smiling about the prayer room. We should love Mr. Humphries even more than we used to for telling us about his son. Instead, no one talks about it, and that only makes it more obvious.

Maya eventually admitted she was the one who bought the liquor, and she got a two-week suspension.

Sometimes there's a whispered recollection, but it's quickly snuffed out, just in case it offends Bernie or reminds Mr. Humphries of the night we let him down.

But today I have other things to worry about, and from the look on Emily's face, she's just as scared.

The class drags on, and ten minutes before the end, I talk myself out of it. But I have to know if Clara goes here.

SIRK has all our photographs. It has our addresses. If I'm right, if Clara is right, I could finally be closing in on some answers.

When the class ends, we leave like normal, only I wait in the hallway, my back pushed hard against the wall, hiding in the corner as my classmates walk the other way.

Emily looks back, waits until the hallway is empty, then screams.

Mr. Humphries is out the door quicker than I expected.

I slip inside and run to his computer. I push a button, but the screen is locked, the password box empty, asking me a question I can't answer.

I hit Enter, even though I know it's useless, then stare around the classroom, wondering how much time I have.

There are more noises outside, and I hold my breath, trying to figure out if the voices are getting closer or further away. But I can't waste this. I might not get another chance.

His lesson planner is on his desk, and I flick through it, looking for words that might mean something or random letters and numbers he couldn't possibly remember. But there's too much in there, pages of notes and reminders and names. It could be any of them.

Except...I think back to Mayfield, to what Mr. Humphries told us that night in the prayer room, and then I type six letters into his laptop—O L I V E R—and hit Enter.

He has SIRK up. He has my page up. I'm shocked to see my own face staring back at me, and I don't move for a moment, then I look for the search function, my heart pounding so fast I'm sure it will give me away.

When I find it, I go to first name and type *CLARA* before pushing Enter. Nothing comes up. Not a single person at St. Anthony's has that name.

"Fuck," I whisper to myself.

I try it again, but it's useless. If Clara is her real name, she doesn't go here.

I've been so focused that I don't hear the footsteps in the hallway until it's almost too late. It's only when I hear another shout outside, a warning, that I quickly type my own name, hit Enter, then step away from Mr. Humphries's computer as he walks into the room.

"Jessica," he says. "Did you forget something?"

Holding up my lanyard, I say, "It was under my chair, sir."

"It should be around your neck," he says, walking behind his desk and closing the laptop without looking at it.

"Sorry. See you next class."

"I just caught your best friend making a scene in the hallway," he says.

"Oh?"

I couldn't sound guiltier if I tried.

He picks up his planner, turns a few pages, then looks at me.

"I should go," I say, and Mr. Humphries holds my stare until I feel uncomfortable, refusing to look away until his next class starts to arrive and I can escape.

106

"Did you do it?" Emily asks, and she can tell by my face that it's not good news.

"She doesn't go here—if her name's even Clara."

Emily sighs. "At least you tried. And we didn't get caught."

"I nearly did. He had my details up. I had to put it back the way it was."

"That's weird."

"Not really. I was just in his class. He was probably making notes or something."

Emily doesn't say anything for a long time. She walks silently next to me until we're back in the homeroom.

"Thanks for helping," I say, and she nods but still doesn't reply.

It's not until Hanna arrives that Emily takes a deep breath and says, "Okay, I have a theory."

We stare at her, waiting for her to explain, and when she doesn't, Hanna says, "Go on then."

"The newspaper articles...what if it wasn't a student?"

"It has to be," I say. "One was here, and the other was at Mayfield Lodge."

Emily takes another deep breath and says, "Unless it was Mr. Humphries."

107

"You're saying our theology teacher is the Magpie Man?" I ask, and Emily shakes her head.

"I don't know. But he could have put both articles in your bag, and he was looking at you on SIRK after class. That's a little creepy."

"He's a teacher. He was doing his job," I say.

She has a point about the articles, though, and the more I think about it, the more pieces fall into place, like how a ten-year-old story could be kept all this time. A kid wouldn't do that. But a man might. Although it still doesn't make sense why he would do it.

I went in there to find Clara and came out with something completely different. But I should be used to that by now.

"I can't think about this," I say. "It's not him. It can't be. I need to find Clara."

"There probably is no Clara," Emily says.

But she sounded so scared on the phone. She sounded like she didn't want to say the words coming out of her mouth.

I believe her. I just need to figure out who she is.

108

I went to Doveton Elementary School, so it's not hard to talk my way past the reception desk and into a conversation with my old teacher Mrs. Maxwell about work experience.

She looks happy to see me, even though I haven't been here for six years.

"How have you been?" she asks, a flicker of something serious behind her smile.

She was here when Mom was murdered. She knows my history. But she's trying hard not to bring it up.

"I'm good," I say. "I'm a junior now."

Mrs. Maxwell looks surprised, although she shouldn't be. She knows when I left. She knows how old I am. And yet somehow, when your elementary school teachers see you, they can't help but express wonder at the passing of time.

"We have a work-experience week coming up soon," I say, "and I was thinking of doing it here."

She grins like she's the reason for my decision, even though being a teacher is the last thing I want to do.

"I'm sure we could arrange that," she says. If she has any idea about the show, she's hiding it well.

The classroom looks like it did when I was here last, just different interpretations of the same displays and the same teacher with a slightly older face.

I feel guilty for lying to her. I could come here, moving from class to class, learning every single kid's name. But I don't have time for that. Instead, as I'm about to leave, I say, "I think I know someone who goes here. Her name is Clara."

Mrs. Maxwell shakes her head. "I don't think so, Jessica. We don't have a Clara here."

She smiles like that's the end of the conversation, telling me to leave my details with the secretary and that she will talk to her boss.

But I leave without speaking to anyone else, quickly running out of ways to find a girl who may not even exist.

109

I call Lorraine, and when she doesn't answer, I leave a message. Two hours later, she calls back.

I could explain on the phone, but it is harder to ignore someone face-to-face, so I ask if we can meet.

"Is everything okay?" Lorraine asks. "Have there been more Polaroids?"

"No," I say, and you can tell by the sound she makes that she's disappointed, unwilling to waste time on me unless it's an emergency.

It already feels like the time I told her about the comment and the newspaper clippings, when she couldn't care less. So I say the only thing that is guaranteed to interest her—the promise of an instant promotion.

"I've heard from someone who knows the Magpie Man," I tell her.

I'm waiting outside when she arrives, and when she opens her car door, I shake my head and say, "Not here."

I don't want Dad hearing this conversation, because I don't want to get his hopes up, so we drive five minutes down the street, then stop.

Lorraine faces me and says, "How have you been, Jessica?"

If she genuinely believed I knew something, she wouldn't be starting the conversation like this. She would say, "So, what have you got for me?"

Instead, she's making small talk because she thinks whatever I have is nothing compared to the photograph.

"I might have found an actual witness," I say.

"How did you do that?"

I tell her about the episode with all the left behind family members, Clara's phone call, and how she said she lived close by.

Lorraine writes everything down, but I quickly realize this is for my benefit, not hers.

"Okay," she says. "We'll look into it."

"I can help."

"That won't be necessary."

"She doesn't go to St. Anthony's or Doveton Elementary. I've done some investigating."

Lorraine sighs and touches my arm, and this is the moment I lose her completely, because she feels sorry for me.

"You shouldn't be taking the law into your own hands," she says.

"Do your job then!" I shout. "I'm telling you—this girl knows something. We need to figure out who she is."

She sighs again, and it annoys me how she's not even trying to hide what she's thinking. She doesn't believe a word I'm saying.

"If she calls again, tell her she should be speaking directly to the police."

"And if she doesn't?"

"We'll continue to do our jobs. I promise we'll look into it as best we can."

But they won't do what's necessary. They won't dig as deep as they need to until they find her.

"You gave me your number so I could contact you when I had something important. This is something important."

Lorraine smiles sadly and says, "No, Jess. The Polaroid was important. And I'm so grateful for that. But this isn't. Do you realize how many people call us every day, saying they know something? We have a lot of officers focused on your case, and we'll add it to the list of tips. But you shouldn't get your hopes up."

I don't know why I thought the police would help when they didn't before. They couldn't catch him ten years ago, and they haven't caught him since, even with fourteen dead bodies and fourteen angry families as motivation. They're useless, even the ones who pretend they care.

"Take me home," I say.

Lorraine looks at me for a moment, then drives back in silence.

As I'm getting out, she says, "I know how much you want to catch him," but I ignore her, because she has no idea.

If she really knew, she would listen. She wouldn't be brushing me off with the kind of things you tell people who are wasting police time.

I always knew it would be hard to catch him, but I genuinely believed she would see the truth in my eyes the way I heard the fear in Clara's voice. Maybe all she sees, all anyone will see, is desperation.

They don't think I'm solving the crime. They see what happens when grief turns you into a mess. When all you have left is pointing fingers at strangers.

If I'm going to finish this, I'll have to do it without them.

110

On Saturday, it's Emily's turn to host a sleepover, but when we arrive, she's not there, so Hanna and I sit awkwardly in the living room while her mom makes nervous small talk.

Usually, Emily makes excuses for us to have it somewhere else. But this week, she was excited, because her dad was taking her out, and he didn't flake at the last minute.

When they arrive, she hugs us and says, "We had the best day."

If you look closely at her, you can see the sadness just below the surface, the way she glances nervously at her father and the wobble in her smile.

It probably wasn't the best day. But it was a day with her dad, and she doesn't get many of those.

"I should go," he says, glancing at me, then away.

"Stay for a while," Emily replies. "We're having Chinese."

Her dad gives me another look, then shakes his head and says, "Maybe next time."

I'm used to people staring, but his look unnerves me.

"Same time next week?" Emily asks.

He says, "We'll see, darling. Enjoy your sleepover, girls."

Once he has gone, she does her best to stay happy. But we can see how deflated she is, so I change the subject, telling them I visited my old school to look for Clara.

"You don't know she lives locally," Hanna says. "What does 'close' even mean?"

"It was the way she said it. She sounded terrified. I think she knows something."

Emily sighs. "I still think you're focusing on the wrong person." She's convinced Mr. Humphries has something to do with it. "Next theology class, we should show him the newspaper articles and see how he reacts," she says.

"And then what?" I ask.

"And then we'll know more than we do now."

If Hanna was pointing the finger at Mr. Humphries, I wouldn't be so angry, but Emily knows what he's been through.

"How can you accuse him?" I ask. "Have you forgotten what happened?"

Hanna looks confused, but Emily says, "I haven't forgotten. I just don't trust him."

When Emily goes to the bathroom, Hanna whispers, "What was that about?"

I tell her about Mr. Humphries's son, then think back to the prayer room and his face in the candlelight, the sorrow that crept out with every word until we wondered how we had never seen it before.

"Emily's wrong," I whisper. "I know what grief does, and it's not that."

"But it *was* someone at Mayfield," Hanna says. "Someone there left the article."

I nod, and just as Hanna is about to say something else, Emily bursts back in and says, "I'm starving."

We eat downstairs, listening to Emily run through every second of her day with her dad, and when she tells us to cheer up, I think about leaving.

But I show her my best fake smile, and she grins and says, "What are you thinking?"

"It's not Mr Humphries," I say, just as Emily's mom walks into the room.

I should hold my tongue, but I need them to believe me, so I move closer, then mumble, "Clara is important."

"I used to have a Clara in my class," Emily's mom says, not looking at us.

She starts clearing the plates and is about to leave when I say, "When was that?"

She stares at me then, her eyes clearing like she was in a daydream, and says, "She's in fifth grade now, so that would have been three years ago. Why?"

"No reason."

No one says anything else. We all stare at one another, then back at Emily's mom, who is a teacher's aide at Harmony Elementary.

Clara does live close, just not as close as I thought.

111

Her name is Clara Farrell. She probably looks a little different from the second-grade photo Emily's mom showed us, but I finally have something solid, even though it might not be her.

The following Wednesday, I go six houses down and ask for Jamie, and his mom looks at me and smiles, then shouts over her shoulder and makes a face when he comes bounding into the hall. When he sees me, he blushes, and his mom's smile gets wider.

I pull Jamie outside, close the door, and say, "I need your help."

"Sure," he says, not asking why or what or when.

I hide the grin pushing hard against my lips and say, "I need you to follow someone."

"Okay."

And then I smile anyway, because he's sweet and loyal, and I realize I love that about him.

"It's a girl... I need to know where she lives. But it means skipping school."

I remember Jamie's hand on my arm when he pulled me back from the alley and when he chased Becca and Taryn and their boyfriends away, although I'd told him to leave.

Jamie nods, and I wonder if he would literally do anything I asked. But it's more than that, because I think if he asked, I would do the same for him.

"When?"

"Friday."

Mrs. Bradley will go bananas if I skip another day for no reason, so I need to be smart about it.

"I'll meet you at the Harmony-side bus stop at 8:30," I say.

As I'm about to leave, his mom steps into the street and says, "Jessica. Would you like to stay for dinner?"

"Mom!" Jamie stares at her until she laughs.

"I'm just being polite," she says.

"Well, I wish you wouldn't."

He looks embarrassed, and I should leave, but something else happens.

"Sure."

It comes out by accident, and when Jamie makes a face, I shrug, think of the microwave meal waiting for me while Dad's at work, and say, "What? I'm hungry."

112

His dad is sitting in the living room, and when Jamie introduces me, he says, "It's an honor to have a celebrity in our home."

I can't tell if he's being sarcastic or weird, but the way Jamie rolls his eyes, it's probably the latter.

I flash back to the moment I first saw him, peeking through the curtains the night I met his son. He seems friendlier than the face I saw that night suggested. But he looks at me with an intensity I'm not used to, like someone who was never told it's rude to stare.

He keeps straightening his glasses and squinting as if he's studying me. A couple of times, I fake a smile, and he nods but carries on staring, his fingers drumming the T-shirt that barely covers his belly.

While we're waiting for dinner, Jamie takes me to his room, and his parents don't say anything. I wonder if taking random girls upstairs is normal behavior for him. But seeing how awkward Jamie looks when we're alone and how long it takes him to decide where to sit, I don't think so.

I look out his window and imagine him watching Michael walk past.

There are binoculars on the windowsill, and when I hold them up, Jamie says, "They're my dad's. It's easier to keep watch...you know...in case anything else happens."

He's perched on the edge of his bed, so I sit on his desk chair and quickly wish I hadn't since it creaks every time I move. I try to stay as still as possible, feeling increasingly nervous and wondering why I agreed to this.

Every time I catch Jamie's eye, he looks away, and the longer we sit in silence, the more awkward it feels.

Almost every time we've seen each other, it's been too manic to focus on the small stuff. But sitting alone in his room, the small stuff suddenly feels enormous.

His walls are covered with posters of *The Umbrella Academy*, his bookcase full of graphic novels and figurines.

When he sees me looking, he grins and says, "What do you think?"

It's not really my thing, but I smile and say, "They're cool."

"This is Diego," Jamie says, holding one of the models up. "He's my favorite."

I reach out, but he looks nervous and places it gently back on the shelf.

"So," Jamie says, "who are we going to follow?"

"Her name's Clara," I say. "She goes to Harmony Elementary"

"Cool. What's the plan?"

"We wait for her to leave school, then I talk to her. That's all."

Jamie nods, like this is usual for him. "Can I ask why?"

I tell him about Clara's phone call and explain why it's a two-person job. I need his help, because even though we've never met, Clara would recognize me in a heartbeat. Plus, if school letting out is anything like St. Anthony's, it'll be chaos.

We could leave later, but that would mean hanging around at home or sneaking out of school during lunch. If we go early, that's one less problem to deal with.

When we're back downstairs, Jamie's dad winks at him, quickly losing his smile when he sees me looking.

"Dinner!" his mom shouts, and the floorboards creak, and a boy and a girl appear out of nowhere.

"Hi," the boy says, just as the girl asks, "Who's this?"

"It's no one," Jamie says, and then, "I mean...it's Jess. She's my friend."

"You're in that show," the girl says, and I nod and give Jamie a look, because I have no idea who I'm talking to.

"This is Erin and Henry."

"We're twins," Henry says.

"Our double delight," Jamie's mom says.

His dad rolls his eyes and mumbles, "More like our double despair."

They look about nine, and I wonder why Jamie hasn't mentioned them before. But we haven't really talked about anything except me since we met.

All through the meal, Jamie's dad talks about the show, and his mom keeps trying to change the subject.

"I knew your mother," his dad says, which catches me by surprise. The way Jamie looks, this is news to him too. "I'm sorry about what happened."

"Thank you," I say, feeling uneasy.

I expect him to keep going, to try to ease the awkwardness by making it even more awkward, but he doesn't say another word.

Eventually, I ask, "How did you know her?"

He sighs and says, "I used to go in the store where she worked. She was very friendly."

When Jamie's mom mentions dessert, I say, "I'd better go. But thank you. It was delicious."

Outside, I remind Jamie about Friday, then say, "Did you know your dad knew my mom?"

"No idea."

"Have you always lived in Doveton?"

"Yep. We've been neighbors all along."

If he knows what I'm getting at, he doesn't let on. He's hopping from one foot to the other, and I suddenly feel nervous for a completely different reason.

Ignoring it, I say, "Do your parents watch the show?"

"Only my dad. Mom thinks it's exploitative. No offense."

I laugh and say, "None taken. I should go."

As Jamie steps forward, I step back and say, "See you soon."

113

After school on Thursday, I greet my nan with a sad face and a sigh.

"What's wrong?" she says, and when I tell her I'm not feeling well, she reaches for my forehead as expected. "You don't feel hot."

"My head's pounding," I say, "and my stomach doesn't feel right."

She pours out the tea and sits across from me while I keep my head down, breathing deeper than normal, my eyes not quite as wide, my smile replaced by a grimace.

If you are going to fake an illness, it's no good doing it on the morning of the day you want to stay home. Effectively skipping school requires preparation. You have to be willing to sacrifice the previous night if you want to get the next day off, so when Nan asks what I want for dinner, I say, "Maybe some soup. I'm not hungry."

She looks more serious then, because I always ask for soup when I'm sick. She touches my head again, and even though the result is the same, she says, "You do feel a little hot."

"I might go to bed," I say. This is at four thirty in the afternoon.

I eat slowly, pretending I can only manage one slice of toast, then kiss her and Dad and go to my room. I get ready for bed right away and read, pretending to be dozing when I hear Nan's footsteps in the hallway.

The next day, when I tell her I'm feeling a little better and should probably try to go in, she's the one who tells me not to.

She offers to come back and sit with me, and I tell her it's okay, I don't feel as bad as yesterday. I just need some sleep.

What makes this plan perfect is that Friday is Nan's busy day—hairdresser in the morning, book club in the afternoon, and bingo after dinner. She hates missing it, and I tell her she doesn't have to.

Any other day and she would ask to speak to Dad or tell me to call her every hour. But instead, she says, "Okay. Get plenty of rest. I'll phone the school."

Downstairs, I greet Dad with a smile and tell him how much better I'm feeling.

It's a risk, but Nan won't call him because she knows he won't answer. And by Tuesday, I hope it's forgotten.

At 8:30, Jamie is waiting for me at the bus stop. He has brought two packed lunches.

114

Harmony is slowly coming back to life after another winter.

Hanna's ice-cream parlor, like all the other shops and restaurants, is dusting itself off before the Easter break, gearing up for another manic summer.

I'd like to go in, because Hanna's dad will give us free desserts, but her mom will ask why I'm not at school, and I can do without a lecture.

The wind coming in with the tide and the overcast sky mean sunbathing isn't an option, not that I would do that with Jamie around. Instead, we walk the length of the beach, then up and along the sidewalk, staring out to where the sea meets the sky.

It really is a beautiful place, so peaceful you can't help but imagine a better life if you let yourself daydream as the waves crash against the rocks below.

I should come here more often, although if I did, maybe

this feeling would wear off. Maybe magical places don't feel magical to the people who see them every day.

We find a bench and eat the sandwiches Jamie made for us, the gaps between our conversations getting bigger as we drift off into our own thoughts.

When I look at him, he's staring out to sea with a smile on his face, and I don't look away until he turns and says, "What?"

"Nothing."

I want to ask about his dad. After what he said about Mom. But there are too many questions in my head right now, and I need to focus on Clara.

Instead, I try to let my mind wander, remembering when we came here as a family, Mom hurrying us from bed to car to beach. She loved it here. She called it her heaven.

Doveton is home, but maybe Harmony could be my version of Mayfield Lodge.

"What do you want to do when you graduate?" I ask.

"I'm going to college to study civil engineering."

He says it so confidently, so quickly, that I can't help but look surprised. I don't know why, but I assumed he was as confused about the future as I am.

"What?" he asks again.

I smile and say, "I didn't expect you to be so…"

"Clever?"

"Grown-up."

Jamie laughs. "It's what I've always wanted to do."

I used to hate people like that, people who could talk you through their entire life before they'd finished school.

There's this saying: "If you want to make God laugh, tell him your plans." And when your mom is murdered, you know exactly what that means.

But I'm starting to see a future through the mess of my life. I'm not planning, I'm imagining, and there's nothing wrong with that.

"What about you?" Jamie asks.

It was a question I always hated, but not today.

I think of Bernie and Reg and Mr. Humphries and Emily's mom—all these broken people I ignored, because I was an acceptable kind of selfish. No one blames the grieving girl for only thinking about herself. But that doesn't make it right.

I remember what Bernie said under the tree, about her therapy sessions, and say, "I'm going to help people. I want to be a therapist."

"You'll be good at that," Jamie replies. "You're so brave."

It catches me by surprise, but I don't feel embarrassed. I feel proud.

I hope he's right, about being good at something, because I've been thinking about it a lot, in between all that's been happening. There's a job for me out there, and I think I can make a difference.

Even when everything has been eaten and I start to feel cold, I sit listening to the sea below and the birds above and the hum of everything in between. I wish Mom were here to enjoy this place with me.

If I close my eyes and think hard enough, I can remember burying her legs in the sand and carving a mermaid tail.

I can remember when she taught me not to be afraid of the

ocean, diving headfirst into its vastness until I laughed away my fears. And I can remember Dad piggybacking me along the boardwalk while he walked hand in hand with his soul mate, in the calm before the storm.

115

I show Jamie the image on my phone of Clara's old school photo, and he stares at it for a long time before nodding and saying, "Got it."

"You sure? She's going to look older now."

"Yep. I'll recognize her."

I need her to be away from the school, away from her teachers and her friends, before I approach her.

Jamie can wait by the front entrance with the other parents without being noticed, but I don't know how many of them watch my show, and I'm not prepared to find out.

When we first arrive, there are only a few moms there, gossiping and paying no attention to us. We hang back until it starts to get more crowded, then Jamie takes a few steps forward while I pull a baseball cap low over my face and hope no one recognizes me.

By three o'clock, the place is packed, and I'm glad I brought help.

The youngest students come out the side entrance, all screams and giggles and hyperactivity. Then the older ones follow, and I try to find Clara without looking suspicious. I think I see her a couple of times, but a quick glance at my phone says otherwise.

There are too many people all crowded together, and I start to panic. I can't even see Jamie now.

I must look suspicious, a weirdo waiting outside a school for someone else's child, but when my phone buzzes, it's Jamie, and he says, "Can you see me?"

"No."

"I've found her. Go left, toward the bus stop."

I do as he says, and when I see him, I follow at a distance, waiting until the group she is with starts to split up.

Jamie looks over his shoulder and smiles, but I pretend we don't know each other. I still think Clara will run if she realizes how close I am. I'm lucky that she's a walker, not a bus rider, and that her parents trust her to come home on her own.

When it's just Clara and one other girl, talking loudly like they don't have a care in the world, I catch up with Jamie, and he grins but doesn't say anything.

The girls turn in to a side street, and we follow until Clara waves goodbye to her friend and continues on alone. She reaches into her pocket, and I hear the jangle of keys, realizing she's almost home, that if I'm going to do this, it needs to be now.

"Stay here," I say to Jamie. Then I shout "Hey!" and speed up until I'm right behind her.

Clara turns, and when she sees me, I know I have the right person.

She looks terrified.

116

"Are you the girl on the phone?" I ask.

When Clara doesn't answer, I say, "I think you are. I think you know something about the Magpie Man."

She shivers and starts moving, fiddling with her keys as she does so.

I chase after her, touch her shoulder, and say, "Please..."

Clara spins around. "I don't know what you're talking about," she says, then opens a gate, runs up the path, and stabs her key at the door.

She's panicking, giving me just enough time to say, "I need your help."

She turns around again, shakes her head, and says, "I'm sorry," then opens the door and slams it shut before I can respond.

But I haven't come all this way for nothing. I look back at Jamie, who is a few houses down, then walk through the gate and up the path and ring the doorbell. Clara doesn't answer.

I'm certain this is the girl I've been looking for. So why won't she talk to me? I need to know what she knows, so I go around the side, where a gate opens with a latch.

I'm trespassing now. I'm not solving a crime, I'm committing one. But I head toward the backyard, then turn and look through the patio doors, directly into Clara's kitchen. It's empty, and I look closer, staring deep into the house.

That's when I see her walking straight toward me, and when she slides the door open, I try my best to smile, to make her know I'm here to help.

But she has a phone in her hand, and already dialing a number, she says, "I'm calling the police. Go away."

"I need to know...did you message me? Did we speak on the phone? Please."

Maybe she was messing with me, just like everyone else. Maybe she was trolling me in her own unique way, not thinking I would actually come looking. But when I see a tear creep down her cheek, I know it's more than that.

"Just go," she says, closing the door and locking it, pulling the curtains closed so I can't see inside.

I walk back around the house and down the sidewalk and away.

"So?" Jamie says.

"She knows something. But she's too afraid to say what it is."

117

Harmony has messed with my mind.

I daydreamed so long about my mother that it feels like I've lost her all over again, while Clara's refusal to help means my sadness is mixed with anger. I feel ready to explode, and I don't know what will be left when I do.

I read the texts Mom sent Dad, over and over again, desperately trying to remember her voice. But I barely remember anything, only fragments of moments that dance across my memory, untrustworthy and chipped away by time.

How has Jess been today? Tell her I'll be home soon.

Was I ill that day? Did something important happen?

I feel a bolt of pain whenever I imagine her writing my name, thinking of me, reassuring me she'll come home.

I need more of her, because I've used up what we have. Eventually, every picture loses its magic; every message is only words on a screen. They aren't her. They're just things.

In the corner of the attic, untouched, is the box Dad asked me to ignore. I always imagined it was full of memories that would break our hearts all over again, so I did what I was told. But not today.

When I open it, I see an ultrasound scan, a black-and-white smudge that must be me. Underneath is a journal of my first year, and beneath that are notes in my father's handwriting. Some are crossed out and rewritten, and I realize these are drafts of messages he wrote to my mother.

Tucked to the side is a digital camera that won't turn on. God knows how long it's been here or how many devices we own that haven't been charged since she died.

I take out the memory card and go back to my room, then bring my laptop to the attic, where the musty smell and twinkling lights calm me in a way I can't describe.

These are photos I've never seen before: not familiar pictures from the albums Nan likes to reminisce over but candid shots, mostly of me, some of Dad, and those few magical moments of Mom, brand-new images that make my heart soar.

I grow up seven years in one hundred clicks of a mouse, and then the images change. They are smudged and unclear, as if someone has focused too closely on something.

There are four of them, each less blurry than the last but still a mystery, and then the final image, of someone holding a camera in front of their face, photographing whoever took this shot.

I look at the date stamp. It was taken the day Mom was killed.

118

The more I stare at the pictures, the blurrier they become. Even the image of the person with the camera is unclear, like someone was moving as they took it, smearing the man's edges.

It is a man—I can see that much, but that's all. It's too close to tell where he is or what he's doing, only that he's returning the favor: two people each taking a photo of the other. But why?

I leave the attic and hold the laptop in front of my dad. "Did you take these?"

He stares at them, then says, "No. What are they?"

"I found them on an old camera. I think Mom took them."

Dad's eyes go wide, and I wonder if I've said too much or if he realizes what box they are from.

It's been a long time since my father got his hopes up, and I don't want to break his heart all over again with "evidence" that turns out to be useless.

"Do you recognize them?" I ask.

"I'm sorry, Jess. I'm not even sure what I'm looking at."

But he looks anyway, staring into the mess of colors, because he's as desperate for this to be over as I am.

If it was Mom's camera, if she took these the day she died, it could be vital.

"It's okay," I say.

Back in my room, I stare at the blurred images, all reds and yellows and greens. They could be anything. I click through, from the graniest to the clearest, over and over again, trying to figure out what it is I'm looking at. And then I focus on the image of someone I can't identify, who is covering his face with a Polaroid camera.

Could it be him? Could this be a picture of the Magpie Man? We now know he took pictures of the women he murdered. He collected his kills. But is there more?

I try to slow my breathing, pushing my fingers against my temples to calm the headache that has come hard and fast.

I could call the police, but what would I tell them? I don't even know what four of the photos are, and I can't risk Lorraine taking them and putting them with everything else they never found a use for.

I could call him out. I could show the world these images and hope it's enough. But you can't see his features. All you can see are blurred lines and a hidden face, just hands and a camera.

119

Again, like every week now, I'm awake hours before Danny arrives. The more I don't tell him, the angrier he'll be when he finally finds out.

I'm supposed to film every defining moment, but there was no way I was going to stick a camera in Clara's face. Whatever she knows, she won't tell me, let alone the whole world.

When I get to school, Mrs. Bradley is at the entrance, ready to do the late list, and she gives me a look but doesn't say anything. If she thinks my nan lied for me, she keeps quiet, although she's obviously suspicious. I smile at her and walk past without stopping.

You can tell Emily wants to talk about Mr. Humphries again, but one look at Danny and she realizes she has to keep her mouth shut.

I feel like I've spent the last few weeks trying to untangle lies from truth, games from reality. All I know for certain is that he watched me the night I dyed my hair, he placed the Polaroid, and he killed Lorna Banks. I should be focusing on that.

Clara knows something, and I need to keep pushing until she tells me. I have to be the one who decides if it's important, not her.

He may have only just killed, but I don't think we have another nine months before he strikes again. He was two months early this time, and I have a terrible feeling his pattern has changed forever.

I daydream all the way to English, telling myself over and over again that it's working, and when I walk past Mr. Collins, I almost don't feel it.

And yet it's there, the tiniest brush of his skin on mine, and when I look down, his hand shoots behind his back, a flash of something black-and-white pulled away from my open bag. I stare at him, and I can see the fear on his face.

Danny almost crashes into me, and behind him, there are groans and shouts, the hallway quickly filling with people trying to get in and others wanting to get past.

I look over the camera, directly into Danny's eyes, and ask, "Did you get that?"

He shrugs and mouths, "Get what?" and when I look back at Mr. Collins, I see sweat forming on his temples while ripples of panic cover his face.

I slowly breathe out, find my voice, and whisper, "It's *you*."

120

All along the hallway, people are yelling, desperate to get past, and I'm so close to him, I reach behind his back and try to grab the article.

I hear it crunch in his fist as the force of everyone pushes me into the classroom. Then he steps in after me, the others following while the other students shout as they walk down the hall.

Danny stares at me, and I wonder how the hell he didn't get that on-camera. But he was focusing on me, and I curse myself for not keeping the head cam faceup in my bag.

I'm standing in the middle of the classroom, and Mr. Collins doesn't ask me to sit. He just stares at me. As I glare back, I see the lines on his face rearrange themselves, and I can't tell if he's scared or amused or angry.

My heart is pounding, and I wonder how I didn't see this before.

The first article fell out of my bag in English class, seconds after I walked past him in the doorway. The second was in my suitcase at Mayfield Lodge, but he was there before we left. He gave us homework while we waited by the bus, our bags left unguarded on the ground.

I look at the camera, wondering what my viewers think is going on, then close my eyes and breathe, trying to figure out what to do.

Has he been this close all along? Is he the Magpie Man or just another Michael?

"Please sit down, Jessica," Mr. Collins says at last, but his voice sounds different.

He's too calm, too quiet. He knows he's been caught, and he isn't running. But that doesn't mean I won't.

"Come on," I say to Danny, and he follows me out of the classroom while Mr. Collins watches in silence.

"What's going on?" Danny asks.

I stare into the camera. "It's him."

I'm not telling my director. I'm telling everyone. He tried to put another article in my bag, and I don't know what that means, but it means something.

I don't have long.

"Jess?" Danny says.

It feels like a question I can't answer, a word that's suddenly too heavy to fit in my head.

"It's him," I say again, the panic rising in my chest, and Danny lowers the camera so it's facing the floor.

"Don't," I whisper, because I need him to film this. It could be my only chance.

He lifts the camera, and I look into the blinking red light, count down from five in my head, then say, "Action."

121

"Where are we going?" Danny asks, not caring that his voice is going out live.

He looks worried, but he should be glad. He used to moan at me for doing this on my own, for not filming the important parts. Now we're a team, and he's still complaining.

"His office," I say, running ahead and not caring how blurry this looks.

I don't have time to explain everything to my subscribers or my director. English lasts an hour. Then Mr. Collins is free. I don't know if he'll run or try to find me, and I'm not sure what's worse.

I stop at the bottom of the steps that lead to the teachers' lounge and the teachers' offices. If we get caught, they won't believe me. But what choice do I have?

As I walk upstairs, Danny touches my shoulder and says, "Jess. This isn't a good idea."

"It's the *only* idea. He put the clippings in my bag. He saved them all these years, and he's been taunting me. Who does that?"

Danny stares at me with his mouth open, and I imagine the sound of thousands of gasps as my viewers catch up.

"Be careful," he says. "You know what happened—"

"This is different," I say, cutting him off before he mentions Michael.

He looks shocked but doesn't say anything else, just follows me upstairs and focuses the camera as I look around the corner, checking that the coast is clear.

The teachers' lounge is at the far end of the hallway, but the door is open, and if anyone sees me, it's over.

"Come on," I whisper, and I'm not only talking to Danny. I'm speaking to everyone watching.

I look through the door to Mr. Collins's office, and it's empty, the desk free of laptops, the signs all good. I push the handle, and it opens, because teachers trust other teachers. But I need to be quick. If any of them are watching me online, they can see exactly what I'm doing.

When Danny has followed me inside, I close the door and go straight to Mr. Collins's desk, searching the drawers for anything suspicious. There's a filing cabinet in the corner, but it won't open, the metal clanging against the wall as I pull.

I turn to Danny and wonder if this is what he means about going too far, but he's still filming me. That's when I see Mr. Collins's ugly green coat hanging behind the door, and when I search his pockets, I find keys and a car fob.

Danny shakes his head, then reaches into his own pocket and stares at his phone.

He holds it out to me, and when I step closer, I see it's from Adrian, just two words: Let her.

He's watching this. They all are. This is the excitement they wanted when they signed me up.

I smile, jangle the keys in front of Danny, then creep back into the hallway.

The voices come quickly, loud and close by, and I shove him back inside, duck below the window, and slowly push the door until it clicks shut.

Danny and I are side by side, the camera turned away from me, and he adjusts it until I'm back on-screen. There's the slightest shake in his hand as I realize how scared he is. But he's still doing his job.

The voices are above us, then past us, fading down the hallway and away.

I stand up, open the door, and listen. "Okay," I whisper. "Let's go."

I run to my right and down the stairs, and only then do I look to see Danny three steps behind.

When we're back in the main hallway, I think about hugging him, because we did it. I thought of a plan, and it actually worked. But it's not over yet.

"Are you sure about this?" Danny asks, and I grip Mr. Collins's keys.

"Absolutely."

122

His car is big and silver, with room for a family I can't imagine him having.

When we get close, I press the fob, and the car beeps and unlocks, and it's as easy as that.

"Stay here," I tell Danny. I don't want him getting in trouble for this.

I open the passenger-side door and pull everything out of the glove box. I don't know what I'm looking for, but if Mr. Collins is the Magpie Man, I'll find proof.

"Jess," Danny says, and when I turn, there's a crowd gathering, students with a free period who look from me to their phones and back again. There's no escaping what I'm doing. It's everywhere, and Mrs. Bradley will kick me out if I'm wrong.

That's why I have to be right.

No one says anything. They watch me like I'm not real, so I continue like they're not real either.

There's nothing under the seats except empty coffee cups and scrunched-up parking tickets, so I open the trunk and push past the junk until I find a laptop bag. It's light but not empty, and when I unzip it, I see her face, over and over again, reprinted on countless newspaper reports. I see my mother and the horrible headlines my dad did his best to hide from me.

That's when I turn to Danny with tears in my eyes and say, "Call the police."

Then I hold the articles up to the camera and say, "I have proof."

123

It's the secretary who comes out first, asking me what I'm doing in the parking lot, but I don't reply. I sit, holding the articles, waiting for the police to take him away.

When the period ends, the crowd grows until kids from every grade are there.

A single beep over the loudspeaker tells me the teachers are coming. It's their not-so-secret code that shit is going down. It usually means a fight or trouble at the front entrance. But this time, it's me, sitting next to Mr. Collins's open car while Danny films every moment.

When the police car arrives, it slowly pushes its way through the crowd until Lorraine steps out, crouches next to me, and asks if I'm okay.

I nod but don't say anything, just hand her the articles, and she passes them to another officer wearing gloves, and I wonder if I'll ever see them again.

"This isn't enough evidence to arrest him," she says, and I point at the rope in the trunk and the shoes caked in dirt.

"You should check those for DNA," I say. Her face says it's still not enough, so I ask, "When was the last murder?"

Lorraine shakes her head, and as she checks her phone, I say, "It was Tuesday, April seventh. Ask Mr. Collins where he was that day."

The pieces didn't fall into place right away. But between breaking into his car and Lorraine arriving, I remembered something important. The day Lorna Banks was killed, Mr. Collins wasn't here. He was at the educator conference in London.

On their own, the pieces don't add up to much, but together, they paint a picture.

He was here all along. The Magpie Man was the one giving me the articles. He was taunting me, and I shudder at the thought.

The crowd starts murmuring, and when I look up, I see him walking toward us. If he wanted to run, it's too late.

"Jessica," he says, but before he can get to me, Lorraine and her partner block him off and say they have a few questions.

Danny is creeping closer, zooming in on Mr. Collins's face as it turns from anger to fear to something else.

They don't put him in handcuffs. The crowd doesn't cheer as they drive him away. There's only a strange kind of silence, full of unspoken thoughts.

When the police leave, Danny turns the camera back to me, and I guess this is where I say something important.

But all I can do is close my eyes and think of Mom, because whatever I say won't be enough.

124

No one tells me off for breaking into Mr. Collins's office. No one blames me for what happened. I've turned their world on its head, and they don't know how to deal with that yet.

"Holy fuck!" Emily says when she finds me in the reception area.

I'm waiting to be picked up, but I haven't phoned Dad yet. I don't know what to tell him.

The secretary tried, but he didn't answer. So I guess he wasn't watching.

Emily sits down and gives me a hug that I don't want. But I let her do what she has to, then smile and hope it looks genuine.

Justice is supposed to feel better than this, but until he's charged, until I know he won't come back, everything feels worse than before.

Danny sits across from me, filming Emily say, "I can't believe it's him."

I wonder if she feels guilty for blaming Mr. Humphries, but how was she to know? Everyone has their theories, and she was only trying to help.

We sit in silence until three o'clock.

I never did call my dad. Instead, I get the bus home, ignoring the stares and the whispers, and go straight to my room.

In the end, he comes to me when Danny has left, knocking gently on my door and sitting on the edge of my bed when I don't answer.

"Do you want to talk?" he asks.

I shake my head, and he touches my foot and says, "I'm here when you do."

"I wasn't scared," I say. "I thought I would be. But when I looked at him, when I saw who he really was, he wasn't anything to fear."

Dad sighs. "It's going to get harder before it gets easier. If it is him, there'll be a trial."

"Do *you* think it's him?"

"I hope it is," he says. "You've been through enough."

"So have you," I say.

He squeezes my hand tighter than ever.

125

The police haven't spoken to me yet. Lorraine said they will eventually, but I guess I've given them all they need.

Hanna and Emily wanted to come over, but I told them I need to be alone. It's easier when I don't have to pretend, when I can stare at Mom's pictures and imagine what she's thinking, when Dad and I can sit in our shared silence.

That night, when my phone rings, I'm not expecting it.

"Have you heard?" Hanna says. "Go online."

The link is everywhere, shared and shared and shared again. The same horrible image stares back at me, no matter where I look: a body marked with the number 15 and below it the word DEAD carved into its stomach.

She wasn't local. A report says she was murdered in Sheffield.

By putting DEAD below the number, he was sending me a message. He was sending it to every single one of the left behind who wore that T-shirt.

We did catch him, but not before he killed again.

126

I stay awake all night while the image of Mr. Collins's last victim goes viral, people sharing it for fun, creating memes they laugh at because it's what they do. Some of them have photoshopped me wearing my ALIVE T-shirt next to her.

I did this. I tried to be clever, and he outsmarted me. He might be caught now, but people will remember his message, and they'll blame me.

I started this wanting to remind everyone of his crimes, to bring him back into the public consciousness. But is that exactly what he wanted too? Was he enjoying being famous again? Was he getting worse to stay relevant?

I feel disgusted that he was there the whole time, teaching me, taunting me.

Whenever I think my tears have run dry, they come again, and I don't even try to wipe them away.

I imagine the left behind, a group that has only got bigger since I started this. As they sat, quietly swapping grief stories in my backyard, I saw how worn down they were. Still alive, still fighting, but missing the vital part that made their smiles sparkle and their eyes shine.

Whenever the conversations stopped, the silence hung so heavily around their necks, the unspoken horror of losing a daughter or a sister or a wife etched deeply into their faces.

And now there are more, a fifteenth family, and how can they not blame me? The image of all of us in those T-shirts accompanies every single report. What Mr. Collins did to her only makes sense because of us.

I was so proud of that picture. Now I can't bring myself to look.

127

My nightmares are collages of corpses and newspaper clippings. There are faces, both dead and alive, and numbers carved into the bodies of everyone I know.

Singsong taunts rip through my ears like razor blades: "*One for sorrow...two for joy...*"

Every night, I dream of Mr. Collins, his hands held tightly behind his back, and when I reach for whatever he's hiding, he disappears. Then he's looming over me, and the crowd from that day closes in, pushing us closer together until I'm swallowed by the hands I can't untangle.

I dream of Mr. Humphries and his stolen son, the boy who died before he could be anything, then Lorna Banks's little boy, broken and pleading for the justice I found too late.

Sometimes, I dream of Bernie, unconscious on her bed at Mayfield Lodge, and then Reg breathes her back to life and she becomes my mom, sitting bolt upright, forcing me awake.

Other times, I'm in a room full of Polaroid pictures, lines of murders hanging on the walls like a sick exhibition.

At the end of every nightmare, I wake up screaming, my sheets soaked in sweat, my room full of shadows that continue the story until I blink them away.

The fear comes first, then the realization, and finally the guilt.

128

I'm ignoring calls from Ross and Danny, but Hanna and Emily force their way into my house, past Sara and the other reporters.

The media shout and shove and aim their cameras at the gap in the door, because I'm suddenly newsworthy again. My teacher killed my mother, and that's a story everyone wants.

"It's ridiculous out there," Hanna says.

Emily says, "I kicked one in the shin, just for you."

She tries a smile, but it quickly falls from her face when she realizes I'm not in the mood.

"It's not your fault," Hanna says.

But I can't even pretend to believe her this time, because it is my fault. I wore the T-shirt, I made the statement, and he responded like only he can.

"It is," I say. "He did it all for me. I called him pathetic, and he reminded me what he's capable of."

"And then you caught him."

"But he was there all along. I looked him in the eye every fucking day. How stupid am I?"

"You're not stupid. He tricked everyone."

"But I always thought I would know the moment I saw him."

I shake my head until the tears fall hard and fast, and then I'm sobbing so loudly that my two best friends don't know what to do. I catch them looking at each other, sending silent signals, wondering how to react.

Have I finally broken like Dad did? Are they deciding whether to fix me or let me fall apart? Then they smother me in a four-armed hug with me wrapped in the middle.

Eventually, when today's tears have run dry and my stomach aches, Hanna says, "We're here," and Emily squeezes me every chance she gets.

But I'm focusing on something else. He tricked a lot of people; that's what Hanna said. He taught for years, and he tutored fifth graders, so what if Clara knew? What if that was what she was too scared to tell me?

If she saw something, she could be the witness who ensures he's locked up forever.

129

I stand at the bus stop, trying to ignore the reporters throwing questions at me and the photographers sticking their lenses in my face. Only Sara stands back, but she can't stop the others from harassing me for a comment. They want to know how I feel, like it's that easy.

I feel all over the place. I feel confused and angry and scared, because catching him and locking him up forever are not the same thing.

"Hey!" someone shouts again, and Jamie barges his way through the crowd, stands in front of me, and says, "Fuck off!"

The reporters don't move. Some ask him questions, and others act like he's not there. But when he starts swinging at them, kicking out at anyone close, they step back until they're on the opposite side of the road.

"Thanks," I say.

Jamie shrugs. "Don't mention it." He stands with me until the bus comes, then gets on and says, "Where are we going?"

"Clara's house. She knew it was Mr. Collins before I did. I think she has the evidence that can end this for good."

130

The driveway is empty, and a quick look through Clara's patio doors seems to say no one is inside. I knew she'd be at school, but I hoped one of her parents might be home.

If I can explain—if they realize how important Clara is to convicting Mr. Collins—they could bring her home early. But I'll wait all day if I have to.

Clara didn't want to speak to me last time, but she must know we've caught him now. She doesn't need to be scared anymore.

I move to the front of the house and stare into the living room, but all I can make out is a TV and a fireplace and some photo frames, and that's when I see it, only it can't be. I jump back, then hold my hands against the glass and peer inside.

"What the fuck?"

"What is it?" Jamie asks, and I pull him around the side of the house.

"I need to get in."

"Now?"

"Yes, now. Have you ever broken into somewhere before?"

Jamie shakes his head. "I don't think we should," he mumbles, but he doesn't know what I saw.

"Please," I whisper. "You said I was brave. Now I need us to be brave together. We have to get in there."

He shakes his head, mutters something under his breath, then starts walking around the backyard, looking under flower pots.

"On TV, people always hide their keys somewhere," he says.

I don't know why he likes me so much to follow my wild ideas. But I'm glad he does.

He gives up and goes back to staring through the windows.

Gently tapping on the patio doors, Jamie says, "We're not getting through these."

He tries the back door before checking the garage, which thankfully is unlocked, and coming out with a crowbar.

"Are you sure?" he asks, and I steady my breathing.

"Yes."

"Will you tell me why?"

"You'll see for yourself in a minute," I whisper. Then, when he doesn't move, "I know this is foolish. But is it more foolish than chasing Michael down the street with a hammer? Or stopping those bullies? I'm not as brave as you think I am. I need your help."

Jamie listens for a moment, then puts the crowbar in the gap between the door and the frame and pulls. The paint is cracking, and it looks old compared to the rest of the house, but as much as Jamie tries, it doesn't open.

Just when I think he's going to give up, he says, "Kick it."

"What?"

"When I yank, you kick, hard. Not the glass part obviously. Aim low."

"Won't that be noisy?"

Jamie shrugs. "Do you want to get in or not?"

For a second, I think maybe I don't, because I'm scared of what I'll find on the other side of the door, but I nod and say, "Okay."

Jamie pulls. "Now," he says, and I kick, then again, and the third time, I hear a crack, and the door swings open.

We pause, waiting for someone to come and investigate, but no one does. We stare at the doorway that leads into the kitchen. I watch Jamie, and for the first time since we met, he looks genuinely scared.

We could still leave, and no one would know it was us. But I step forward, the smell of an unfamiliar house hitting me harder than it ever has before.

The house is quiet, too quiet, just the hum of a huge fridge and the sound of birds singing coming through the broken back door.

I leave Jamie in the kitchen and go straight to the living room, and there she is, staring at me from a family portrait—Bernie.

I feel dizzy and sit heavily on the sofa.

I stare at the photo, at Bernie smiling that perfect fake smile as she stands with her mother, stepdad, and Clara.

It's the same look I saw in the hospital and on her first day back at school after Mayfield Lodge.

She wasn't happy then, and she isn't happy in the image her

new family has chosen to show the world. Next to her, Bernie's mom has the same smile, while her stepdad looks straight-lipped and serious.

I don't understand what's happening, and when Jamie comes in, he sees what I'm staring at and says, "Isn't she in your class?"

I nod, unable to speak. None of this makes sense.

Bernie left Doveton after her mom married her boyfriend. She moved to Harmony. She moved here.

But that still doesn't explain Clara's phone call.

I think back to our walk, when Bernie talked about her little sister—her half sister.

"What now?" Jamie asks, but the room is spinning, and I can't reply.

Part of me wants to stay until Bernie comes home, to find out what the hell is going on, but we shouldn't be here. And yet I can't shake the feeling that something's not right.

"We should check upstairs," I say, and as we walk into the hall, a noise behind us makes me jump, and I swear we've been caught.

Jamie's eyes go wide with terror, then just as quickly, he sniffs and smiles.

He reaches down and picks up an air freshener, whispers, "Motion sensor," and then, after another deep breath, "Bali sandalwood and jasmine." I stare at him, and he says, "My mom loves these things."

I should smile, because this is typical Jamie, making light of dark situations, but my heart is pounding, and I can't get the image of Bernie out of my head.

He sniffs again, then he walks upstairs, and I follow.

Clara's bedroom looks a lot like mine, her parents' is neat and tidy, and the third room, Bernie's, is almost empty. I know it's hers, because her schoolbooks are on the floor. One small dresser stands in the corner and an unmade bed, but nothing else.

While Jamie goes into her parents' bedroom, I head straight for Clara's, doing my best to put Bernie out of my mind.

I open Clara's desk drawers and her bedside table, but there's no diary, no laptop, nowhere that a name could be written in secret.

I think back to when I was ten, trying to figure out where I would bury something so big. But there's nothing here.

When I've looked everywhere, I go back to Bernie's room. I can't help myself. If Clara knows something, maybe her sister does too. That's when I notice Bernie's bedroom door. There are dents on the outside, the wood caved in and splintered.

"Jamie," I say, "I think we should leave."

I reach out and touch the door, the paint coming away in clumps, like someone has put their fist through it, and when I look closer, the hinges are bent, and there are more dents at the bottom.

The rest of the house is immaculate, but this looks like a battleground.

I feel my chest tighten and back away, then turn and walk into the main bedroom where Jamie is quickly moving from drawer to closet and everywhere in between.

"What are you doing?" I ask.

"Looking for clues. If Clara knows Mr. Collins, maybe her parents do too."

"No. We should go."

Who smashes up someone's bedroom door? No one good. No one whose house we should be breaking into.

Jamie starts going through the dirty clothes basket, reaching into the pockets of trousers and jeans and pulling out whatever he can find.

"Come on," I say, but he's holding something out to me with a strange look on his face.

"What is it?"

"Where was the last murder?" he asks.

"Sheffield."

"You should see this receipt," he says. "Look at the address."

It takes me a while to find it. But when I do, I gasp. It's from a supermarket in Sheffield.

At 3:14 the morning after someone carved DEAD into the fifteenth victim, Bernie's stepdad bought a coffee near the crime scene. He paid in cash, but he kept the receipt.

"It wasn't Mr. Collins," I say. "It was him."

131

I hold the receipt tight but not too tight, terrified it's going to rip or I'll lose it or it will vanish from between my fingers. It feels so fragile.

I should be wearing gloves, slipping it into a sealable bag, and handing it to the forensics team. Instead, I gently fold it and put it in my sock.

Jamie starts going through the bedside table, pulling out bank statements and bills.

"Maybe there's more," he says, handing me piles of paperwork.

Bernie's stepdad is named Elliot Farrell. He's Clara Farrell's father. He's the secret she was too scared to tell. But we don't have time to check all this. We need to leave.

Before we go, Jamie gives me a strange look, nods, and hugs me. It feels weird, and then it doesn't, and we stay like that for longer than we should.

At some point, my arms copy his, and we hold each other.

And as we stand there, slowly feeling less awkward and then more awkward than ever, we hear the front door open and realize we are trapped.

132

"Shit," Jamie whispers, stuffing the clothes back in the dirty clothes basket. He turns and looks at me, his eyes conveying something I've never seen before.

"When you get the chance...run."

"What?"

He walks back to me, holds both my arms, and says, "Just run."

I expect him to move, but he doesn't. Instead, he stands in the doorway, waiting for whoever is down there to come up. They must have discovered the broken back door by now, but the footsteps below are slow and calm.

I swallow my nausea and look behind me, trying to find another way out. The windows are big enough to climb through, but they won't open. The only way out is down.

We hear someone walking up the stairs, but they stop halfway, and I suck in my breath and hold my hand over my mouth, desperate not to make a sound.

Jamie sees me and copies, his eyes wide, his arms shaking, and I want so desperately to be anywhere but here.

A step creaks, then settles as whoever is out there waits for us to give ourselves away. They aren't panicked by the broken back door. They want to find us.

After ten long seconds, we hear movement, and when they are almost at the top, Jamie darts into Bernie's room.

I hear a creak on the top step and slip behind the bed, then look to see Mr. Farrell walking slowly after him.

He looks nothing like he did at the hospital. There, he was smiling, friendly, grateful. But in the moment before he disappears into Bernie's room, I see something that terrifies me, a calm sort of anger, a devil with no need to hide.

My mind is racing, but my legs are frozen to the spot. I should help Jamie, the way he always helps me, but he said run, and I have the only proof I'm ever likely to get, so I step forward, the noise from the next room loud and terrifying.

I walk out to the hallway and take each step slowly and carefully, not knowing which ones creak and which don't.

What happens when you break into the house of a monster and that monster catches you? I imagine it and quickly block it out.

I'm still not running. I hold my foot above every step, gently placing it down before steadying myself and going again.

Over and over, I creep down the stairs, then past the family portrait with Bernie's fake smile and her stepdad's dark eyes.

I think back to the hospital, when he thanked me for finding Bernie at Mayfield. He was mocking me.

I walk as quietly as I can to the back door and am about to step through when I see the crowbar.

In a flash, I feel Jamie pulling me back from the mouth of the alley. I see him creeping up on Michael with a hammer in his hand, attacking him when he had no idea Michael was harmless. I remember him agreeing to everything I have ever asked, like skipping school and following Clara home and coming here today.

The crowbar feels cold in my sweaty palm. It feels like a decision I have to make. It feels right.

That's when I hear movement, and before I can turn, I feel something pushed hard against my mouth, one gloved hand muffling my scream and the other wrapped tight around my waist.

Behind me, almost in a whisper, Mr. Farrell says, "You should have run."

133

I refuse to cry in front of him, no matter how much I want to. I stare into his eyes until he's the one to look away.

We're upstairs, my back pushed against the side of his bed, when he reaches into his pocket and says, "You like being recorded, don't you, Jessica?"

"What?"

Holding his phone out to me, he says, "Smile for the camera."

It takes a few seconds to understand what I'm looking at, then I realize it's me, here, now.

I look up, scanning the four corners of the bedroom, and there it is, a camera like the ones in my house. Only this one isn't streaming my life to the world; it's going straight to Mr. Farrell's phone.

"You can't be too careful," he says. "I had a feeling your persistence would pay off. How old were you when your mom died...five?"

"Seven," I say, and he grins.

"Time flies." He walks over to the camera and pulls it off the wall. "I'll have to get rid of these now...along with everything else."

He smiles, and there's nothing fake about it. He looks like the monster I once imagined him to be.

"You made me do something I haven't done for a long time, Jessica. You made me kill quickly."

"I didn't make you do anything."

Mr. Farrell crouches in front of me and says, "But you did. You challenged me, all those grieving families with their T-shirts. It gave me an idea I couldn't ignore. I had fun playing with you. It's a shame it has to end."

He grabs me under my arms and pulls me up, then opens Bernie's bedroom door and pushes me inside.

I look at Jamie and hate myself for getting him into this. I want to tell him I'm sorry. I want to go back in time and do things differently. I want to ignore Mr. Collins and force Lorraine to believe me about Clara and have the police find the receipt.

But if I had a time machine, there would be no need for any of this.

"Did you like my messages?" he says.

Then, as if realizing something, he pulls me up and forces his hand into my pocket, pulling my phone out, then does the same with Jamie. He looks at them, then smiles.

"Call me paranoid," he says, "but I thought you'd be recording my confession. Who else knows you're here? Have you got your little director friend hiding in the closet?"

He knows we don't, because he's been watching on his

phone, but he still looks worried for a second, the sneer slipping just long enough to show something worse underneath.

He can pretend all he wants, but I know he's terrified of being caught, no matter what he's done to protect himself. And that scares me even more, because how far will he go to stay free?

He needs to think we wouldn't be stupid enough to break into his house without telling someone.

"The police are on their way," I lie.

He stares at me and says, "I don't think so. They're too busy talking to that poor teacher of yours. How does it feel to have an innocent man arrested, Jessica?"

But something in his eyes suggests he's uncertain, and that's what I focus on.

He starts pacing the room, then takes the SIM card from his phone and snaps it.

When I think he's not listening, I lean toward Jamie and whisper, "I'm sorry."

Mr. Farrell yanks me up and pushes me on the bed. "Do not talk to each other," he says. "It's time to end this."

I imagine every murder is perfectly planned. It has to be for him to always escape unnoticed. He can't kill us here in his stepdaughter's bedroom and expect to keep living his lie. But he can't let us leave.

This might not be his usual trap, but it's still a trap.

We need to figure out how to escape before he figures out how to kill us.

134

Mr. Farrell grabs Jamie and says, "If you scream, I'll kill him."

He forces Jamie out of the room and closes the door, and when I turn the handle, it won't budge.

I think of the dents in Bernie's bedroom door. What must it be like living with him? Does she know what he is? Or is he different types of evil in different situations?

There are clues all over the place if you look hard enough, and I wonder if Clara suffers the way her sister does.

Her room looked normal, messy like mine, more clothes on the floor than in the closet, the bulletin board above her desk covered in Post-its and selfies. But Bernie's room is the complete opposite.

I hear something downstairs and put my ear to the floor, trying to figure out what's going on. Then I move to the door and listen, praying he isn't hurting Jamie.

This is my fault, and if anyone dies, it should be me. Jamie doesn't deserve any of this. He did one good thing, and I pulled him into my messed-up life, and now he's trapped in a madman's house. He told me to run, but he should have been the one running. He shouldn't have been here in the first place.

I hear footsteps on the stairs, the handle turns, then Jamie is pushed into the room, and Mr. Farrell reaches forward and grabs me.

"Your turn," he says, and I see Jamie has his arms tied behind his back.

Mr. Farrell is holding the rope, and he forces me to the floor, then wraps it around and around until it cuts into my skin. He yanks it hard, making sure there's no way I can escape, then he sits me down next to Jamie.

"Okay," he says. "Now I can think."

He looks scarily calm, his eyes flicking back and forth between us like he's doing eeny-meeny in his head, picking which of us to kill first.

This isn't what he had planned, even if he did prepare for the worst with the camera. If he'd known we were coming, he would never have left the house.

I'm desperately trying to use that somehow, because I don't want to die. I have to fight. I have to beat him.

"Remember," he says, "no talking."

When he leaves, he doesn't close the door, and the creak of the floorboards suggests he is only a room away.

And that's when I realize I've got another phone, stuffed somewhere he would never think to check.

"Shit," I whisper, and Jamie looks at me, his eyes wide, and shakes his head.

I had the perfect chance to call for help, and I didn't do it. How many times can I screw up on the same day?

My secret second phone is in my bra, and I was three numbers away from rescue, and it slipped my mind. Who does that?

We had him. All I needed was to dial 999 and tell them where I was, and we would be the proof they needed. And if they still didn't believe me, I would pull the receipt out of my sock, and Mr. Farrell couldn't lie his way out of that.

Plus, somewhere in this house is the worst photo album imaginable.

I only need one chance to make a call. But no matter how much I struggle against the knots behind my back, I can't loosen them.

He knows the police aren't coming. We're alone in this fight.

135

Every now and then, we hear movement, but he doesn't come back.

Every bump and bang downstairs makes my heart jump, yet after what feels like hours, he still doesn't put us out of our misery.

When I'm sure Bernie's stepdad isn't listening, I say, "We need to do something."

Jamie stares at me, his eyes bloodshot, and says, "No shit." He looks terrified.

"He's not going to kill us here," I say.

Jamie shivers and shakes his head. "I don't want to talk about this."

"We *have* to. We don't have much time. We need a plan."

But it's hard to plan when you have no idea what's going to happen.

Is he going to keep us here until his wife gets back? Will Bernie come home from school to find us trapped in her room?

How long does it take a serial killer to figure out how to murder two people who willingly walked into his house?

It feels like another hour or more has passed when Mr. Farrell comes into the bedroom, a weird smile on his face, and says, "I know what to do with you."

He pulls Jamie up, then me, and bundles us down the stairs. In the kitchen, he rips a dish towel in half, then gags us with it, and I have to focus on breathing through my nose as my chest tightens.

Then he pushes us through the broken back door, points to the garage, and says, "In there." His car is inside, the trunk open, and when Jamie looks at him, he says, "Get in. Now."

Jamie climbs in, and even though I'm sure there won't be enough room, I follow.

I was right. But Mr. Farrell doesn't care, slamming the trunk.

I hear the front of the garage slide open, the car door slam shut, the engine rumble, and the car slowly move forward.

Mr. Farrell gets out and pulls the garage door closed with a clunk, then starts driving.

It's hard to breathe, but I do my best while simultaneously trying to wriggle free of the rope without kicking Jamie in the face.

We don't attempt to communicate. We work with the space we've got, struggling helplessly to untie ourselves before the trunk springs open.

Wherever he's taking us, that's where he'll do it. That's where we'll die. But I'm not ready to. There's no way this bastard is going to kill me. There is no way he's going to win.

I think of Mom and wonder if the people at Mayfield Lodge are right, if she really can hear the prayers I say inside my head.

Is she scared? Does she know I'm going to get out of this somehow? Or is she already planning my welcome party?

I try to shake the thoughts away, because they are not helping.

The car stops before I expect it to, but Mr. Farrell doesn't come for us.

In the darkness, Jamie's finger grips mine, and I pray that we'll figure out a way to stay alive.

136

I try to keep track of time, but it's impossible. It feels like we've been in here for hours. Finally, I hear a car door open, the jangle of keys, then the trunk springs up.

It takes a while for my eyes to get used to the moonlight, and when I recognize where we are, I start to retch, and Mr. Farrell pulls the gag from my mouth just as I throw up.

When I look up at him, he smiles, and I notice he's head to toe in black, with only his face visible. I look at his hands and wonder if those were the gloves he used to strangle my mother.

He doesn't say anything, just waits for me to take a few deep breaths, then pulls me forward. I know exactly where we are going, and he doesn't disappoint.

Mr. Farrell keeps pushing us along until we reach my mother's gravestone.

Only then, when he forces us to the muddy ground, does he say, "Surprise."

137

"Are you impressed?" the Magpie Man says. "I don't know where they all are. But she was special."

I want to smash his face in. I want to kill him right here, where we buried my mom.

Jamie is breathing fast, and I look at him, telling him to settle down with my eyes.

The Magpie Man stares at him and says, "Calm down, little man," but that only makes him worse.

He unzips a bag and pulls out a kitchen knife, the biggest in those five-set collections that sit in blocks of wood on the countertop, the one you only use on special occasions.

When Jamie sees it, he starts making whimpering noises through the cloth, and I guess this is it. The Magpie Man is going to murder me next to my mother's grave. So what harm is there in talking to him if he has already decided my fate?

"This is your big plan?" I say. "You're going to kill us here. They'll find you, you know."

He laughs, so loud it echoes in the darkness, and says, "I'm not going to kill you, Jessica. You are going to kill each other."

"What?"

"Well, technically, I'm going to force you to kill each other. But they won't know the difference."

"You're sick."

"Maybe. But I'm also smarter than you. If you and your boyfriend make a suicide pact, if you slit your wrists by your mother's graveside, that's not suspicious—it's just sad."

"I won't hurt him."

The Magpie Man smiles and says, "We'll see about that."

"This won't work," I say. "The police will figure it out."

"They didn't last time."

He pushes me onto my front and cuts through the rope holding my hands behind my back. Rolling me over, he leans down and stares into my face until I have to look away.

"You look just like her," he says.

"Fuck you."

"No, Jessica. Fuck you. You thought you could catch me. But I'm always one step ahead. Did you really think that dressing up like your mother or standing in that alley was going to be enough? Did you really think I would come? I kill when I want to. You don't choose. I do."

His smile makes my skin crawl, but I need to focus on the phone he doesn't know I have, the hands he has freed, the space into which I will run if I have the tiniest chance.

"I liked your T-shirt," he says. "Did you like mine?"

I imagine the picture of his last victim with her fate carved below her number.

"You're sick," I say again.

He smiles. "You made me more creative."

"Why did you kill my mother?"

For a moment, I don't think he's going to answer, but then he sighs and says, "I've been watching your show, Jessica. You know that. How could I not? You're a strong girl. I like to think I'm the reason."

I take a deep breath to stop myself from spitting in his face, then he stands and walks over to Mom's gravestone and touches the words.

"I killed her because I had to."

I stare at his face, trying to match it with the hidden image Mom took the day she died.

Is he the man in the photographs? Was his blurry image sitting unseen in a forgotten camera all this time?

"She changed everything," he says.

I could run now, but I need to know. I need to hear what only he can tell me.

"You were there all along," I say. "You weren't a monster. You were our fucking neighbor."

The Magpie Man smiles and says, "I was both."

When I was seven, when my whole world fell apart and my dad chose to live in the wreckage, I didn't pay much attention to the man who replaced Bernie's dad.

Even before that, he was just a shape, just a noise next door, another stranger in a world full of them.

"Why?"

"She saw," he says. "I had no choice."

I glance at Jamie, his tears soaking the rag in his mouth.

"She was taking photos, snooping on me. She hated me living next door, in *his* house, moving in with *her* friend. But she picked the wrong day to spy."

I think of the four blurry images, the mixture of colors that has now seeped into my dreams.

"What did she see?"

The look on his face chills me. "She saw what I was burning."

I don't think she did. I think she was trying to, but whatever it was, she couldn't get it clear enough. She tried, she failed, and he killed her anyway.

"I should thank you," he says. "It seems right that we end it here, back where it started."

I don't understand what he's talking about, and then suddenly, I do.

"What did you mean when you said this worked last time?"

The Magpie Man smiles and says, "I think you know."

The suicide in the cemetery on the day before Mom died wasn't suicide. It was murder.

"You'd killed before," I say.

He crouches down next to me and says, "It wasn't the same. I felt nothing. And there was so much blood. I had to burn my clothes."

The reds and yellows and greens—the backyard fire Mom was trying to stare into. He saw her watching, he took her photo, and that night, he took her life.

"She didn't see anything," I say. "It was blurry. She didn't know what she was looking at."

He looks confused, then says, "I got rid of her phone."

"It wasn't on her phone. It was a camera."

For the first time, the Magpie Man looks genuinely scared, and as he turns away, I seize my chance.

I stand and run, and for a few seconds, there's no sound except my breathing and my feet against the ground. Then he's shouting, and I start weaving between the gravestones, running as fast as I can.

Not stopping, I reach into my bra and pull out Dad's phone and dial 999.

I hear the Magpie Man behind me, his own heavy breathing ripping through the darkness, and I dart to my right and start moving slower, trying not to make a sound.

"Nine-nine-nine. What's your emergency?"

I hear him stop, the crunch of the leaves on the ground slow and deliberate, as if he heard the operator speaking into my ear.

If I reply, he will hear me, and I won't have time to tell them where I am, let alone why.

The woman starts to repeat herself so I hang up, feeling my way between the stones, praying that I'm moving away from him with each careful step.

"What do you expect to happen, Jessica?" he calls. "I *will* find you."

I hear him walking toward me, too slowly to know exactly where I am.

I stick to the shadows, terrified the moonlight will give me away. Every sound feels louder in the darkness, each snap of a twig like thunder in my ringing ears.

His footsteps crack against the uncut grass, and I freeze,

my fists balled up so tight my fingernails dig into the skin. The pain focuses me, and I close my eyes, listening for his movements, figuring out exactly which part of the darkness he's coming from.

I'm too scared to breathe deeply. Instead, my breath comes out small and jagged, my chest growing tighter until I'm sure I'll explode.

He isn't calling anymore. He's listening as closely as I am. He's hunting me.

I hold my breath, ready to fight, until the noises fade slightly. He's walking away from me.

This is my only chance, so I push a different number, hearing it ring once, twice, three times, then I hang up.

I call again and count one, two, then stop.

And then again, three rings this time, the end of a pattern I pray Dad remembers.

And then I call for a fourth time, and before the first ring has even finished, he answers, "Jessica? What's wrong?"

"Mom's grave," I whisper. "He's here. Help me."

Before Dad can reply, I hang up and throw the phone into the darkness, and it can't be more than five seconds before the crack behind me is too close to be anything except the Magpie Man.

"Found you," he says.

138

I swing around and hit him as hard as I can in the face, and as he steps back, I run.

I'm praying Dad will come, but I need to give him enough time. With no traffic, with no red lights, he could be here in less than ten minutes, and I use that as my motivation to run faster, dodging between the gravestones, fighting against my beating heart and my aching legs.

I hear him behind me, feel him reach out and touch my shoulder just as I find another gear and slip out of his grasp.

I turn quickly to my right and run deeper into a cemetery that stretches farther than I ever imagined.

I want to look back, but that's the first mistake they make in movies. You look back and you fall and you're caught. I keep my eyes forward, trying to make out every obstacle a few seconds before I have to dodge it.

The second mistake is that people always run in a straight

line, so I weave through the gravestones, then turn sharply to my left and go harder and faster than before. My heart's pounding, but I keep going.

The third mistake is stopping, thinking you've outrun them, believing they aren't as desperate to kill you as you are to survive. Once you hide, it's only a matter of time before you're found.

So I run until my legs burn...and then I keep running.

Except there's one thing I don't see until it's too late: the metal railings forming a border around the cemetery. Keeping people out...and in.

I'm about as far away from the only entrance as I can get, and if Dad does come, I'll be dead long before he finds me.

I touch the railing for a moment, trying to take in a few deep breaths as quietly as I can.

It's darkest in the corners, but there's no way out. I focus on the silence and the cold tickling my fingers while my body burns with adrenaline.

And then I start running around the edge of the cemetery, where there are no stones blocking my way, just a clear path back to the gate. My legs are on fire, and my heart hammers in my head, but I don't stop.

I see the entrance ahead and feel a surge of hope. I'll get help and save Jamie and catch the Magpie Man. I see everything fall into place.

And that's when I hear him behind me. He's getting closer with every step. And this time when he reaches out, he grabs my shoulder and pulls me back, and I have no energy left to fight.

He pushes me to the ground, then leans over with his hands on his knees, panting.

I could try to run again, but maybe I don't have to, because Mom's grave is not far from Dad's only way in.

I could piss him off so much that he kills me right here. Or I could submit, just long enough for a savior to arrive.

He waits until his breathing has slowed, then grins and says, "I like a challenge."

I clench my fists and go for him, but he knocks them away, forcing them to my sides.

"Enough," he snarls. Then he pulls me back to Jamie, who looks dazed, like he's just come to.

The Magpie Man sits us next to each other and pushes the knife into my hand.

"Here's what's going to happen," he says. "I'm going to make you slit his wrist, and then, very quickly, I'm going to make him slit yours. And when the police find you, it will look like you snapped and went to join your mother.

"That's how they'll remember you, Jessica: as a weakling who couldn't handle it when your little show didn't work and ended it in the most terrible way."

There's that grin again, the evil dripping off him. How did he go so long without being found out? How can he be two such different people at the same time? But maybe he isn't. Maybe Bernie knows how bad he can be and that's why she did what she did. Maybe Clara finally thought enough was enough.

"How can you do this to your daughters?" I say.

He looks angry and says, "I only have one daughter."

"Bernie tried to kill herself because of you."

"You have no idea," the Magpie Man says, and I'm hoping

he's about to explain, because the longer he talks, the more chance Dad has of finding us.

"Have you hurt her?" I ask, but he doesn't reply, forcing my fingers around the handle of the knife.

What will Jamie's parents think? Will they believe the lie the Magpie Man leaves for them, or will they see the truth below?

I try to let go of the knife, but he wraps his hand tightly around mine and moves my arm toward Jamie.

With his other hand, he grips Jamie's wrist and holds it out, then forces my hand down toward his skin until the blade is resting there.

"I'm sorry it had to end this way," the Magpie Man says. "It was never my intention to hurt children."

I can't help but laugh, even here, even now, and he tilts his head and says, "What's so funny?"

"It was never your intention to hurt children? You murdered their mothers. And I know what you do to Bernie. I saw her bedroom door."

He doesn't respond to that. He nods and grips my hand even tighter, then pushes until the knife breaks Jamie's skin, directly over the rope burn.

I try to fight back, to pull the knife up as he's forcing it down, but he's stronger than me, and I see the blood start creeping out.

I look at Jamie, his eyes wider than I've ever seen them, his face white in the moonlight, and I hate myself. He deserves so much better than this. He only ever wanted to be my hero, and he is.

I pull back more, refusing to do this, fighting against the

Magpie Man's grip even as Jamie's cry escapes from behind the cloth still stuffed in his mouth.

And that's when we hear the noise, feet pounding toward us, the shape arriving so quickly, I can't believe my eyes.

It smashes into the Magpie Man and knocks him backward, the knife falling to the ground, and my first instinct is to pull the cloth from Jamie's mouth and wrap it around his wrist.

Only then do I turn and see my father on top of the Magpie Man, beating his fists on his chest.

He came. He actually came. The man who gave up, the man who barely leaves the living room, he caught the monster.

But the Magpie Man rolls away, leaps up, and punches my dad between the eyes. Then he grabs the knife and lunges forward just as Dad jumps back, the blade slashing the air between them.

Blood trickles from Dad's nose, but his eyes are locked on the Magpie Man.

He sways slowly from side to side with his arms out while the Magpie Man wipes his own blood from his lips, smearing it across his cheek.

He sneers and says, "You can't beat me. I'll kill you just like I killed your wife."

I see something crackle under Dad's surface, but he doesn't move. He waits, watching the knife and the monster holding it.

"Come on," the Magpie Man snarls, but Dad doesn't respond.

He waits until the knife moves again, then spins to the left, steps forward, and punches him in the side of the head. Then again, until the Magpie Man's legs give way and he falls.

Then Dad is pinning him to the ground, punching him over and over again, taking out ten years of anger on the only person who deserves it.

He looks so big, towering over the man who ruined his life, and I see who he was before Mom died.

"Are you okay?" Jamie says, and I nod, even though I can feel tears streaming down my face.

I should be asking him that, and I touch the cloth covering his broken skin and say, "I'm sorry."

"It isn't your fault."

It is. Jamie is only here because of me. But if that was my fault, then so is this. So is my dad tilting his head back, taking deep breaths into the sky as the Magpie Man lies beaten on the ground, his face bloody, his eyes closed.

I stand up and touch Dad on the shoulder. "That's enough."

139

The sirens drift through the night air, growing louder until they shatter the silence of the cemetery as flashing red and blue lights repaint the scene.

Elliot Farrell is handcuffed and pushed into the back of a police car.

I've pictured this moment so many times. But it doesn't feel like I'd imagined. I don't feel elation. We don't celebrate. We just watch as the man who killed my mother is driven away, his eyes focused on us until we're out of sight.

I used to have nightmares about those eyes, before I knew who they belonged to.

Now I hope he has nightmares about mine.

While Jamie is taken to the hospital, Dad and I sit by Mom's grave, watching detectives unwind yellow tape, slowly barricading us in.

Dad stares at me, a look on his face I've never seen before.

It's a mixture of anger and fear and hatred and sorrow and everything in between.

"Thank you," I tell him. "I wasn't sure you'd remember the code."

"Of course I did," Dad says. "You should be proud of yourself. The show worked." The smallest hint of a smile flickers across his face before he says, "I was paying more attention than you thought. I always have."

I don't visit Mom's grave enough. Nan does. She comes once a week, removing the dead flowers and replacing them with whatever's in season. This week, there are bright pink gerberas to keep Mom company.

"We should come here more often," I say.

"We should," Dad replies.

I wonder if this is the change I've been so desperate for, if catching the Magpie Man will bring my old father back.

The early signs are good.

140

It's not until we're home that I remember the receipt.

I pull it out of my sock and stare at it, wondering what would have happened if the Magpie Man's plan had worked and they'd found it when I was dead.

Would they have realized, or would they have thrown it away without a second look?

It doesn't matter now, but it's nice to think I might have got one over the Magpie Man from beyond the grave.

Lorraine doesn't answer when I call the number on her card, so I leave a message, telling her I have one last piece of evidence for her to collect.

Nan comes over that night and holds me tight, and it's not until I try to end the hug that I realize she's crying. For ten years, she kept us together, and now, finally, she can break down.

"Thank you," she whispers. "She would have been so proud of you."

This time, I know this isn't Nan's way of saying *she's* proud of me. I know it's true.

I don't say anything back. I hold her extra tight and wait for her to let go.

Later that night, the three of us sit in the living room, mostly silent, mostly happy.

I would be lying if I said catching him made everything all right. In a strange, cruel way, I feel sadder when I think of Mom. The terrible certainty of never seeing her again is more powerful than the satisfaction of getting justice. But now we can grieve.

And I am happy too. I'm happy that he will never kill again, that Lorna Banks's baby boy will grow up knowing her murderer rotted in jail.

I'm happy that somehow this ridiculous idea of mine actually worked.

The biggest moment of the show happened when no one was watching. But that's life, I guess. Most of our defining moments take place when no one's paying attention.

I didn't know I was having my last conversation with Mom when she kissed me goodbye the day she was murdered.

She didn't know those photographs would rob her of a happy ending.

Dad didn't know he would lose his soul mate on a random Friday.

And Elliot Farrell didn't know he would be caught because of a secret second phone and an emergency ring I never thought I would use.

141

"I always knew he was an asshole," Bernie said. "But I didn't know he was a monster."

It took a while before she would talk to me, and when she finally did, I didn't ask why.

Maybe she was embarrassed, maybe she hated me a little bit, maybe she couldn't look me in the eye once she knew what her stepdad really was, or maybe she needed some time to repair her own broken family.

We all have our reasons...for everything we do. I just didn't know Bernie's reasons were quite so horrible.

When we spoke, the tears came first, then the words, then both.

She apologized, over and over again, even when I said she had nothing to be sorry for.

"I should have told someone that he hurt my mom," Bernie whispered. "But he told me if I ever said anything..."

She didn't need to finish the sentence. I had seen for myself what he was, and I didn't blame her for a second.

I never got the chance to talk to Clara again. Maybe one day, I will, because I'd like to say thank you.

But the three of them are supporting one another. They're free, and, I hope they'll eventually be happy.

"The only one of us who he actually loved," Bernie said, "and she saw right through him."

I didn't ask what it was like to live with a man like that. I could guess, but I think I would still come up short.

Sometimes Bernie gave me glimpses, explaining how it felt to be on the other side of the door while her stepdad punched and kicked from the hallway.

"I'd turn up my headphones so much it hurt my ears," she whispered. "But I needed to block out the noise."

In the end, the Magpie Man didn't pretend to be perfect to the people I once imagined were keeping him safe. He didn't have that in him. He simply hid what he really was by being a different kind of devil.

I was too young to realize how close my mom and Bernie's mom had been, that they were neighbors who grew to be friends.

Mom helped her through her divorce. She looked out for her the way she looked out for us.

If I concentrate, I can picture them sitting in the living room, whispering over mugs of tea. I can remember them talking over the backyard fence.

And not then but now, I can imagine Bernie's mom buying my mom perfume to say thank you. That's how he knew.

When Elliot Farrell came along, Mom watched a little closer. But she would never know that she'd caught him burning clothes covered in the blood of his first victim. She had no idea she would change the way he killed, becoming the first he was proud of, the first he took credit for.

142

At school, I lost my celebrity status quickly, if I ever got that far. There were celebrations, congratulations, smiles from teachers who had bought new equipment with money from the show, and then there was nothing.

It was back to the three of us, trying not to think too hard about anything, not senior year, not saying goodbye, not college or whatever comes after that. We still have a year and a few months, and for now, we're desperately clinging to the few months.

The only thing left to think about until the summer is the prom, which is a bigger deal for some than others. Emily comes under "some."

Prom doesn't mean as much in eleventh grade, because it's a party rather than a farewell. But I'm going because Mom would want me to. I'm going because I don't have an excuse not to anymore.

"I'm getting this one," Emily says, waving her phone in my face. "It comes in royal blue, baby pink, or merlot red."

Hanna rolls her eyes, and I can't help laughing, but Emily doesn't care.

She just grins and says, "Juniors usually wear party dresses. It's not until senior year that we need to think about ball gowns."

We let Emily talk while quietly having our own conversation.

"Have you asked him yet?" Hanna whispers, and I try to play dumb while feeling the butterflies flutter in my stomach. We each have a guest ticket for prom, and there's no rule saying that your guest can't be from tenth grade.

Next to us, totally oblivious, Emily says, "It's got capped sleeves and a lacy overskirt, but the lace looks silly in pink. And I haven't decided between sandals or heels."

She could go on like this for hours.

"Speak of the devil," Hanna says.

Behind me, with no clue what is happening, Jamie nods and says, "All right."

Emily stops talking about herself and exchanges a look with Hanna that Jamie catches but pretends not to.

When the bell for next period rings, his fingers brush mine, and I think of the night he pulled me back from the alley and everything that came after.

My life is not a love story. But there's no harm in trying.

143

Mr. Collins and I sit across from each other while Danny sets up the camera.

This interview has been a long time coming, but even now, my former English teacher looks like he has made a mistake.

He never came back to St. Anthony's. He has another job now, at another school in another town.

When I ask how it's going, he says, "As well as can be expected."

"I'm sorry," I say.

He shrugs. "It was my fault."

That's why we are here, to find out his story.

According to Adrian, if I want to end my contract early, my audience needs everything resolved. He calls Mr. Collins a loose end.

Danny nods. "Ready when you are."

So I look into the blinking red light and say, "I made a few mistakes along the way, and I'm trying to put that right." Turning to Mr. Collins, I ask, "Why did you put the articles in my bag?"

He looks ashamed, nothing like the man he was at school, and glancing at the camera, then the floor, he says, "I knew your mother. We grew up together. We were friends."

I thought only Dad and Nan had stories about Mom. I never expected an English teacher I hated to have a treasure chest filled with his own.

"She was the first person I spoke to in eighth grade," he whispers. "She sat next to me in class and smiled the biggest smile, and I wasn't scared anymore. We were friends from that moment on." He is silent for a while, then he mumbles, "I'm sorry about the articles. I was trying to help. I realize now that wasn't the case. What kind of person puts stories about a murdered woman in her daughter's schoolbag?"

Before, I would have said a terrible person, but listening to him speak about my mother, I'm not so sure now.

"I should have spoken to you," he says. "But what would I say? I know the kids see me a certain way. I thought it was better to stay anonymous. I wanted to motivate you, to ensure you never forgot what you were fighting for."

I don't tell him I could never forget, for a single second, what happened to her.

But thinking back to that first night after Mayfield Lodge, when I came home, convinced I was quitting the show before the article in my suitcase and Sonia's coup pulled me back, I realize he did help me.

"You made a difference," I say, and he offers me a relieved smile.

I want him to keep talking long after he's stopped. I want him to tell me everything he can about Mom, because he was her friend when she was my age. He knows things no one else does.

When he's gone, Danny sits next to me and says, "So that's it."

"I guess."

"It's been an honor. I'm proud of you."

I used to hate it when people said that, but not anymore.

"What are you going to do next?" I ask.

"I don't know. Something will come up."

"You were a good director."

"It was the luck of the draw," he replies, and I don't know if he means for me or for him.

144

It would be wrong to think Dad had some remarkable transformation that day. In so many ways, he's still broken, just not as much as before.

There are times now when he gets carried away with a conversation, when his eyes start to shine, when he laughs and actually means it. These are my favorite times, even though he looks like he feels guilty afterward.

That is a curse of the grieving: to feel ashamed of our brief moments of happiness.

On the day Elliot Farrell is found guilty of sixteen counts of murder, the day he's told he will spend the rest of his life in jail, a shadow leaves my father's face. The receipt, the Polaroids, the photographs my mother took, they were all used as evidence.

The man Mr. Farrell killed was named George Hanson. His family was the first to suffer but the last to realize why. He went to school with Bernie's mom, and they reconnected online. When Mr. Farrell found out, he snuffed out the threat.

On the news, after George Hanson's suicide was changed to murder, his family's tears were a combination of horror, heartbreak, and relief. In time, they can find closure like the rest of us, but for now, they have another grief journey to complete.

When Dad hugs me, I wonder if he will ever let go. When he does, he pulls something from the side of his chair, but it's not Mom's photograph; it's an envelope. Inside is a check with my name on it.

"For the future," Dad says.

It's a word we can finally think about.

"I paid off the mortgage with your mother's life insurance," he says, "and there was plenty left over for bills. When I work the night shifts, that's for you."

"I thought you did it so you could get out of the house."

"I did," he says. "And it helped. But the money was always for you. So what are you going to do with it?"

"I might go to school to be a therapist. I want to help people."

Dad smiles and says, "You'll be good at that." And for the first time, I'm not afraid to move on. I'm not worried to leave him alone while I find my way.

That night, we do what I have been planning for weeks.

As I light the candle, I think back to the prayer room, to the time I silently spoke to a woman I will never truly know.

Dad knew her in ways I can only imagine. He fell in love with her, he trusted her, he lived for her: a stranger who became his entire world.

The flame sends shadows flickering across the walls, my dad's face looking unfamiliar in the half-light.

Before, I whispered into the deepest, darkest corner of my mind. Now, I share those thoughts with both of them: my mother and my father, the left and the left behind.

When I'm done, I pass the candle to Dad, who stares at it in silence.

I see a hundred different emotions dance across his face, the flame steered back and forth by his breath.

For a long time, he doesn't talk, and I imagine the words in his head, the silent memories I hope he is recalling, the words he has kept hidden, slowly unwrapped and passed to the only person he ever wanted to hear them.

When he clears his throat, I stand and leave, whatever he wants to say best shared in secret.

I go to my room and record my final statement, repeating a script I've been working on for weeks, the one that ends the show.

Sometimes I wonder if this is real, if we really did catch him. But I only need to close my eyes to remember.

I'm not live online anymore. But Adrian has granted me an epilogue: one final statement to satisfy my audience.

"My name is Jessica Simmons," I say, "and I caught the Magpie Man. That's what we called him before we knew better. But his real name is Elliot Farrell. His crimes and the people whose lives he destroyed should never be forgotten..."

I hear a creak in the hallway and see Dad's reflection in my bedroom mirror. He stands for a few more seconds, not-so-secretly listening to me tell the world what justice feels like.

Then he looks at me through the reflection and smiles.

AUTHOR'S NOTE

If you have experienced something similar to the events in this book, there are resources available to you.

The National Domestic Violence Hotline is a twenty-four-hour confidential service for survivors, victims, and those affected by domestic violence, intimate partner violence, and relationship abuse. You can reach them through the National Domestic Violence Helpline at 1-800-799-7233 and on their website at thehotline.org.

The National Center for Victims of Crime is a nonprofit organization dedicated to providing information, resources, and advocacy for victims of all types of crime as well as the people who serve them. You can visit their website at victimsofcrime.org or call their support line at 1-202-467-8700.

A Q&A WITH VINCENT RALPH

14 Ways to Die **is your debut novel. What inspired you to write it?**

I've always loved scary movies and wanted to do something similar with this book. I used to take a shortcut home after nights out, through an alley I really should have avoided. I remembered that alley when the first line of the novel came to me, and it grew from there.

Why did you choose to base *14 Ways to Die* around social media?

It used to be the case that if you locked your doors and windows, the monsters stayed outside. Social media has changed that. But we can also use it for good, which is what Jess does. She knows that while her story has been forgotten, YouTube offers her a chance to reach the whole world.

How did you create the Magpie Man?

Like many people, I grew up being told that seeing a single magpie is bad luck unless you wish them well. I took that idea and changed it slightly: a dad telling his daughter a story to disguise a terrible truth. Magpies collect precious things, so it fit the character perfectly.

Do you think Jess should have gone to the lengths she did to catch the Magpie Man?

Jess has spent a decade defined by her mother's murder. For a long time, she felt powerless, but now she has a chance to solve the crime. On occasions, it could be argued that she goes too far, yet she is driven solely by her quest for justice. As she says, she's spent her life hiding, and now she wants to seek.

What other books would you recommend to fans of your book?

A Good Girl's Guide to Murder by Holly Jackson is a great book that is brilliantly executed. I'm also a big fan of Karen M. McManus's books. While she's not a YA author, Gillian Flynn was a huge inspiration for *14 Ways to Die*. All her books are superb, and after reading *Gone Girl*, I was inspired to sit down and write a thriller of my own.

Who is your favorite character?

I love Emily as a character. She isn't afraid to speak her mind, and she was a lot of fun to write. She brings some light to a dark story, and some of her lines still make me chuckle now.

Did you find it challenging to create a sense of mystery? What tips would you give to budding thriller writers?

When you know who did it, it's a lot easier to draw suspicion elsewhere. I think creating mystery comes in the later drafts, when you can have fun with red herrings. I try to picture every chapter as a scene in a movie. By working in a more sensory way, I find the suspense comes easier.

Which was the most enjoyable scene to write?

The cemetery scene and the moments leading up to that were a lot of fun. I also loved writing the chapters at Mayfield Lodge. The change of setting and pace allows Jess some much-needed time to assess what she's achieved so far, and it offers her a glimpse of life after the show.

Are you scared of anything?

I'm still a little bit scared of that alley!

ACKNOWLEDGMENTS

Thank you to my incredible agent, Claire Wilson. You champion my writing with such enthusiasm, and I'm so grateful for your advice and support. You changed my life the day you offered me representation, and this book would not exist without you.

I am incredibly grateful to Steve Geck and Sourcebooks for bringing my novel to the United States. Seeing this story cross the Atlantic is a dream come true. Thank you to marketing manager Beth Oleniczak, production editor Cassie Gutman, art director Nicole Hower, and creative director Kelly Lawler.

Tig Wallace: Your passion for this story was clear from our first meeting and your eye for detail is superb. You coaxed a far better story out of me, and I will never forget that.

To my UK editor, Carmen McCullough, your fresh eyes and feedback were vital as we got this book over the line. Thank you for taking the reins from Tig with the same passion for Jess's quest for justice.

Thank you to everyone at PRH Children's UK who has played a part in this journey so far, especially Michael Bedo,

Anne Bowman, Amelia Lean, Wendy Shakespeare, Jane Tait, and Harriet Venn.

A huge thank you to my wife, Rachel. You are the love of my life and my inspiration. You were the first person to read this book, and you approached each new draft with the same excitement as the last. I will be forever grateful for your unwavering support.

To our gorgeous son, Charlie: You weren't around when I wrote this but I'm delighted that you saw its publication... although it will be a few years before you can read it.

Thank you to Miriam Tobin for all your work behind the scenes at RCW.

Thank you to Barry Philpott: one of my earliest readers and most enthusiastic champions. Your support and feedback were invaluable, and you always believed I would achieve my dream...even when I wasn't so sure.

I am grateful to each and every person who reads this novel. I have imagined this moment for most of my life, and you are now part of that story.

To my grandmothers, Ivy and Patricia: Thank you for everything. I wish you were here to hold this book.

The biggest thank-you goes to my mother. This only exists because you always encouraged me to dream.

ABOUT THE AUTHOR

Vincent Ralph has been writing in one form or another since his teens and always dreamed of being a novelist. He owes his love of books to his mother, who encouraged his imagination from an early age and made sure there were new stories to read. Vincent has lived in London, Cornwall, and Chester, but he now lives in his home county of Kent with his wife, son, and two cats.

#getbooklit

Your hub for the hottest young adult books!

Visit us online and sign up for our
newsletter at FIREreads.com

 @sourcebooksfire

 sourcebooksfire

 firereads.tumblr.com